Loyalties

Uncertain / Mixed / Fanatical

by

Richard Davidson

Richard Davidson

Books by Richard Davidson:
Self-help:
DECISION TIME! Better Decisions for a Better Life
Mysteries:
The Lord's Prayer Mystery Series:
Lead Us Not into Temptation
Give Us this Day Our Daily Bread
Forgive Us Our Trespasses
Thy Will Be Done
Deliver Us from Evil
Imp Mysteries:
Implications
Impulses
Impostor
Impending
Impasse
Historically Based Fiction
Loyalties
Anthology: (Editor)
Overcoming: An Anthology by the Writers of OCWW

Loyalties, by Richard Davidson
ISBN 978-0-9976381-4-1
Uncertain / Mixed / Fanatical

Loyalties

This book is dedicated to those who appreciate unusual ancestors but aren't encumbered by them.

Richard Davidson

CHAPTER 1 - 1776

Martin Weatherford heard a thump at his front door as he was preparing to go upstairs to bed. The house slaves had retired to their small rooms over the kitchen, so Martin went to the door himself. When he opened it, he found his son John sitting on the top step, examining an unopened bottle of whiskey.

"You've had enough to drink, John. Come inside and go to bed."

"I don't think you realize how significant this bottle is, Father. I received it as a bonus when I signed up for the Continental Army. You may still consider yourself a subject of the King, but I've chosen to be a free American."

"You're out of your mind. You spend too much time at the tavern with those rabble rousers. There will be no country of America, just the thirteen colonies. The British Army will put down the rebellion within months. You and your upstart band of commoner friends will end up dead or in prison. Sober up and realize how fortunate we are to have ample property protected by British law. Your brothers and your sister aren't talking rebellion foolishness. They know how to appreciate our land holdings and our place in colonial Georgia society. New Englanders and Pennsylvanians are

1

the main ones preaching separation from England. It's the impossible dream of poor tradesmen and farmers. It will never happen. Be reasonable, John."

"I can't agree with you, Father. People came here from England and other countries to get away from class systems that limited their potential. You like the King because you've done well under his rule, but I'll cast my lot with the majority of people over here who want to live free and succeed based on their skills, not their class position in society. I'll be leaving to join the Continental Army tomorrow. There are scholars and politicians working right now in Philadelphia on a Declaration of Independence from England. I'll be supporting them and reinforcing troops that have been fighting since last year."

"You'll be living on scraps like the rest of your rabble friends. If you leave this house, you won't be welcomed back. I'll disown you and remove you from my will. How well will you cope with poverty?"

"If that's your attitude, I'll pack a few things and leave tonight. Goodbye, Father. This war may not treat you as well as you think."

CHAPTER 2 – PRESENT-DAY AWAKENING

Sarah Louise Kittleson slipped out from behind the dilapidated red barn and tucked two wild daisies into her finger-combed hair as she checked the unpaved road for traffic. Seeing none, she turned right toward home, skipping three times in a burst of energy. Four minutes later, just after Sarah Louise rounded the road's curve and disappeared, Todd Weatherford, a round-faced, shaggy-haired teenage boy in patched blue jeans approached the road from the opposite side of the barn and turned left. He didn't skip, but trudged along the roadside with an unusual gait, smiling so broadly that his dimples were deeper than ever.

Todd felt special for the first time in his life. He had always been an uninteresting background person, but today, for once, he was a star. During his past childhood and adolescence, nothing extraordinary happened to him. He had a placid nature and remarkably limited ambitions, but he definitely wanted to continue feeling as special as he did today. Sarah Louise had teased him for months at school, but now everything had changed. He had glimpsed a new world. He wouldn't settle for a continued introverted future. It was time for Todd to open his eyes to new possibilities.

CHAPTER 3 – TODD WEATHERFORD

Todd was the last of four children born to a modest but hardworking couple in a small Kentucky village. If he had been a dog, he would have been labeled the runt of the litter. He was shorter than his two brothers, Carter and Hampton, and even shorter than his sister Amy. His unusual gait as a child and adolescent, rocking forward and backward as he walked, earned him the nickname of Odd Todd at school where he had more than a few fights with taunting bullies. He countered the teasing by studying enough to become an academic star.

The elder Weatherfords, George and Judy, operated a small grocery and sundries store huddled next to one of the two gas stations in what barely passed for a town. This mom-and-pop enterprise actually made a small profit for the couple through the first ten years of Todd's life because transient customers bought supplies and souvenirs while they stopped for fuel at the adjacent gas station. When Todd was eleven years old, the new interstate highway opened up, bypassing the village, and the store had to survive on the purchases of local people. There wasn't nearly enough business to make a profit, and the store closed when Todd was thirteen. Dad Weatherford took a job as a mechanic at the gas station, while Mom brought in occasional cash by making and selling colorful quilts. Neighborhood chatter was that the Weatherford family kept their bills paid only because Todd's older siblings, Carter,

Hampton, and Amy, finished or quit school and commuted to the larger town of Winchester, where they worked in the lamp factory.

When Todd finished high school, he left home and moved to Lexington, Kentucky, where he taught himself how to play the guitar and joined a local band. The band work didn't bring in much money, but verbal give-and-takes with listeners taught Todd how to fit in with an audience of strangers. That skill would later earn him several jobs as a sightseeing guide. He eventually ended up in Chicago, where he met Lori Vinci, who would become his wife, and the other woman who would threaten his destiny.

CHAPTER 4 – CAREFREE TIMES

Being a tour guide in Chicago was a party on steroids if you were a young single guy. Once you learned the facts of each tour route and developed your personal patter speech, you were free to enjoy the effects you had on your audience and to single out female tourists deserving your personal attention.

For the first time in his life, Todd Weatherford felt that he was accomplishing something that other people considered important. During his tours, people of all ages gathered close to him and took his every word to be meaningful. Todd had been smart enough to stay away from drugs, but he attained highs without them. What could be better than a child handing him a drawing of him pointing to an architectural detail on a building or a beautiful woman trying to get close enough to concentrate on his entertaining patter speech? The first nine months of tour guide work passed in a flash, but then a new development dampened his enjoyment of his work.

One day, Todd told his boss he'd have to skip his normal tour assignment because he had intermittent pains in his leg joints and an accompanying itchy rash. His boss excused Todd from work but said that he'd have to see a doctor and get a medical release before he could return to his job.

Todd had never liked doctors and had rarely visited one at home because his family couldn't

6

afford medical expenses. As a child, the only medications he'd ever taken were sold over-the-counter in his parents' store. Despite this, he asked a friend for the name of his doctor and made an appointment for an examination.

Dr. Kanden turned out to be a no-nonsense woman in her forties who wanted her patients to treat her the same way they would if she were male. Humorous remarks bounced off of her with no effect, and she made it quite clear that she expected Todd to follow her medical directives precisely. He felt intimidated by her, and due to his lack of experience, Todd assumed that all doctors were dictatorial like her. He didn't enjoy being badgered one bit, but when Dr. Kanden diagnosed him as having the early stages of lupus, Todd figured his problem was serious enough for him to pay attention. Dr. Kanden gave Todd a note for his boss, saying he was well enough to work and sent him away with prescriptions for a steroid and an antimalarial drug. Todd made a pact with himself to take the medications and make the required follow-up appointments, but to tell no one about them. He would resume his carefree lifestyle and hope for the best.

He was convinced he had found the best a month later when he met Lori Vinci, at an early-season Chicago Cubs baseball game. This dark-haired, moderate height, slightly older woman wearing blue jeans and a short tartan jacket accidentally dropped a blob of mustard on his jacket sleeve while they were both decorating their hot dogs. She offered to pay for dry-cleaning his jacket and gave him her phone number. Todd kept the mustard-spotted jacket as a trophy, used the phone number as an opening for dating Lori, and asked her to marry him four months later.

CHAPTER 5 – MARRIAGE

The ceremony was short, but sincere, held at a Las Vegas wedding chapel during their first cohabited vacation. Todd was thrilled that an attractive, well-educated high school teacher said she loved him. For her part, Lori enjoyed his country boy attitude and accent. They hit the casinos and celebrated when they flew back to Chicago $286.30 richer than they were when they arrived in Las Vegas. Todd and Lori figured they were the luckiest people on earth.

Their luck continued when they revealed their marriage to Lori's parents. Joe Vinci was a vice president in a medium-sized bank with branches in several Chicago suburbs. He welcomed Todd into the family and announced that he would set the couple up in a small foreclosure house that the bank had recently acquired. He added that he and his wife Martha would give them the down payment as a wedding present. Lori and Todd were overjoyed by the news that they would start their married life in a house rather than a tiny apartment.

When Todd called his parents to share his good news, he wasn't sure how they would react to the high-value gift from the Vincis. He hoped they wouldn't feel threatened because they couldn't afford to make such a grand gesture. Todd's Mom relieved his fears by congratulating him and Lori and by inviting them for a visit to Kentucky in a few months, by which time she pledged to have created two special quilts, one for each of the bedrooms in the new house.

It was the best of times, but it was more fragile than either Todd or Lori realized.

CHAPTER 6 – COMPATIBILITY

For six months, Lori and Todd explored the joys of honeymoon-frequency sex plus spontaneous outings to sporting events, zoos, and campgrounds. They had a lengthy vacation trip to Kentucky, where Todd's parents heartily welcomed Lori into the Weatherford family. While there, Todd taught Lori camping skills, animal tracking, and the fine points of walking through woods and understanding the local ecosystem. Lori taught him about the evolution of different animal species and guided him to a surprising skill level at sketching landscapes.

Lori's first mistake came as the summer ended and she prepared for the new school year. One evening, as they sat on their patio where Todd played folk songs on his guitar, she said, "Todd you might want to think about going back to school. I'll be tied up with teaching and lesson preparation for a large portion of my time. You could register at the local community college and take some classes, perhaps even earn a two-year degree."

Todd responded with a stare that should have made Lori switch to a different subject.

"I don't need that stuff for my job. I get on fine with everyone in the tour groups, even college professors."

"Do you plan on guiding tours forever? You'll probably want to move up to something better in the future."

"Lori, you're trying to change me. If I wasn't good enough for you when we met, why did you marry me?"

"Of course I love you just the way you are. It's just that we might need more money in the future, especially if we have children."

"Are you trying to tell me you're pregnant?"

"No, and we've only been half trying for children so far. It's just that our expenses will go up with time, and we should prepare ourselves for that by learning new skills that bring in more money."

"What new skills are you going to add?"

"I've already started working on learning Spanish so that I can teach children who don't have a good grasp of English."

"Fine; tutor me in Spanish as you learn it. It's good for a tour guide to be bilingual."

"That's not what I meant. Spanish is good, but it's not enough to get you a real career job."

"Lori, I'm just a poor country boy from Kentucky. I appreciate having things, but I don't absolutely need them. I'm happy doing tours. Why should I want something more?"

"It would give us a better lifestyle and make me proud and happy."

"So, you're ashamed of me. I have to do what you want in order to make you proud."

"That's wrong. I'm all mixed up." Lori didn't know how to untangle her thoughts so she got up and ran into the house.

Todd thought back to a conversation he once had with his father. *Dad was right. Women do try to change you. What am I supposed to do now?*

CHAPTER 7 - RISING STAR

As schoolwork took more and more of Lori's time, Todd started to join the other tour guides after work for a drink or two at their favorite tavern, the Rising Star. He knew enough to minimize his drinking because of his secret medications from Dr. Kanden, so he learned how to nurse a drink slowly, while making it look as though he had consumed more. His favorite trick was to steal an empty glass or bottle from an abandoned table and then position it near his own drink to make it look as though he was on his second or third round. He took the precaution of confiding in Sally, the bartender, and slipping her a tip so that he didn't get charged for the drink that matched the extra glass or bottle.

One day, shortly after Todd and his co-workers entered the tavern, he noticed a woman who had been on one of his tours come in and sit at a vacant table. He thought it strange that a tourist would know about this local watering hole, so he took his beer and approached her table.

"Hello. I'm Todd Weatherford. Weren't you in one of my walking tours today?"

"I was indeed. I'm Emma Read. Please sit down and join me."

"Gladly, but first I'll get you a drink from the bar. What would you like?"

"Thanks; I'll have a Guinness if they have it on tap."

He set his Sam Adams bottle on her table and turned toward the bar. "One Guinness coming up."

13

Todd studied the new arrival as he waited for the bartender. She was blond, tanned, well-proportioned, athletic-looking, and not much older than him. He remembered that she hadn't had any problem keeping up with him on the tour, even when they climbed two flights of stairs to reach the ornate mezzanine of a financial building. She didn't sound as though she was from the Midwest, but he couldn't place her accent.

Todd returned to the table with the Guinness and set it in front of her. "How did you happen to come to this out-of-the-way place?"

"I followed you."

"That's either flattering or threatening. What would you want with a Kentucky lad like me?"

"So that's where you're from. I didn't recognize your accent."

"I can say the same for you."

"I'm a transplant from everywhere. My dad was in the RAF – we're British originally – but he was based overseas ever since I was small, so I grew up with many accents influencing me. My current home is in the West Indies, but I'll be here on business for a while."

"And you collect tour guides for amusement?"

"Just one, so far. Would you like to show me more of the area?"

"That might be fun, but I'm married."

"I might be married too. I'm not declaring my status yet. I'll bet you can still enjoy yourself."

"We have a racehorse saying in Kentucky. 'Sometimes you win; sometimes you learn.'"

"I'd be glad to teach you a few things."

"Interesting way to put it. My wife's a teacher."

"If we spend some time together, you'll have to stop talking about your wife."

Loyalties

"Then, you'll have to keep me occupied by telling me about Emma Read."

CHAPTER 8 – EMMA READ

"As I said earlier, my dad was a career RAF flyer. He served at bases all over the Commonwealth, and in more than a few hotspot assignments in countries where the British were supporting their allies or the United Nations."

Todd looked impressed. "Did he fly bombers or fighters?"

"Neither, he flew transport missions, getting the troops and their gear to wherever they had to be. He had his share of scary close calls, but he had to depend on others if he got shot at. His aircraft weren't armed."

"That wouldn't be my cup of tea, as your family might say. If I had to fly, I'd want to carry lots of firepower with me."

"You said 'if I had to fly'. I assume that means you wouldn't want to be a pilot."

"It would never be my thing. I don't mind being a passenger, and in a mid-air emergency, I might even take over for an unconscious pilot and try to land a plane with coaching over the radio, but for the most part, I choose to keep my feet on the ground."

Emma finished her Guinness, and he went to the bar to get her another one. When he returned he said, "I'm glad I didn't grow up a military brat. I like to stay in one place and learn all I can about it."

"That's why you're a good tour guide. You're genuinely interested in the buildings and places you show us tourists."

"Thanks for the compliment, but we're getting away from your talking about yourself."

"What do you want to know?"

"Why are you in town, and why do you think I'm some easy guy you can pick up for a fling?"

"I'm here to negotiate some additional funding for a resort I'm building along with a few partners."

"In the West Indies?"

"Correct, but I won't say exactly where it is. We're developing an area that has been overlooked in the past. If I openly discussed the location, real estate costs would increase, and we might even get a lot of static from nature lover groups that are against developing pristine locations."

"That's fine, but why the interest in me?"

Emma glanced around the room to be sure no one was overly interested in their conversation. "I need a lover, and I need a host for the new resort."

Todd laughed. "That's the most ridiculous thing I've ever heard. A woman like you doesn't have to travel thousands of miles to a strange city to find a lover. The host aspect of your comment is also weird. You'd be much better off with someone who knows about that part of the world because he grew up there."

"I have good reasons for selecting you, but I won't reveal them until we're a lot more familiar with each other."

"Sorry, Emma. I don't get thrilled by the prospect of being recruited to be a lover with a job interview. It's time for me to go home and get back to reality. I may or may not see you again, but I wish you luck. You're the most distracting thing that's happened to me in a long time."

Todd left the tavern. As Emma finished her second Guinness, she smiled. *The first step is a*

*success. He won't be able to stop thinking about me.
I'll give him a week for his thoughts to simmer into
lust.*

CHAPTER 9 – LORI

Lori noticed a slight change in Todd's attitude over the next several days. She had grown up playing poker with her father and brothers, and that experience helped her assess the outlooks and motives of those around her. Todd was acting as though he had an ace in the hole. He was more confident and less willing to have a lengthy discussion with her on any subject. For the time being, she would attribute his new manner to that conversation about his not wanting to be changed by her. She would avoid suggesting improvements to Todd for a while.

Todd's reaction to her recommendation that he get additional education had seemed childish to her. A good wife should do everything she could to improve her husband's opportunities for success. Todd should be mature enough to see that his Kentucky mannerisms and country boy outlook stood in the way of his finding a job that would be more permanent than tour guiding. That was a young person's starter job, not a career vocation. Even though she told herself she would avoid the subject, Lori began to picture Todd as a teacher in the lower grades. She mentally nodded to herself that he might do a good job of inspiring first and second graders to think about imaginative goals for the future. She would file that thought away for whenever she felt it was safe to again make suggestions for Todd's future.

Lori turned her immediate attention to preparing Todd's favorite supper: bacon, pepperoni, mushroom, anchovy and onion pizza baked on a large rectangular cookie sheet. She'd par bake it and delay the final baking until he was due to arrive home. She'd have to guess when to finish baking the pizza. Since he started going out with the other guides after work, she couldn't accurately predict his schedule. Lori tried to avoid thinking about the number of tour guides who were female. That was another reason to nudge him toward a different occupation. The problem was that women would be his co-workers in almost any job.

After Lori completed her preliminary pizza preparations she decided to call her mother. Mom was always good for a long detailed telephone conversation, usually devoted to the events in her older generation schedule. Lori needed to listen to someone else's problems for a while so that she wouldn't dwell on her own.

CHAPTER 10 – SECOND COMING

When Todd entered the tavern with fellow guides Frank and Sylvia, he did a double take. He thought he had removed the potential problem of Emma Read by rejecting her advances. Yet, here she was again, sitting at a small round table with two untouched drinks, a stein of Guinness and a bottle of Sam Adams Boston Lager. The invitation to him was obvious. Instead of going over to her, he headed for the men's room. He needed a few minutes to decide how to react to her presence. If he simply left, his friends would think there was something wrong with him, and Emma might follow him anyway. If he confronted Emma, Frank and Sylvia might think he was rude and moody.

Todd decided he would have to play it cool. He left the men's room and walked to Emma's table. "I'm surprised to see you here again. I made it clear that I didn't like the idea of being interviewed for a romance."

Emma smiled up at him. "I completely understand. How about joining me for a drink for old times' sake?"

"That's a laugh. I met you here once before. That's hardly an old times situation."

"Todd, shut up and sit down. Let's have our drinks and then get out of here. I have a rental car outside. We'll head to my hotel and get to know each other better. After that, I'll get out of your life if you still want me to."

Todd realized that she had taken control and sat as directed. It would be late before he got home tonight.

By the time Todd left Emma's hotel room, he realized he would have to do some serious thinking about the future. Neither Lori nor Sarah Louise Kittleson, back in Kentucky, had ever made him feel the way he did tonight. Emma was a master of every trick in the sex book, and she had showcased many of them in order to snare her prey – him. When he arrived back home, he discover three quarters of his favorite pizza sitting on the table. Lori had gone to bed. He grabbed a beer and ate the rest of the pizza cold. Two Alka-Seltzers later, he stripped to his underwear and slipped into the bed alongside Lori.

CHAPTER 11 – MEMORIES

Lori vividly remembered that night and the following morning. As a peace offering, she had made Todd's favorite pizza, and then he hadn't shown up to eat it. She had ended up eating part of it despite those hated anchovies, and he finished the rest cold when he came in long after she went to bed. His arrival woke her. She checked her alarm clock and saw that it was two-thirty in the morning. Then she rolled over and went back to sleep without giving him the satisfaction of an argument. She woke up before her alarm triggered, and smelled another woman's scent on him. That unpleasant surprise had been the first of many times with the result that the woman's odor became as familiar to her as the much preferred aroma of morning coffee.

On many subsequent occasions Lori wondered whether an all-out fight that first night might have headed off the impending disaster, but in her heart she knew that any action on her part would have been futile. Theirs was a classic tragedy ungraced by iambic pentameter verse.

Lori lied when her best friend, Beverly, another teacher at her school, asked her why she suspected that Todd had been untrue to her. Lori had listed stereotypical clues, but not the fact that Todd had slapped her in the face with that woman's scent so many times. He hadn't even had the decency to wash before sliding between her bedcovers. Their own sex became a brief and infrequent charade having little lingering effect on either one of them. At least she hadn't become pregnant during the period of Todd's unfaithfulness. How would she later explain to their child that his or her mother and father had tried to kill each other?

CHAPTER 12 – THANKSGIVING

The inevitable climax came on the Thanksgiving holiday. As she reviewed it in her mind, Lori promised herself that she would never again look forward to that annual harvest-time gathering.

Friends and relatives from both sides of the family were at our house that day. They all meshed with each other pretty well and were looking forward to the traditional festive overeating. It was the usual setup where extended family members from opposite sides see each other only a few times each year. I was working in our kitchen. The grownups were in the front room and my three young nieces were playing in the basement. Todd drank more than anyone else. ... Lori took a deep breath and trembled as she began to relive her ordeal.

Todd charged into the kitchen while I was working and slammed the door behind him. The loud crash and his sudden presence so startled me that I dropped the pan of sweet potatoes into the sink. As I started to clean up the mess, he told me he wanted a divorce. I kept my cool and said we could discuss our relationship after the company went home. That wasn't good enough for him. He said that I had to agree to split up right then and there.

Todd wanted children. We had casually tried to get me pregnant, but it didn't work. I suppose one of us had a problem. We didn't take any tests to check on that. Todd refused. He hated doctors and hospitals. This might have been his problem, but then there was that woman who left her scent on him.

He was completely serious and adamant about the divorce. Maybe it took all that drinking to build up his courage to confront me. The violence started after I told him for the second time to relax and wait until the company left before discussing divorce.

The word 'wait' triggered his rage. Todd shoved me against a counter. It was the first time he ever struck out at me. I gasped and shoved him back. I thought that would be the end of it and said I had work to do to feed our guests. Then he slapped me on my left cheek really hard and threw the turkey onto the floor. At that point I screamed at him and called him a bastard and a vicious animal slob.

Todd pushed me back against the counter and started to strangle me. He pushed both thumbs into my throat. He stared at me like a demon. I felt the sharpness of the daggers in his stare. I thought it would be the end for me. A few of our guests, responding to all the noise, opened the kitchen door as he was squeezing my throat so that I couldn't talk or breathe. I made only strange sounds when I tried to call out to them. Most of the others pushed in behind them. I waved my arms for help, but I knew I couldn't wait for someone to react. I had to do something fast before I blacked out. I groped for something on the counter behind me to use as a weapon and found the carving knife handle. I grabbed it and shoved the blade into his left arm just as I started to lose consciousness. As the knife plunged in and I withdrew it, he released his grip on my throat. As soon as I could breathe and talk, I shouted, "Here's your divorce!" I stabbed him a second time, this time in his left thigh, pushing the blade in harder and twisting it. I couldn't allow myself to kill him, but I wanted him to suffer. He staggered and turned toward the guests as he tripped over the turkey on the floor. He landed on top of the oversized bird, and they both skidded across the kitchen floor as though he was belly-flopping on a sled. Todd's blood spurted everywhere. I was soaked with it, and several of the guests got splattered too. It even hit the ceiling. I dropped the knife from my shaking hand and collapsed onto the floor.

One of the guests called 911. The paramedics took us both to the hospital, while the police took statements from those guests who had entered the kitchen early enough to see the last parts of our fight.

CHAPTER 13 – HOSPITAL

When Lori woke up in the hospital on the morning after Thanksgiving, she had trouble recognizing her surroundings. As she brought her room and her near death experience into focus, she thanked God for her survival but also begged forgiveness for what she remembered doing to Todd. She wondered whether he had died in their kitchen or if he was in this hospital with her. Were the police outside her room, and would they arrest her when she was well enough to leave this place? She pressed the call button.

"Good morning. How may we assist you?"

Lori didn't know how well the intercom picked up voices, and she hadn't said one word since her battle with Todd, so she yelled rather than spoke her response.

"I need someone to come in here and tell me what happened since I blacked out in my kitchen. I also need to know whether my husband is dead or in this hospital with me."

The disembodied female voice said, "I'll hear you better if you don't yell. Dr. Raskin will visit you as soon as he finishes with his current patient. After he sees you, I'll arrange for some food for you. You probably haven't eaten in seventeen hours."

Lori didn't know why, but she wondered whether that voice was robotic or human. Then she realized that she hadn't been a patient in a hospital since they took her tonsils out as a small child. It was all bare walls and hard surfaces here. The only decorations were electrical sockets, colored lights, plus cables and tubes connecting her to some kind of scientific instrument. She felt a bit like a puppet dangling on its strings. Her neck and her head hurt when she moved. She found that she had no pain when she wiggled her toes or the fingers on her left hand. The right hand and arm were a different story. They were stiff and didn't want to move at all. *That could be a problem. I'm right-handed.*

The pale green steel door with its small glass window opened, revealing the arrival of Dr. Raskin. Lori felt reassured that he followed the rules and used the hand sanitizer as he entered.

"Good morning, Mrs. Weatherford. I'm pleased to see you awake and functioning after your ordeal. I'm Ralph Raskin, and I'll be your primary physician while you're here. Would you do me a favor and greet me using a full sentence?"

"Hello, Dr. Raskin. How long was I unconscious?"

"That's very good. May I call you Lori? We gave you some medications to relax you when you first arrived. You were out for about sixteen hours after we first treated you. Now, would you raise both arms as high as you can?"

Lori had no trouble raising her left arm above her head, but her right arm refused to lift more than about six inches from its horizontal position.

"That's all right, Lori. Don't keep trying. You may lower both arms to the bed again."

"What's wrong with me, Doctor? Am I paralyzed?"

"Your system had quite a shock during that struggle with your husband. You may have suffered a minor stroke, or the resistance of your right arm to movement may be an emotional reaction to your ordeal. I don't believe it will be a permanent condition. Can you move your right foot?"

Lori did so without difficulty.

"There you are. I suggest that you have a temporary emotional reaction affecting only the arm that you used to strike out at your husband. A stroke would tend to affect your whole right side. Is your neck bothering you from the choking?"

"Just a little. I can handle that. What about my husband? Is Todd dead? Will he recover from his wounds?"

"Todd lost a lot of blood, but we replaced it during several hours of emergency surgery. He's alive, but in an induced coma while we wait for his vital signs to approach normal values."

Lori started to cry uncontrollably. "I didn't want to stab him, but I had no choice. He had me down to my last few breaths. I didn't want to die. I never saw him so angry. It must have been adrenalin giving me the courage to do it. After it was over, I lost all my strength and slipped into darkness. I'm still shaking when I think about it."

Dr. Raskin did his best to sound reassuring. "Lori, we're here to heal your body and ease your mind of negative thoughts that may be affecting your body. You don't have to torment yourself with bad memories. The sooner you separate yourself from thoughts about your trauma, the more rapidly you will heal.

"I see from your file that you're a teacher. There's no reason why you shouldn't be able to return to your school and career after we release you, but it will take much longer to adjust to the absence of your husband. Assuming he survives, it would be dangerous for you to continue living together."

"Doctor, do you consider me a potential murderer?"

"I try to stick to medical matters in my professional opinions. If you'll take my words as being personal and not based on any special training, I'll say that I also would have fought back against someone trying to kill me. Life is sacred. You have every right to try to preserve yours."

"Thank you, Doctor."

"One other question. You said that Todd was drunk when he attacked you. Would you say he was drunker than you had seen him before?"

"I hadn't thought of that. Yes, Todd was further gone than when he came home after drinking with his work buddies. Why did you ask that question?"

"He may have struck out at you because he was taking medications and drinking at the same time. He didn't completely regain consciousness before we put him into an induced coma. We'll check the medication question with him when he wakes up."

"I don't remember ever seeing him take pills. He was afraid of doctors and hospitals. Anyway, medications wouldn't have been an excuse for his strangling me. Whatever his condition, I had to defend myself. I had no choice. He was trying to kill me." Lori started to cry.

"I don't mean to upset you. I only inquired because his medical condition may influence our selection of procedures for treating him. Please relax. The staff will bring you some food shortly. You're free to eat anything that is available. I'll check back with you in a few hours."

After Dr. Raskin left, Lori lapsed into an uneasy sleep that lasted for more than three hours. She saw herself walking down a narrow alley. Every few feet, a pair of hands would reach out from the wall on either side trying to choke her. She tried to run, but she had to dodge snakes that were slithering along her path.

When Lori awoke, she felt sweaty but relieved, and her thoughts came more freely. She considered what would have led up to Todd's attacking her. *Had he been on medications while he got drunk, as the doctor suggested? She knew he hid things from her. It was possible. Did he have an illness he had never revealed to her? Todd wouldn't have hidden his marriage from that woman. She must have gone after him with full knowledge that she was destroying a family. What kind of bitch would do that? The damned thing is that I probably would have agreed to a divorce if Todd hadn't badgered me for a decision while I had a house full of company and Thanksgiving dinner to prepare. Whether Todd recovers or not, I'll be all alone in the future. Nobody wants to live with a violent woman.*

CHAPTER 14 – FLASHBACK: TODD AND EMMA, PART 1

After their third sexual binge together, Todd rolled over and stared into Emma's eyes.

She looked back at his and saw something other than adoration. "What?

"This is a fancy hotel, and I enjoy having sex with you, but why did you pick me out of all the men in Chicago for your bed partner? You followed me to that remote bar when you could have found someone else much closer to home. I'm not Adonis or a movie star, just a Kentucky guy who reads a lot and likes to impress tourists."

"I'm not Aphrodite either, but I do get something unique out of sex with you. You're right, though. I did select you for special reasons. I can't give you the whole story yet, but you have the appearance and personality to fit into a larger adventure in my life. You, Todd, if you're willing, can help me achieve my destiny."

"That sounds as though you're using me as a tool and only because I have the look you want. Would Todd Weatherford ever become an essential part of Emma Read's life and destiny?"

"Possibly, I already mentioned that I'll need a host and lover at the resort I'm building. Even so, there will be many strides up the road before I can say for sure how you might fit into my future."

"What's the first stride? Tell me that much."

"You have to get me pregnant."

"Wow! I didn't expect that one. Do we then go to your place in the West Indies and live happily ever after?"

"Maybe, but only if you're willing to divorce your wife."

Todd realized that this woman was more complex than anyone he had met before. "You move in on me with the obvious expectation that it will break up my marriage, and then you say there's something long term only if I want to leave my wife? Dammit! You undermined my marriage from that first night in the tavern. I don't want to leave my wife, but you're pushing me in that direction. How could I get you pregnant and not leave my wife? I'm back to thinking you're using me, and I won't be anyone's tool."

"Cheer up, Todd. Women have been using men since time began. It's our job. The difference here is that if you help me, you'll end up living a much more luxurious and satisfying life than you ever could here."

"So, you are aiming to move me to your part of the world. I assume there's more to your scheme than my getting you pregnant. I wouldn't have to leave town to do that. Who else is involved in your mystery, and where does the luxury come from?"

"You'll have to wait before I can tell you much more. For now, let's say that I have to have a child and be married by a certain date in order to come into a large amount of money."

"And you don't care whether the child or the marriage comes first?"

"Not at all, but the potential husband has to be free to marry and the father of the child. There will be DNA testing."

"So, before I get you pregnant, I have to commit to not just leaving, but divorcing my wife, marrying you, and moving to the West Indies."

"That's pretty much it."

"I'll bet you have a few other commitments you'll require of me."

"I can't swear that I won't."

"Emma, you do realize the easiest and sanest thing for me to do is to walk out on you right now."

"I wouldn't blame you at all if you did."

CHAPTER 15 – TODD AND EMMA, PART 2

The next evening, as Todd and Emma separated and rolled to opposite sides of the king-sized bed, Todd asked, "Where did you learn your techniques? They're always different and unlike any I've experienced in Kentucky or Chicago. How many times will we have sex before you start repeating yourself?"

"As many times as it takes for you to decide to hook up with me for the long run."

"I've enjoyed hooking up with you so far, no question about that. The problem is that I think of a life with you, and I see myself flying high but then going down in flames. You said your dad was an RAF flyer. Did he have a long retirement, or did he flame out?"

"Our relationship has nothing to do with Dad, but if you must know, he got lost in a fog bank in Guatemala and crashed into a mountain."

"What the hell was an RAF transport pilot doing in Guatemala?"

"They refused to tell me. Something hush-hush, no doubt. Anyway, the powers that governed his life gave me a whole lot of money to keep quiet about the incident."

"They took your father away from you and called it an incident? How old were you at the time?"

"Nineteen and finishing up at the local college. It hardened my outlook as I set out to face the world on my own. Don't feel sorry for me, though. Dad left me with lots of family and government connections plus material goodies."

Todd propped himself up on his elbow and tried to read her thoughts. "Wouldn't you rather have your father than all he left you?"

"Sure I would, but he prepared me for a sudden end to his life. He was in a dangerous business, and he knew it. He was a swash-buckler from the word go."

"And you think you're a swash-buckler too. I can feel it in this fabric of mystery you're weaving around yourself. If we do have a child together, are you prepared to be a good long-term mother, or would that child be a pawn in the strange game you're playing?"

"I honestly can't answer that question."

"That may have been the first thing you've said that I can trust as the truth."

"Here's another truth. I'm up against an absolute deadline, so I'll need you to commit within one week to fathering my child, plus living and working with me, or I'll have to move on and find someone else."

"That one week deadline is Thanksgiving. Lori and I will have a bunch of company over for dinner. It will screw up both of our families if I ask for a divorce before Thanksgiving. Extend that time limit, and you're more likely to get me to break off with Lori."

"No extensions, Todd, and no more sex until you make your commitment to me. Get dressed and get on your way. I have to take a trip for a few days, so I won't be at this hotel unless you contact me within the next couple of days. Then I'll be gone

Richard Davidson

until after Thanksgiving, when I'll be at the Rising
Star in the early evenings."

CHAPTER 16 – SOLILOQUY

The next day, as Todd prepared for his first walking tour amidst the many posters for events going on in Chicago, he found himself fixated on an announcement for the new production of Shakespeare's *Hamlet*. The poster featured an actor in the middle of a bare stage with red letters going diagonally upward asking, "To be or not to be?" For Todd, they read, "To go or not to go?"

Is this a bizarre temptation? Is it my one opportunity to make myself someone special? Lori thinks I'm not special now. She wants me to go back to school and train for a different career. My dad never had a career. He ran a grocery store and then worked in a gas station, but he's happy. Emma's dad was a swash-buckling RAF pilot, but he ended up crashing into a mountain. Is Emma trying to change me just as Lori was?

Even if I decide to go with Emma, I'll have to tell her about my health problem. That might screw up the whole deal before it gets started Dr. Kanden scared me with her talk about lupus meaning my immune system was turning against me. She said I could die from it but she could help me control it – probably. That gets me back to 'To be or not to be?' and all its worries.

One thing's for sure. If I commit to Emma's project it won't be for the sex. I'll show Lori that I can be someone and accomplish something. I'll go into this with my eyes wide open and give myself a guarantee of some reward.

I'll call Emma and meet her for a serious talk tomorrow.

CHAPTER 17 – NEGOTIATION

Todd knocked loudly three times on Emma's hotel room door to show he was firm in his outlook toward this meeting.

Emma answered the door wearing filmy pajamas and invited him in.

As she reached to extend her arms around Todd's neck, he pushed her away.

"This isn't a sex visit. I'm here to negotiate our future – together or separate. Go put on your street clothes so that I won't get distracted."

Without saying a word, Emma took some clothes and went into the bathroom to change. She returned wearing blue jeans and a yellow blouse.

"Is this satisfactory for formal discussions?"

"Fine. I've thought about everything you said, and I decided to join up with your project if you agree to some conditions. If you don't agree, I go back to Lori, and I won't see you again."

Emma sat on the bed and patted the mattress, inviting him to sit next to her. Todd shook his head and sat on the desk.

"I have to be sure that I get some real benefit out of this deal, no matter what happens in the future. My folks, my brothers and my sister have always been poor, just barely getting along. If it's as important as you say for me to get involved, I want four Certificates of Deposit for fifty thousand dollars each in the names of my father and mother, my sister, and my two brothers. They'll have to be issued by a Chicago bank today so that I can mail them before you leave for that several-day trip you mentioned."

Emma smiled. "I agree. What else do you need?"

Surprised by how easily Emma had agreed to his money request, Todd added something he didn't think she would like. "If I get you pregnant as requested, the child must be raised with the family name of Weatherford." He thought this stipulation would show whether she wanted him rather than any convenient guy.

Emma hesitated slightly before responding. "That was a surprise requirement, but I agree to that too. Now tell me why it's important to you."

"I have two reasons. First, because you promised luxury and achievements down the road, and no Weatherford in my family has ever had such status. My second reason is that I may not be with the child while he or she grows up, and I want my family name to continue."

"What do you mean? Are you planning to bail out on me?"

"Not intentionally, Emma, but I'm not well. I discovered a while before I met you that I have lupus. I take medications for it, and it will require long-term doctoring."

She stood and hugged him. "I'll make sure you get proper treatments, but your health problem requires me to demand a few protective steps."

"I said this was a negotiation. What do you need?"

"I told you that the father of my child must marry me and prove by DNA samples that he is the father."

"Right. So?"

"Just in case you die from your disease before we marry in the West Indies, I'll need a large number of DNA test swabs from you plus a letter telling anyone who thinks otherwise that you are alive and living with me."

"That's fine, but if I die, who will you marry and pass off as being me?"

"I already have a backup candidate at home who looks quite like you but is impotent and can't have children. That's why I latched on to you so quickly after I met you."

"You would marry him, but supply my DNA samples?"

"Only if necessary because you died too soon. So long as you are alive, I promise to be a good wife to you."

"But if you have to marry him, you'll have him change his name to mine so that our child is raised as a Weatherford?"

"Absolutely."

"Then I think we have a deal with protections on both sides. It's time for me to get you pregnant and tell Lori on Thanksgiving that I need a divorce."

"Don't worry too much about the first item. You already got me pregnant."

CHAPTER 18 – DIVORCE PAPERS

Two weeks after the Thanksgiving battle, Todd sat in his hospital bed exercising his left arm by squeezing a soft rubber ball. He heard a knock on the door; it opened, revealing Lori and another woman. The stranger spoke first.

"Todd, I'm Rebecca Warren, and I'm here today with Lori to discuss the divorce you wanted. If you and Lori can be calm with each other at this point, we should be able to get matters settled quickly. If not, this may become a hostile action requiring a lengthy amount of time."

Todd motioned with his right hand for them to come closer. "Please come in. I'm sorry, Lori. That disaster was totally my fault. I was worse than high on prescription medicines combined with booze. Thanks for not killing me. Most people in your position would have struck at vital organs, but you held off doing that."

"I thought for sure you would have killed me if I didn't strike back, but I could never be a killer, especially with you."

"You're amazing. I screwed up terribly. At this point, there's no return, so we should make the divorce go as smoothly as possible."

Rebecca said, "We were hoping you'd feel that way. I've drawn up a set of divorce papers. Look them over. Then discuss them with an attorney to determine any changes you want. After that, we can get back together and settle things quickly."

"Lori, did you read these papers?"

"I did, Todd. Rebecca says they're pretty standard. We don't have a lot to split up. Dad would insist that I keep the house."

"The house and everything valuable is yours. I ruined our marriage, and now I should pay for it. I'll give your papers a quick read, and I'll sign them here and now if they don't contain anything weird. Give them to me."

Rebecca handed Todd the papers. He started to read them.

"Todd, ethics require that I strongly suggest you have your own lawyer review the papers. I can't represent both of you."

"Back where I come from, we decide for ourselves whether a deal makes sense, and then we shake hands on it. That's good enough for me. How about you, Lori?"

"Keep reading the papers, Todd. If you agree with them, we're good, but I'm not the best at shaking hands right now. My right hand doesn't move well yet."

"That does it. Give me a pen, and I'll sign. You sign as well as you can, Lori, and Rebecca can be a witness. Do we need to call a nurse to be a second witness?"

Rebecca nodded. "That would be a good idea. We should have someone who is impartial."

Todd pushed his call button.

The speaker came to life. "Do you need assistance, Mr. Weatherford?"

"Please come in here. I need you to witness my signature on a legal paper."

A minute later, a nurse in her early forties entered. She addressed the visitors. "Hello, I'm Maria Diaz. Let me know what you need me to do."

Rebecca introduced herself and Lori. "Mr. and Mrs. Weatherford have consented to a divorce. They will each sign these papers to indicate their agreement. Then you and I will sign to witness that we saw them add their signatures to the document. Is that clear, Maria?"

"Perfectly clear, and I know Mrs. Weatherford from when she was here with us recently."

Todd signed the papers first and then gave them to Rebecca to hand to Lori, who was sitting near the window. Maria gave Lori a clipboard so that she could sign the papers on her lap without having to lift her right hand very high. Maria and Rebecca added their signatures as witnesses. Maria left the room, and then Rebecca addressed Todd and Lori.

"I'll file these papers with the court. It should be a formality, and you won't be required to appear there. I'll emphasize that Todd is still in the hospital if anyone raises the question of an appearance. You'll probably want to minimize contacts with each other until your traumatic memories have faded. I wish that you both have fortunate separate futures. Are you ready to leave, Lori?"

"One moment." Lori walked over to Todd and kissed his forehead gently. "Now I'm ready. I had to clear my heart of any remaining hatred toward you, Todd."

CHAPTER 19 – RISING STAR

When Todd entered the Rising Star tavern, he looked first at the table where Emma Read usually sat, waiting for him. She wasn't there, but as he scanned the rest of the room, he spotted fellow guides Sylvia Troon and Frank Giustini sitting at their usual table by the emergency exit. He approached them leaning on his crutch and walking slowly.

"Hello, you two. If you saved all the money you spend in this place, you could get married or open up your own bar."

Sylvia got up and kissed him on his cheek. "Welcome back, Todd. It's good to see you back on your three legs." She nudged his crutch lightly with her toe.

Frank stood and shook hands. "Todd, you're the last one who should recommend marriage to us. You barely survived that battle with your wife."

"That was my fault. I got super drunk and attacked her. Now Lori will have to face life on her own. I hope she finds someone better than me real soon."

Frank looked at Sylvia. "I know I won't ever find someone better than Syl. I've talked about marriage a bunch of times, but she's holding out for me to change my name to Troon. She doesn't like Giustini."

"You two could get married but keep your own names. Hold off the name debate until you have children."

"That's a good point, Todd. Syl, what if I agree to have the kids be Troons? Would that change your mind?"

"It might, but let's see if we can come up with a different name for all of us that we can both live with."

"Then, you're saying you'll marry me?"

"Of course I am, Frank. It was only a question of when I got tired of badgering you. After seeing what happened to Todd's marriage, I think it's time for us to mellow out and take the big step."

Todd extended his right hand palm down over their heads. "Bless you, my children, and congratulations."

After Sylvia and Frank finished several rounds of hugs and kisses, she asked, "Todd, what are you going to do? Are you running off with that witch who broke up your marriage?"

"I won't give Emma that tag, but I am wondering where she is. Has she been in here looking for me?"

Frank shook his head negatively, his red beard and long hair standing out from his head. "Watch your step, man. I agree with Syl. That woman is dangerous, and she's been setting traps for you all along. She came in here the night after Thanksgiving, and when she heard us talking about the battle you had with Lori, she asked whether you had killed each other. We said we didn't know, and she left without showing any emotion, except for a cynical smile. If you leave town with her, you'll have no backup. Make her stay around here for a while so that we and your other friends can help you with any problems. You're not ready to travel yet anyway."

"Thanks for the support, Frank, but I'm enough of a big boy to be cautious in my dealings with her. Besides, if I let her take me to her home in the West Indies, I'll be in position to set up a great honeymoon for you two."

Sylvia put her hand on Frank's arm. "Listen to Todd. That honeymoon could turn into a gig as tour guides in a much warmer place than Chicago."

CHAPTER 20 – DISAPPEARING ACT

Todd wasn't particularly bothered by Emma's absence from the Rising Star for the first two evenings after his return to that watering hole, but during the following few days he began to realize that she had lied about being in a rush to fly back to the West Indies with him. He felt justified that he had insisted on those certificates of deposit for his family, but sad because he had lost Lori and might never see Emma again. Todd didn't know what kind of game Emma was playing, but he knew it was time to act instead of waiting for her to take advantage of him again. He barely noticed how quickly he shifted from picturing Emma as his second wife to viewing her as his enemy.

During a final evening visit to the Rising Star, Todd met with Frank and Sylvia and arranged for them to call him if Emma Read showed up again. In the meantime, he would go home to Kentucky for some family support and thinking time to develop future plans, with or without Emma.

The shock of her double cross and disappearance hurt, but it had also changed him. Todd would no longer lack ambition and settle for the minor blessings of life. Emma had wronged him and driven him to ruin Lori's life. He had faced death and survived. If Emma wanted war instead of love, he would be ready for her next move. He was sure she wouldn't settle for the damage she'd already caused.

CHAPTER 21 – FAMILY DISCUSSIONS

The elder Weatherfords welcomed Todd home and told him that they had left his old bedroom unchanged since his last visit with Lori. The older siblings, Carter, Hampton, and Amy had all married and moved away, the boys to Lexington and Amy to Louisville, so nobody would disturb Todd while he worked on his future plans. Although Todd's crutch and divorce were surprises, his mom and dad accepted the news calmly. They would wait for their son to feel comfortable about discussing the missteps that had driven him to the sanctuary of home.

After supper on the third evening, Todd asked his father to join him for a beer in the back yard. They sat on the old stone wall that had played a major role in Todd's childhood adventures. A loose stone led to a large internal space where young Todd had hidden his treasures.

Todd started the conversation by asking, "Did you receive the Certificate of Deposit I sent?"

"We did, and so did your brothers and your sister. You must be doing really well to be sending us all that money. Thanks for thinking of us, but you didn't have to do that. We get along, no matter what comes our way."

"There's a strange story behind that money, and I want you to hear all of it because I'll need your help and guidance going forward. I thought I'd better tell you outside to keep Mom from getting upset by my screw-ups."

"Hold it right there, Todd. There's nothing going to make your ma more upset than having you leave her out of this conversation. The wellbeing of both of us depends on including her. Uncap a third beer while I get her. Then give us the whole story."

When George Weatherford returned with his wife, Judy, they sat on the wall, toasted their son with their beers and waited for him to gather his thoughts.

Todd looked first at them and then off across the field as he related everything that had happened since he and Lori had visited them several months into their marriage. He omitted nothing, not even Dr. Kanden's diagnosis of lupus and the medications he had taken secretly. "... and then, after I finally got out of the hospital after signing the divorce papers for Lori, I discovered that Emma had left town without any concern about me or my condition. She manipulated me into getting angry and attacking Lori. One or both of us could have died; we were both tagged as critical in the hospital. Emma probably would have laughed at that result. I don't know how I could have thought she was my future."

George nodded. "Todd, Son, you've been had, and don't think for one minute that Emma Read ever really cared for you. She wanted something, to get pregnant by you. Having accomplished that, she went home."

Todd nodded. "Wherever home is. If she was at all truthful, it's somewhere in the West Indies, but I don't have any idea where to look for her."

George looked at Judy and gestured for her to respond.

"Todd, we know exactly where to look for her.

"Where, Mom?"

Loyalties

"It's a long story."

CHAPTER 22 – THE WEATHERFORDS

George Weatherford packed and lit his pipe before beginning. "Before we directly answer your question about Emma Read's whereabouts, we'll have to give you some family history. Our family is an old one in this country, dating back to before the Revolutionary War."

Todd interrupted. "I never knew that. I could have used that information in some of my tour guide speeches. Inserting a little family pride makes you part of the show."

"The reason for our downplaying the history of our family is that most of them were on the losing side in that war. They were almost all Loyalists. They enjoyed a privileged life under the King's rule, and they weren't about to join the American rabble and rock the boat by fighting for change. We weren't proud of their position and never talked about it."

"Give me some details. Who was the head of the family back then?"

"My incomplete knowledge of the family history goes back to Martin Weatherford. He was unusual for his time because he had an interracial marriage. His first wife was listed in the genealogies as Mary Jane Halfblood. She was descended from Creek Indians. They had five children: Charles, William, James, John, and Catharine. John was the only one of them who supported the American rebels. His father cut him off without a penny of support when he joined the Continental Army. Because of his courage to break with his family and support the American side, we choose to think of him as our ancestor; but I'm not even sure he had children. Sometimes, people interpret incomplete genealogy information to fit their own preferences."

"I never would have guessed that if our family was here that long ago, they would have supported the British or been descended in part from Indians. Interesting stuff. Where did they live?"

"Martin was born in Virginia and had quite a bit of land there, but most of the family moved to Augusta, Georgia around 1757. That land and family wealth was the key to why they were Loyalists. They were happy with the British government because they thrived under it. John was only three years old when the family moved to Georgia and must have moved to Augusta with them, but when he grew older, he argued with the others over politics and the importance of freedom over wealth. When John couldn't convince the other family members to back the rebellion against British rule, he chose to live in South Carolina, when he wasn't actively serving in the Continental Army. He probably lost contact with all the Loyalists in the family.

"I don't know when John's mother, Mary Jane Weatherford died, but Martin married for a second time around 1775, to a woman named Isabella. She would have been Martin's wife when John left for the Continental Army."

"Did they have children?"

Todd's mother laughed. "They sure did. The Weatherfords were very fertile, but not at all creative. What messes up the family tree is that they had favorite names that they used over and over again. Martin's second batch of children with Isabella included Henrietta, John William, William

Henry, Catherine (Caty), Charles, Richard, Charlotte, and Sarah."

"Mom, you're saying that Martin had two sons named John, two named Charles, two named William, and two daughters named Catherine. That certainly is weird. Isabella must have been much younger than Martin to have had that many children during that second marriage."

"He would have been close to fifty years old when he married her, so he was still siring children at an advanced age."

George said, "The use of repeated names is unusual, but something more unique is that Martin's first son Charles, whose mother was Mary Jane Halfblood, married a Creek Indian woman named Sehoy III. The Creeks had a female-dominated society, and she was high up in it. Their son, William, became Chief Red Eagle of the upper Creek towns in Alabama and led warrior groups that were known as the Red Sticks against the Lower Creek towns and the United States Army during the Creek War of 1813-1814. He was an angry man who wanted to push the Americans out of Creek territory. Chief Red Eagle was backed by the British during the War of 1812 because they wanted the Americans to be fighting two wars at once. Red Eagle finally had to surrender to General Andrew Jackson, but went on to become a wealthy slave-owning planter."

"Let's get back to the Revolutionary War Loyalist aspects of the family, George."

"Right, Judy. Even during that war, our family was involved with the Creek Indians. During the siege of Augusta, Martin and most of his sons served in the Augusta Loyalist Militia. That was a terrible battle where the Loyalists were defeated, but not before the King's appointed commander, Thomas Brown, hanged thirteen rebel prisoners and burned others alive. Martin was appointed conductor of the Creek Indians. Later, he led three hundred Creek warriors in an attempt to push back the American rebels when Savannah was under attack. They put up quite a fight, but Savannah fell to the Americans anyway."

CHAPTER 23 – 1778 SIEGE OF AUGUSTA

In the woods outside Augusta, American Lieutenant Commander Elijah Clark spoke to four of his key men.

"Some of our soldiers were captured in the Mackey House when we had to retreat. The enemy hanged some of them and has since burned that house. Our scouts report that prisoners were alive and still inside during the fire. Their screams were agonizing to hear. These people aren't wealthy landowners; they're beasts. We have to strike back at such viciousness. You four are our best sharpshooters. I want two of you to approach what remains of the Mackey House from the east and two from the west. Shoot as many of the Loyalist bastards as you can, and then slip away during the confusion. We'll have long memories about the way our fellow colonists treated prisoners. This war won't last forever. Treachery will be punished."

A short while later, Benjamin and John silently approached the burned-out house and observed a group of enemy militia soldiers discussing the day's events. One tall individual stood apart from the others, leaning on a fencepost to write in a diary. As they prepared to shoot, John Weatherford grabbed Benjamin's arm. "On my signal get as many in that group as you can, but don't shoot that tall man by the fencepost. He's my father. I hate what he represents, but I can't be responsible for his death."

Benjamin nodded and shifted several paces away so that they would shoot from two different angles. He waited for John's signal and then fired, hitting his target in the head. He reloaded as quickly as possible and heard John fire during the process. A second man fell. Benjamin fired again. He knew John would be reloading. The targeted group of militia soldiers started to run away while he reloaded. He heard John's second shot and saw one grab his thigh and fall. Benjamin fired a third time and saw his target fall to the ground and unsuccessfully attempt to crawl away. Then he heard John's signal to retreat. As Benjamin turned to filter back into the woods, he saw the man with the diary crouching behind that fencepost, unhurt. John would be relieved that his father survived.

CHAPTER 24 – BANISHED

Todd shifted his seat to escape the smoke from his father's pipe when the wind changed direction. "So, the Loyalist family members fought for their beliefs, but I'm sure they equally wanted to preserve their wealth. What happened to them when the British lost the war?"

George Weatherford took the hint when his son moved farther away from him. He knocked the ashes out of his pipe. They fell onto the bare ground and he stepped on the remaining glowing embers. "After the war ended, it wasn't safe to be out in public in Georgia if you were a Loyalist. Many people were beaten, hanged, or murdered because of their political stance. One day Martin, Charles, and a friend were walking toward town when they saw a crowd approaching.

Martin scanned the front rank of the approaching people. Most of them were men, but a few were lower class women. All of them had sided with the American rabble in the war. "Boys, this doesn't look good. We'd better make a run for it to avoid contact with these people. They look angry."

Martin and Charles had lived in the area for years, and they knew every path through the woods and every rocky obstacle. They left the road and darted into the thickest part of the surrounding woods. Charles' friend, Robert, followed them, but being a stranger to the area, he couldn't keep up. Charles kept yelling for him to go faster, but soon Robert could no longer hear those calls. Robert did the best he could, but he wasn't even sure he was moving in a single direction. The tangle of thorn bushes and vines made him take multiple detours.

Just when he thought he had gone far enough to lose his pursuers, Robert heard voices coming from several directions. He didn't know which way to run, so he hid in a gap beneath a fallen tree and prayed that he wouldn't be seen.

The voices were all around him now, and he realized he hadn't escaped the mob. Several people passed within a few feet of him, but didn't detect his hiding place. Robert began to hope he wouldn't be found. The sounds of the people moving through the woods grew fainter.

Then, Robert heard different noises. Several children had followed their parents in the crowd, but had lagged behind. The hike through the woods was play time for them, and they called out to each other as they dodged obstacles. One of the boys had a dog he called Doodle. That animal hardly noticed the obstacles that sidetracked people, as he followed scent trails. When he came across an unfamiliar smell, Doodle followed it, leaving the paths the children had taken. He ignored his master calling, "Doodle, come here!" Then he heard something moving. Surprise! He found a man curled up in a hiding place under a fallen tree trunk. Doodle barked long and loud to show how proud he was of his discovery. The man said some words to him that he didn't understand, but soon his master and the other children came running. They were followed by adults who had heard the barking. Doodle felt like a hero.

When the adults arrived, they pulled Robert from his hiding place and tied his hands behind his back. One asked, "Should we hang this Loyalist pig right here? We have plenty of rope, and some strong branches."

Another said, "No, you know the plan. We have a surprise brewing for him at the Taylor farm. The others are coming. Bring him along, and we'll have a party."

At the Taylor farm, behind the barn, the crowd, singing patriotic songs and cursing their prisoner, approached a large metal tub, heating on an open fire.

A man who appeared to be the leader said, "Take off his clothes."

Many people, male and female, responded, tearing the prisoner's clothes as they removed them. Soon, Robert stood in the center of a circle of jeering onlookers, naked as the day he was born. He dreaded what would happen next.

Robert's screams were ghastly as people rushed to cover him with hot tar.

One joked, "Now you'll be even warmer than you were with those clothes we took off you."

Then women ran up with bags of chicken feathers and threw them over the sticky tar. Robert looked more like a stuffed toy than a human by the time they finished.

As a final act of degradation, they tied Robert to a long fence post passed between his legs, then had two strong men pick up the ends of the post and parade the tarred and feathered Robert around the bonfire and then down the road to the center of the nearest village. There, they dumped him in the middle of the square. A sign around Robert's neck read *THE KING'S GARBAGE.*

The Weatherfords kept to themselves and hoped that hatred for the losers would soon blow over, but it didn't. In 1782, the Weatherfords were included in a list of people from whom the state of Georgia would confiscate lands and property. This edict was followed in 1783 by a proclamation banning them from the state of Georgia. They had to abandon all their former property and leave the state. Our family, along with most of the other Loyalists, could hardly believe how badly they were being treated by their neighbors and former friends."

"Where did they go? Loyalists wouldn't have been any more welcome in the other states."

Judy had mostly listened up to this point, but now she took over the narrative. "Florida was divided into two parts in those days. The Peninsula was called East Florida and had its capital at St. Augustine. It had been taken by the British after early exploration and settling by the Spanish. Many in the British government considered it their fourteenth colony in America. Spain retained and governed West Florida, which included the current Florida panhandle, but extended all the way to the Mississippi River. The American rebels had never gained a significant following in East Florida, so Martin's family moved there, hoping that the British would reward their Loyalist followers with Florida land grants."

"Did they end up doing well in Florida, Mom?"

"You get a yes and a no on that one. They had to leave everything behind in Georgia, but the British government in Florida gave them modest tracts of land. While they lived in Florida, Martin Weatherford learned that the new governor of Georgia had taken the Weatherford property as his personal prize. Martin vowed that he would sue to regain his property once a postwar legal framework had been established.

Within a year of the Weatherfords arrival in Florida, the Treaty of Paris officially ended the Revolutionary War, and its terms changed the family's future once again. East Florida had been Spanish territory until a previous treaty gave it to Britain following an earlier war between those two countries. Spain had joined France and a few other countries in supporting the American side against the British. As a reward to their ally, the Americans insisted that the treaty require Britain to return East Florida to Spain. In exchange, Britain negotiated that Spain would leave their outposts in the Bahamas. As soon as the Spanish took over in East Florida, they demanded that the British Loyalists leave, although they gave them a transition period of one year."

"Where did they all go?"

"A whole bunch of places. Some went to England, some to Canada, some disavowed their loyalty to England and stayed in Florida under Spanish rule. Our branch of your dad's family decided to head west into the wilderness areas, where relationships would not be based as much on support or opposition during the Revolutionary War."

"Where did Martin Weatherford and his immediate family go?"

"They were among a large group of Loyalists who went to the islands of the Bahamas."

"Were they British colonies?"

"That's a very good question, and it caused problems for the British."

CHAPTER 25 – FIXING THE BAHAMAS

Todd's father, George, continued the story. "In the early 1600's the Bahamas had a small number of European settlers, but they were mostly a haven for pirates. Much earlier, Spanish Conquistadores had slaughtered and enslaved the indigenous Lucayans, removing the survivors to other Spanish colonies. At various times, the British, Spanish, and French attempted to control the islands, but no country succeeded for very long.

"As British colonies were settled in North America during the middle of that century, King Charles II awarded the Province of Carolina to eight insiders whom he called Cousins and Counselors. Six of the eight received the extra grant of all the islands in the Bahamas two years later. These so-called Lords Proprietors were supposed to govern and settle the Bahamas, but they mostly ignored the islands and occasionally sent scoundrels and misfits there to assert their authority."

Todd said, "That sounds strange. You're saying that the Carolina colony had the islands as their own colony."

"The King's buddies as a group owned both territories and could sell real estate or issue land grants. The Carolinas and the Bahamas were their private countries, to the extent that they could control them. They certainly couldn't control the Bahamas, and during the Revolutionary War, the Spanish captured and governed New Providence Island and Nassau. Ships carrying a force of American Loyalists and Out Island Bahamas

65

settlers called conches recaptured New Providence and the Abaco Islands in 1783, but they did so nine days after the signing of the Treaty of Paris that gave the Bahamas to the British in exchange for East Florida. It was a battle that never needed to happen.

"In order to control land grants following the Treaty of Paris, Parliament bought the interests of the Lords Proprietors, knowing that the many of the Loyalists moving to the Bahamas expected land in recognition of their past steadfast support."

Todd stood without his crutch and started limping back and forth. "All of this family history is interesting, but I thought you were going to tell me where I should expect to find Emma Read."

George stopped Todd by grabbing his shoulders. "Think it through, son. Martin and his offspring went to live in the Bahamas. They received significant land grants from the Crown for their loyal support. Some of that land is still in the family, and many younger relatives are hoping to get a share of it when their older relatives die. Emma manipulated you into getting her pregnant. That child will have Weatherford DNA that will give her a claim on family property. Now, tell me where you think she is."

"In the Bahamas, but where – which islands should I check? I still don't understand why she wanted to have my child. Our immediate family doesn't have any land there; do we, Dad?"

"I never talked about it, but we do."

CHAPTER 26 – ENTERPRISE

Todd looked at his father in disbelief. "You're telling me that we have land in the Bahamas, when I've spent my whole life thinking that we had nothing but our Kentucky house and the pay we received from our various jobs?"

"I guess I am."

"Why did you keep it a secret?"

"We've always enjoyed living in this area, and I never wanted to be more than a small town businessman. We felt that if our neighbors knew we had property elsewhere, they'd treat us differently. We don't have a lot of land in the Bahamas, but it has a prime location."

"Is it land that has been sitting vacant since Martin Weatherford's time?"

"Nope. My ancestors were smart enough to realize that Crown land grants were conditional upon doing something with the land. If your land sat idle too long, the government took it away from you."

"So what did your ancestors do, rent it out for farming?"

"Nope. It's had a store on it for a very long time. It started out as a general store when imported goods were hard to get. Back then, they did a good part of the business through bartering. More recently, it grew into a home improvement store. We're silent partners in it. Our family has been working with members of a different family for a very long time, almost two centuries. I wouldn't want your friend Emma to sabotage our business or our relationship with our partners."

"Let's not call her my friend anymore. I may have been seduced into becoming her lover, but it's clear now that she targeted me to father a child who would have a claim to our property. Tell me more about the business, our land, and its location. I'm going to have to go there and resolve this problem."

Judy said, "However you go after her, don't harm your unborn child. He or she is part of our family, intentionally or not."

CHAPTER 27 – PARTICULARS

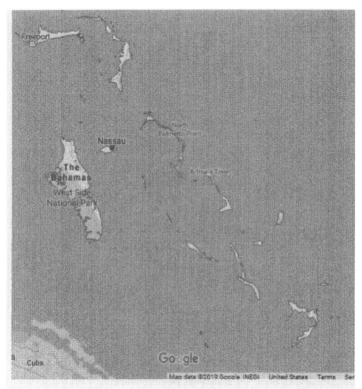

After lunch, George and Todd went into the family room, where George unfolded a map of the Bahamas and laid it on a card table.

Todd studied the map. "There are many more islands than I realized. I've only heard of a few of them."

"There are more than seven hundred islands, and the smaller islands are called cays. Most of the American Loyalists settled on three of them, so the important ones for land grants and government are New Providence, Abaco, and Eleuthera. Nassau is the capital, and it has the same borders as New Providence Island. It's also the seat of national government and where most of the legal maneuvering over land takes place."

"They could have just named that island, Nassau."

"Some people think of it that way.

"Where is the Weatherford family land and ours in particular?"

"It won't mean much to you until you get familiar with the Bahamas and Abaco Island specifically, but Martin received grants for 200 acres in Little Harbour on Abaco and the entire Bridges Cay. That's a tiny 29 acre island across the bay from Little Harbour. Our own family land is a sixty acre tract in Marsh Harbour. That's farther north from Little Harbour, and it's the most highly developed town on Abaco Island. It has an airport if you'll be flying in there. Our land is on the coast of the Sea of Abaco, the body of water between Great Abaco Island and the Out Islands or cays that form a barrier to the open ocean. People refer to our island as Great Abaco because there's a small semi-detached part at the extreme north end that is called Little Abaco."

"Dad, tell me more about the family you're in partnership with, and the person who's in charge of the store."

"We'll have to go deep into history for me to give you that background, and some of it might make you feel uncomfortable. When Martin Weatherford came from East Florida to claim his land, he brought six whites and twenty-five black slaves with him."

"I never thought of the possibility that he was a slave owner."

"All slaves in the Bahamas were freed between 1834 and 1839. Many, of course were free when they first arrived or were freed before British law required it. One English titled Lord, John Rolle, had plantations named Rolleville and Steventon on Exuma Island. When Britain decreed the end of slavery, Rolle gave the Exuma plantations to his former slaves and their descendents. Most of them took the family name of Rolle, which is now very common in the Bahamas. We've worked with one of the Rolle families for many years at the store, and my current partner there is Sandy Rolle. He's about ten years older than you. His dad, Tim, retired last year, but Sandy worked with him more than long enough to learn the business."

"So we have a business run as a partnership between a former slave-owning family and a former slave family. That's appropriate. I don't remember you being away very much. Do you ever go there?"

"I've been making an average of two short visits each year for a very long time. All those buying trips for our local store to Louisville and Atlanta were actually buying trips for both the Kentucky and Abaco stores. During those trips I also flew to Marsh Harbour in the Bahamas to meet first with Tim and later with Sandy."

"I wondered why you continued those trips, even after we closed our store in town."

"If you had asked, I had a cover story ready, about going out of town to take flying lessons and put in my required flying hours to remain active at it. You didn't ask, so I kept quiet about where I went."

"Dad, are you telling me you're a pilot?"

"I am, but I never bought a plane. I don't fly enough to warrant getting one. I drive to Lexington and rent a Cessna out of Blue Grass Field when I need to make a trip."

"Do you fly your rented plane to the Bahamas?"

"Sometimes, when I have a rush schedule, but mostly, I take commercial flights. The best airline flights are Lexington to Atlanta to Nassau to Marsh Harbour, but they're expensive and take a long time because of the stops."

"That's good info, Dad, but I think my first trip to Marsh Harbour will be by boat. It's not that far from Florida, and I'll want to get a feeling for the ocean and the islands."

"You may want to wait until you're rid of that crutch. The ocean can get rough."

"Don't worry, Dad; I'll be rid of it next week. Just tell me everything I should know about Sandy Rolle and your business there."

"I will, Todd, but consider it our business. I've wanted to get you involved for a long time. It's your turn to run our interests now. Tomorrow, I'll arrange for a company charge card in your name, and I'll email Sandy to watch for your arrival."

Loyalties

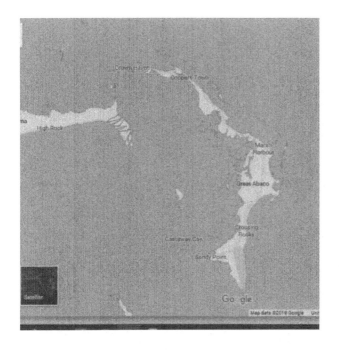

CHAPTER 28 – CREW

Sally, the bartender, took the phone call at the Rising Star. After a few minutes of conversation, she laid the receiver on the bar and walked to a table near the emergency exit.

"Frank, pick up the phone on the bar. It's for you." As Frank walked away, she winked at Sylvia. "Todd's on the line. I think you're going to like what he has to say. He gave me a hint or two."

"Is he coming back here? He went home to Kentucky."

"No more clues from me. I'll let you wait for Frank to give you the story." Sally walked away mumbling something about the luck of the Irish.

Frank picked up the phone anticipating something unusual based on Sally's attitude. "Hi, Todd. What's happening?"

"I wondered whether you and Syl had worked out your name revisions so that you could go ahead and get married. I gave your marriage my blessing, so I feel as though I have a stake in this process."

"You do indeed. When we get hitched, I want you to be my best man."

"Thanks, Frank; I'll consider it an honor."

"In answer to your question, we did morph our names to something we both like. Very shortly, Frank Giustini and Sylvia Troon will become Frank and Sylvia June."

"Have you filed the legal papers for that yet?"

"Yup. We have a certified copy of a Name Change Court Order signed by a judge, but it will take a while to get all our records changed to the new name."

"Great! You're all set for us to get you married and honeymooning in the Bahamas."

"You're moving pretty fast there, Todd. Slow down and tell me the whole story."

"I'll save the long version until I'm with you and Syl in person. The crux is that I've learned that I have property and a share in a business in the Bahamas. My dad kept it hidden for a long time. I'm going to the Bahamas, and I want you two to go with me. The honeymoon will be my wedding present to you, but in return, I may ask you to play a role in my future adventures."

"Gotcha! You're going after that Emma, and you want us to provide backup in case you run into trouble. That sounds like fun, but I'll have to run it past Syl when I tell her that you're pushing us toward that ceremony. I'll call you back in a little while. Thanks for the honeymoon offer and the promise of some excitement. I haven't had any since Special Forces days."

Before Todd finished his can of Blue Stallion beer, his cell phone rang. He answered while walking to loosen up his leg muscles, now free of crutch support.

"Hi, Frank; are you ready to move forward?"

Sylvia's voice soothed his ear. "Todd, you honey, of course we're with you. I'm looking forward to island living already. Frank and I have our passports. My only hang-up is that I promised my mom that I'd get married in a church when the time came. Dad always downplayed church, but it would mean a lot to Mom. Frank and I aren't worried about a particular denomination. Can we work that into your plans?"

"That won't be a problem at all. How much time will you need before you're ready for your ceremony and honeymoon? When we get to the Bahamas, I'll be nearby, but I won't interfere with your honeymoon privacy."

"Can you give us a week to quit our jobs and get ready?"

"The week is fine, but maybe you should take temporary breaks instead of quitting."

"We've already decided that we're done with Chicago winters. If you take us to the Bahamas, we'll stay there and find new jobs. It may take us a while to get a long-term work permit, but we'll do whatever the government there requires."

"That's an optimistic move. Once I get involved in the family company, I'll give you paperwork that says we need you. We'll be going by boat from Palm Beach, Florida. I just scanned the map. There are several churches within a convenient distance from both the airport and the inlet where we'll board our charter boat. I'll pick a church that looks good and make arrangements for your ceremony."

"That sounds perfect, Todd. Thanks for everything. We'll be ready in a week. After you make your arrangements, let us know where and when we'll meet."

CHAPTER 29 – DEPARTURE

Sylvia answered Frank's phone while he was in the shower. "Hi, Todd; is everything set?"

"I thought it was, but I didn't realize you'd be bringing a bellowing animal with you."

"That's the way Frank sings in the shower. I haven't had the guts to tell him his voice isn't beautiful. Besides, I'm getting to enjoy laughing at his singing."

"You may want to take notes on this. Try to arrive at Palm Beach International Airport by noon on Thursday. Phone or text me your flight number, and I'll be there to meet your plane when you arrive. Then we'll have an hour or so to relax and freshen up. At two o'clock, you two will meet with Father Michaels at St. Mark's Episcopal Church, north of the airport in Palm Beach Gardens, to discuss your outlook toward marriage and your preparedness for it. It will be a shortened version of their usual counseling requirement. The ceremony will follow at four o'clock. I don't know whether you and Frank are Episcopalians or some other denomination, but that's my church, and they're getting to be more open about backgrounds. Then, I have you booked in an almost-but-not-quite fancy hotel for your honeymoon night. We have a charter boat leaving early Friday from Palm Beach Inlet for Marsh Harbour on Great Abaco Island in the Bahamas. How does that all work for you two?"

"I have one question. What did you do with the old humble Kentucky tour guide we used to know? I never realized you could be this efficient at planning a trip and an event."

"Before I was a tour guide, I played in a band that did a lot of traveling. As the youngest guy in the group, I was stuck with making all the trip arrangements. It was hard work, but I learned the tricks required to coordinate ticketing, events, and sleeping spaces."

"It sounds as though you could get a job as a travel agent. Thanks for handling everything. My bellowing baritone is out of the shower now. I'll give him the schedule, and then we'll arrange our flight and contact you with the flight number. I can't believe that after all the time I spent sparring with Frank about marriage possibilities, we're actually taking the big step this week. I can hardly wait."

"Is there enough time for you to shop for a wedding dress?"

"Todd, I'm not that kind of girl. To me, the husband is the important part, not the dress. Don't worry about our not having enough time. I'll bring Frank up to date on the plans and then arrange for our flight."

Forty-five minutes later, Todd's phone rang. He picked it up and saw Frank's name. "Hi, which future spouse is using Frank's phone this time?"

Frank's voice answered. "I heard about your comments on my singing. It must have been distorted by the bathroom acoustics."

"Sure. That was it. Once we get to the islands, we'll let you give us a concert."

"I agree with all of your plans, and I have flight information for you."

"Go ahead; I'm ready to write it down, but remember to say 'we' instead of 'I' from now on."

"Good point; I need all the brownie points I can get. Anyway, our flight is American Airlines 4494, arriving at Palm Beach International at 11:59 a.m. That was as close to noon as we could get. Actually, with a smaller airport like that, we didn't have many choices."

"That's fine. I'll meet you at the airport. Have fun preparing for married life."

"You do realize we've been living together for fifteen months?"

"Trust me; being married makes it different. I'll see you soon."

As Todd drove the rental car toward the church from the airport, Frank, now with short hair and no beard to make the wedding special, chattered about the weather delay they barely avoided, but Sylvia was unusually silent. Todd took his eyes off the road long enough to see the tension in her face.

"What's wrong, Syl? You're not getting cold feet about the wedding, are you?"

"It's not that. I'm up tight because thanks to my atheist dad, I didn't grow up as an active churchgoer. He didn't consider religion important, so the only times I went to church were when my girlfriends or dates took me. I don't know whether this priest will consider me sufficiently Christian."

"Don't worry about that. There aren't any requirements. They say Christianity is about love, and you and Frank qualify on that score."

"Just the same, I'm going to be on my best behavior during our discussion session to avoid any chance that he'll refuse to marry us."

"If there's any snag, we'll get you married in the Bahamas after we get there. We could even have the captain of our charter boat do the honors. Boat and ship captains are supposed to qualify."

"Not on your life, Todd! I want my marriage to be as official as possible. It can be a church in the Bahamas after we get there if necessary, but from here on out, I'm hooked on church."

When they arrived at St. Mark's Church, they walked into the large sanctuary with its slightly arched ceiling and scanned the wide worship space from one end to the other, focusing on rich wooden pews with maroon carpet and accents.

Frank said, "This place is huge and empty. I'm not sure I'd feel comfortable having our wedding ceremony in here."

A voice came from behind him. "I feel the same way. That's why we'll use our chapel. It's small, bright and colorful."

The three visitors turned around to see a man wearing clerical garb standing behind them.

"Welcome to St. Marks. I'm Father Michaels. The gentleman who felt uncomfortable with a ceremony in this large space must be Frank. I'm very pleased to be able to assist you and Sylvia into the state of Holy Matrimony. The other gentleman would have to be Todd Weatherford. We spoke on the phone, and you impressed me with your sense of organization."

Todd shook hands with Father Michaels. "I'm pleased to meet you in person. Surprisingly, your appearance matches my image of you from our telephone conversation. That doesn't usually happen."

Frank and Sylvia shook hands with the priest, and then they all followed him to his office.

Father Michaels gestured at the cups and drinks on his side table. "Help yourself to coffee, soda, or bottled water. We're lacking in tea or fruit juice, but I'm sure drinks aren't the main thing on your minds right now. You appear to be close friends, and I'd like to get to know all three of you. Unfortunately, our time together is limited, so let's start with the more important discussion. Todd, I'll ask you to take your drink and spend some time anywhere you like in the church or the neighborhood for the next hour. Sylvia, Frank and I will be getting to know each other and privately exchanging views on marriage during that same period."

Todd left, and Father Michaels addressed Frank and Sylvia. "The first point we should discuss is that of your names. You aren't related to each other, are you? I see you both have the same last name, June."

Sylvia's tension disappeared as she and Frank roared with laughter. "It's all right, Father. I'm not marrying my first cousin. Frank's family name is Giustini, and mine is Troon. I didn't want Giustini as my married name, and Frank was a little cool to Troon. We solved that conflict by merging our two family names and legally changing them to June. We'll be as close to each other in our relationship as possible, but through marriage, not genetics."

The tone of the pre-marriage counseling session lightened as the bride and groom relaxed and cheerfully responded to each topic Father Michaels placed on the table for discussion: backgrounds, beliefs, views on children, goals for the future, understanding of the binding nature of marriage, and many other subjects. By the time Todd returned, Sylvia and Frank were on a first name basis with Larry Michaels, and he had told them why he had chosen religion as his career.

Richard Davidson

During the counseling time, Todd located the main office and spent the hour with Rose Shannon, the church secretary. By the conclusion of their chat, Rose volunteered that she had close relatives on Great Abaco Island and promised to shop at Todd's store when she visited them in a month or so.

CHAPTER 30 – WEDDING

Sunlight streaming through the mosaic stained glass windows brightened the modern chapel and lifted all of their spirits. Frank was taken by the large rough-hewed stone slab sitting on a sturdy stand behind the altar rail. It had a cross extending out of its top surface. Frank saw it as his personal Sword in the Stone. Through marrying Sylvia, he was about to gain his own Excalibur and become her hero for life. Sylvia saw herself surrounded by brightness and color and mentally vowed to avoid boredom at all times during their married life.

Sylvia turned to Todd. "We've known each other for a relatively short time, but in addition to your being Frank's best man, I'd like you to take the place of my father and give me away."

Frank looked as though he was having a crisis. Todd grasped his shoulder.

"What is it, Frank? You look startled."

"I'm always afraid I'll forget something, and I did this time. In all the rush, I left our wedding rings in Chicago."

Sylvia hugged him. "I guess we'll just have to have our ceremony without rings. They're only symbols of our love. We still have the love itself."

Todd smiled. "Remember the old Mighty Mouse cartoons? That mouse would fly to the rescue saying 'Here I come to save the day!'"

Frank stared at him. "Are you Mighty Mouse?"

"I may not look the part, but I do have a matched pair of silver just-in-case wedding rings in my pocket." Todd withdrew a small box, opened it, and showed the rings to Sylvia and Frank. "I tried to cover all the bases. Use these for the ritual. You may keep these or substitute others later as you wish."

Sylvia faced the priest. "Larry, let's start the ceremony before anything else goes wrong."

Larry Michaels led them to the altar rail and started the traditional service.

Dearly beloved, we are gathered together here in the sight of God, to join together this Man and this Woman in holy Matrimony ...

Frank, Wilt thou have Sylvia to thy wedded wife, to live together after God's ordinance in the holy estate of Matrimony? Wilt thou love her, comfort her, honour, and keep her in sickness and in health; and, forsaking all others, keep thee only unto her, so long as ye both shall live?

"I will."

Sylvia, Wilt thou have Frank to thy wedded husband, to live together after God's ordinance in the holy estate of Matrimony? Wilt thou love him, comfort him, honour and keep him in sickness and in health; and, forsaking all others, keep thee only unto him, so long as ye both shall live?

"I will."

Who giveth Sylvia to be married to Frank?

Todd stepped forward. "I do."

Then, Father Michaels had Sylvia and Frank face each other, clasping right hands, each in turn vowing commitment to the other. Then came the exchange of rings and prayers for their future life together, ending with

Those whom God hath joined together let no man put asunder.

Forasmuch as Frank and Sylvia have consented together in holy wedlock and have witnessed the

*same before God and this company, and thereto
have given and pledged their troth, each to the other,
and have declared the same by giving and receiving
a Ring, and by joining hands; I pronounce that they
are Man and Wife ... Amen.*

Larry Michaels nodded. Sylvia and Frank hugged each other and exchanged a record-breaking kiss. Then Frank turned to Todd and said, "You're absolutely right. Marriage does make it different."

CHAPTER 31 – OPEN OCEAN

As the sun peeked over the eastern horizon, the charter boat, *Sweeney's Queen*, captained by Steve Sweeney, surged out of the protected inlet in a challenge to the open ocean, powered by its throbbing inboard engine. Lashed to the railing were six large cartons. Todd concentrated on the controls as Steve guided his *Queen* eastward. The honeymooners were enjoying the privacy of the cabin. Steve commented on his operations and outlook for the voyage.

"Glad to have you and your friends on board, Todd. We should have a relatively smooth crossing today – no storms predicted. As we head out into open water, the trick is to be wary of sandbars. All the inlets tend to generate them as water moves in and out. It's a process called shoaling. The water movement builds sand ridges below the surface. This inlet is deep and can even handle cruise ships, but when the traffic is heavy some vessels wander off-channel, especially in bad weather. We have had fatalities."

"But you know our course well?"

"To use the old expression, I know the ocean bottom for our trip like the back of my hand. You know how your knuckles and bent fingers keep the back of your hand from being smooth? That's how it is with the ocean bottom. Surface photos show smooth water and widely separated islands, but the Bahamas are actually peaks of a vast underwater ridge system. It pays to know which islands are steep peaks and which have extended shallow slopes around them."

"I'm curious, Steve. What do you have in the cartons lashed to your railing?"

"That's one of my other businesses. As soon as you start shopping in Abaco or one of the other islands, you'll realize that everything is more expensive than in the States because of transportation costs. I have a deal with a couple of stores on Abaco to bring in merchandise when I have a charter. You're charter is paying for this voyage, so I can sell the retailers goods with just a normal markup and avoid extra freight charges."

"Knowing a little bit about the history of these islands, I have to ask; does your side business fall under the heading of smuggling?"

"The thought did cross my mind when the stores first approached me, but I play it straight and clear all the merchandise through Customs."

"You said that was one of your other businesses. What else is there?"

"In between charter voyages, I do fishing and scuba diving trips, especially on the Bahamas end. Keep me in mind if you'll be looking for adventure outings while you're on Abaco."

"I'll do that. I'm also involved in a home improvement store business there, so I'll discuss your freight-free import business with them."

"Thanks, Todd."

As Todd scanned the horizon and realized that he wouldn't be seeing any land for quite a while, he asked, "Will this be a non-stop crossing?"

"We'll have one stop. When we're sixty miles along our course, we'll put in at the nearest point of Grand Bahama Island, Old Bahama Bay Marina at West End. You'll be able to stretch your legs there while I top off our fuel tank to give my *Queen* extra range. After that, we'll have another hundred miles to Turtle Cay, where we could stop for sightseeing, or twenty miles beyond that to Abaco directly."

"Let's save the sightseeing for another time and head directly for Marsh Harbour on Abaco."

"When you arranged this trip, you told me that members of your family settled in the Bahamas around 1800. With that background, you should definitely hit Turtle Cay sometime. They have a museum there chronicling that early period, and the place looks like Cape Cod or the Massachusetts islands."

"I'll work it into my schedule, Steve."

Sylvia and Frank emerged from the cabin stairway, squinting at the bright sunlight.

Todd smiled and took Sylvia's hand to steady her. "Welcome. I'm glad you two came up for fresh air. There's absolutely no pollution here."

Sylvia scanned the horizon. "I guess we missed all of the scenery. I see nothing but water and sky."

Frank said, "We're seeing the planet the way it was before land masses formed."

Todd laughed and turned to Steve. "You can tell that man works as a tour guide."

"Frank, if you and Sylvia do some serious studying and get a boat, you'll build yourself a good business. There are more than seven hundred islands in the Bahamas, and only something like thirty of them are populated. Guided tours to the Out Islands and cays are a great visitor attraction if you know your stuff."

Sylvia purred, "Steve, how would you like to share in that business by buying a boat for us."

"Do your homework of learning all about the islands, and I might take you up on that. I do have some leads on used boats that wouldn't cost that much. You'd also have to study sailing and the charts for all of the waters around the islands. Those waters can be treacherous. For many of the early years, the biggest business in the Bahamas was wrecking, salvaging whatever was valuable from shipwrecks."

Todd added, "Learn everything you can about weather forecasting too. You wouldn't want to be at sea, alone or with passengers, when a sudden storm came up. Don't jump at a tempting opportunity. Do your homework first."

Sylvia hugged Todd. "Thanks for the advice, Teacher. We'll take our time on that project. I believe you're planning to have some assignments for us in the early days of Bahamas living."

"That sounded like a cue to fill you in on adventures that may lie ahead. If you didn't leave the cabin in a total mess, we'll go down there and discuss possibilities over a beer. Steve, I assume you won't be lonely without us."

"Nah. I have a job to do on the bridge here. If I do get involved with Frank and Sylvia on that touring business later on, I might want to join your team and learn about those assignments Sylvia mentioned."

"That's a pleasant surprise. Wait and see. We might take you up on that. Exploits in the Bahamas might require a navy."

Sylvia went down into the cabin ahead of the men to straighten up. By the time Frank and Todd arrived, the cabin was neat, and three Kalik beers were open and sitting on the table.

Todd looked around. "Nice recovery, Syl; the cabin looks shipshape. I had Steve stock Kalik beer in the fridge so that we'd have an early taste of the

Bahamas. Relax, and I'll fill you in on what I expect we'll be facing."

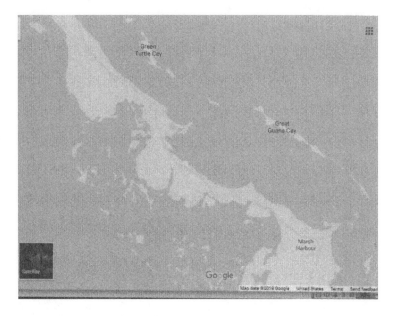

CHAPTER 32 – ABACO

Sweeney's Queen turned southeast, following the coast of Little Abaco Island and then passed between the northern end of Great Abaco and Spanish Cay. Steve set a course into the protected waters of the Sea of Abaco, bounded on the east by small cays and on the west by Great Abaco Island. He decreased speed as he approached the barrier island of Green Turtle Cay.

"Listen up, everyone. We have about twenty miles to go to reach Marsh Harbour, but if you do ever find yourselves sailing these waters, be cautious at this point. There's a shallow sandbar reaching eastward from Treasure Cay toward Whale Cay. If your boat has appreciable draft, you'll want to swing outside of Whale Cay to avoid this sandbar. I'm going to do that in order to show you the procedure."

Steve increased engine speed and turned the boat eastward until it skirted the north end of Whale Cay. Then he followed the coastline of that small island but kept offshore of it by several hundred yards. *Sweeney's Queen* rocked side-to-side as it continued this course. To compensate, Steve turned the bow toward the open ocean to drive the boat into the aggressive waves.

"You have to be careful in taking this course, because once you maneuver around Whale Cay, you have no shelter from the ocean. There's no cay farther out to protect you. If you skirt that island too close to land, you could be pushed aground on the shoreline by waves, especially in bad weather."

Frank nodded. "Now, I'm starting to understand what you meant by cautioning us to do our homework before getting a boat. Thanks for the lesson."

Steve slightly increased engine speed. "That's all the schooling for now. Last leg of the voyage. Marsh Harbour, here we come."

At 3:35 in the afternoon, they arrived at Marsh Harbour, Steve docked *Sweeney's Queen* at Harbour View Marina. He told his passengers he would stay in Marsh Harbour for two days before his next trip, a fishing excursion to the waters off several of the Out Islands. He would be docked on board *Sweeney's Queen* for the next three evenings if they wanted to contact him.

Todd, Sylvia, and Frank took a taxi to U Save Auto Rentals, and selected a Dodge Caravan for greatest flexibility during their initial activities. Frank grabbed the keys when the clerk offered them.

"Todd, you'd better let me take the first shift at driving. In the Army, I was based in London for a while, and I've done some driving on the left side of the road. You should practice a bit before you take over."

"That's fine, Frank, but don't set yourself up for a long drive. Our first destination is just down the road."

Frank drove the black minivan out of U Save Auto Rentals, turned right on Don Mackay Boulevard, passed a few buildings and open lots, before Todd said, "Turn right here."

Frank hit the brake. "I've only gone a thousand feet or so."

Sylvia looked down the driveway at their destination. "Oh, my God, Todd, it's you."

Beyond the paved parking area stood a large white concrete block building bearing the sign, Weatherford & Rolle, Home Improvement & Building Supplies. At least two dozen customer cars were parked near the front double doors, while a delivery van and employee cars lined a driveway to the left of the building.

Frank parked the Dodge Caravan near the front doors keeping a few spaces away from the other cars in case they needed to load something into the minivan. As they walked to the store entrance, Todd noted mentally that the parking lot paving was in good shape and that the building had been painted recently. Upon entering the store, the trio faced a large poster displaying the image of a confident-looking dark-skinned man and bearing the captions, *Welcome* and *Sandy Rolle, Managing Director.*

Todd smiled. "That saves me the trouble of having to identify Sandy. I know what he looks like, and I can see an office partitioned off to the left of us in the corner of the building."

As they opened the outer office door and walked in, a receptionist greeted them. "Good day. May I help you?"

Todd said, "My friends and I would like to see Sandy Rolle."

"He's very busy this morning. May I ask your names and why you want to see him?"

"My name's Todd Weatherford."

"I'm Joyce White. Just one moment."

Joyce ran to the inner office door and opened it without knocking. "Sandy, he's here!"

Joyce stood aside to let Sandy pass her. He saw two men standing with a woman. *Which one was Todd?* He extended his hand slowly, first toward

Frank and then swung it over to give a firm handshake to Todd. "I wasn't sure for one moment, but then I remembered that George said you were shorter than I am. You do look a bit like your father. Please introduce me to your friends."

"I had the advantage on you, Sandy. Your picture greeted me as I entered. These fine folks are Sylvia and Frank June, and they're newlyweds."

"Wonderful news; I'm pleased to meet you both. Are you here on your honeymoon, or will you be staying?"

Sylvia kept her hand on Frank's arm as she answered. "It's a honeymoon that I hope will last forever. We'd like to stay and work here, but we have to learn what will be required for us to do that."

Sandy said, "I'm sure we'll be able to work things out with the government people. This store pays a lot of taxes. Joyce has many contacts and will work with you. For today, we'll be sure to give you some gifts from the store to help you get started here."

Todd walked Joyce into the conversation. "I'm sure Joyce does many things to handle day-to-day problems. Sandy, she did her best to protect you from time-wasting strangers when we first arrived."

"That's part of my job. I hope it didn't give you a bad impression, Todd."

"Just the opposite. I admire efficiency in all its forms. Now, would someone be available to give us a tour of the store? If not, we could wander on our own and then come back here with a better understanding of the business."

Sandy stepped forward. "I'll take you, and then we'll split into two groups for dinner. Joyce will show Frank and Sylvia one of our colorful dining spots, while Todd and I will go to a quieter place where we'll have some privacy for business discussions."

The tour revealed that Weatherford & Rolle was a smaller version of an American home improvement store that stocked dedicated hardware and building supplies, but it was very light on consumer goods and gift items. As the group walked up and down the store aisles, Todd noted that tall, thin, but muscular Sandy moved easily, like a dancer or an athlete in the early stages of a marathon. Along the way, Sandy gave side comments and greetings to customers and workers. The relaxed comfort of these interactions reminded Todd that he would have to acclimate himself to the slow but determined pace of the Bahamas.

When Todd commented on the lack of consumer items, Sandy explained that Abaco wasn't a consumer society. Local people limited their purchases to their needs, while tourists and visitors on brief trips rarely shopped at home improvement stores. He added that he would leave the matter open for discussion as Todd involved himself more with the business.

Following the tour, Joyce drove Sylvia and Frank to the Chef Creole café for an informal meal, while Sandy took Todd to Angler's Restaurant. There they would eat in a secluded corner next to a potted palm tree while viewing the waterfront.

After they placed their orders, Sandy said, "Your father wants me to tell you about the history of our partnership, and he tells me that your mission here extends beyond business. I'll help you with any and all projects. We are partners, after all."

CHAPTER 33 – BUSINESS QUESTIONS

Todd saw energy in each conversation or action involving Sandy. "One thing I have to ask, how do you stay so upbeat all the time? You have many responsibilities, but they seem to stimulate you and make you want to do more, rather than wear you down."

"The answer to that is that I've seen too many people who fail to get the most they can out of life. Tourists see the Bahamas as a great place to sit in the sun, relax, and recuperate from the work they do at home. That's all fine, but for many people who live here, the beautiful weather and scenery is an excuse for not accomplishing anything. They do the minimum required to get by. I can't live that way. I want my life to be an adventure, and I'm pleased to have you and your father as part of it."

"That's a great outlook, Sandy, and it's not too far from mine. People expect a country boy from Kentucky to be a loner who doesn't reach out to other people and places. Ever since I played in a band when I first left home, I've sensed a rhythm in life, and I want to make that beat a positive driving force, not to make money, but to feel that I did something and affected other people."

"Your father said you were working as a tour guide, like Frank and Sylvia."

"We were all doing that in Chicago. It was fun for me because I met lots of people, and I didn't have to seek them out. They all came to me and seemed to enjoy the show I gave them. They learned about Chicago from me, but I learned a lot about them and their lives too."

"What are your first impressions of our business?"

"It fits the needs of Abaco. It's well maintained and managed. It has the aura of being traditional and modern at the same time. In other words, I'm impressed by what you've done with it. I do wonder how you keep customers happy while making a profit, given the high costs of importing goods."

"That's a battle. You may not have noticed it, but we have a corner of the store where we sell used materials. This is aimed at local customers with little cash. Whenever a building is torn down or a boat is wrecked, we hire local people to reclaim whatever materials are still useful. The local folks earn some cash; we get materials and hardware free of major shipping costs; and we end up with lower priced products to sell. Our customers appreciate it."

"I may be able to give you a bit of help on shipping costs, Sandy. Steve Sweeney, the owner of the charter boat that brought us here, transports cargo without shipping costs when he has a charter that pays his way. I told him we might be interested in working with him."

"See, Todd; you're already becoming more active. Thanks for thinking of me when you saw an opportunity to reduce costs."

Todd moved his chair closer to Sandy's to hear him better. "What I need to learn from you is the story of how the partnership between our families got started. I was surprised to learn from Dad that back in Revolutionary War days, the Weatherfords owned slaves. How did former slave owners and former slaves become partners?"

CHAPTER 34 – PARTNERSHIP

Sandy tilted his chair back as he composed his thoughts to respond to Todd. "First, let me say that I'm surprised that George, your dad, didn't answer your question, but he always was stingy with his words. I think his branch of your family must have come from New England, where they're tight-lipped about almost everything."

"It may have been my fault. I didn't get around to asking him that question, with all the surprising news he was giving me about the partnership and you. Dad doesn't volunteer unnecessary stories."

"That's what I meant. It's also why I never played poker with him. He holds his cards close to his vest and shows no expression on his face. I'd never be able to pull a successful bluff on George. He knows my thoughts before I do."

"But I heard you get along well together."

"Absolutely; George and I completely trust each other. I hope we'll develop those same feelings. Anyway, in answer to your question, our partnership dates back to about 1850. The British government outlawed slavery here in about 1834, but it took a few years to cover everyone. Almost all the slaves were free by 1839, and many of the Loyalists who came here after your Revolutionary War were free black people. Many of them were former slaves who earned their freedom by fighting on the side of the British during that war."

"So, slavery became illegal here well before Lincoln acted on it in the States."

"It was inevitable, and in case you haven't noticed, you're in the minority group here nowadays."

"No problem with that; people's actions count a lot more than their skin color."

"Getting back to the beginning of our partnership, the Weatherfords and their former slaves continued to work together on several building projects, but on an employment basis. As in all cases where people work together, they had close friends on both sides. Some friendships became closer than others."

"Are you telling me that there was intermarriage?"

"There may have been a degree of informality about it. I'm not sure. Several versions of the story have been handed down in my family. The common fact in all those stories is that my greatest grandmother who lived in post-slavery days had a daughter named Gwendolyn, whose father was a member of the Weatherford family."

"Gwendolyn's parents may have been married. It wouldn't have been the first time in our family."

"What do you mean, Todd? Do you know something that I don't?"

"I didn't know anything about my family's genealogy until Dad filled me in. He told me about my Loyalist ancestors and their flight to the Bahamas when they were no longer welcome in America following the war. The patriarch of the family was Martin Weatherford. He came to Abaco with his second wife and children plus 25 black slaves. His second wife, Isabella, was white, but his first wife, Mary Halfblood, had Creek Indian ancestry. I'm a little confused as to whether I'm descended from the first wife or the second, but I may have a bit of Creek Indian blood in me, while you have Weatherford blood in you. It's a mixed bag of DNA that we probably should study someday. How did you get to be part of the Rolle family?"

"On the island of Great Exuma, Lord John Rolle had extensive plantations operated by his slaves. When the slaves were freed under the new law, Rolle gave his plantations to his former slaves after a short apprenticeship. The plantations became the towns of Rolleville, Steventon, Mount Thompson, Ramsey's, and Rolletown. All the former slaves on Lord Rolle's plantations took the surname of Rolle, and even today, any person who can trace his genealogy to a former Rolle slave, can get a subsistence plot to farm on those lands. Gwendolyn, my greatest grandmother's daughter, married a former Rolle slave named Nathan. They lived and worked a small plot of land in Rolletown, but one of their sons, Rodney Rolle, left Great Exuma for Great Abaco because he didn't want to be a farmer. Gwendolyn told him to contact John Weatherford, who had been her friend growing up. After some discussions, John started this store with Rodney and his own son, Albert. John wanted a continuing business on his land grant parcel so that the government couldn't take the land away from him due to its being unproductive. In those days, Marsh Harbour was called Maxwell Town after a former governor. That's the whole story. Our families have been partners ever since."

"But you're saying that because of Gwendolyn, you may actually be a distant relative of mine."

"That's true, but someone really smart about DNA analysis would have to decide whether we're related or not."

100

"Sandy, the thing that amazes me is that after all those generations since Gwendolyn, your name is still Rolle. You must have traced your lineage through all male ancestors."

"You weren't listening, Todd. Every person with ancestry traced to a former Rolle slave can take the name of Rolle, even if the ancestry falls on the female side of the bloodline."

CHAPTER 35 – SYLVIA AND JOYCE

After eating at Chef Creole, Frank decided to explore the waterfront and shop for fishing equipment, leaving Sylvia and Joyce to spend some time together. The two women walked toward the Marsh Harbour Boatyard, chatting along the way. It was a pleasant walk, and Sylvia thought she might get some feeling for whether there were older boats available that could be reconditioned on a tight budget.

As they walked, Joyce responded to Sylvia's earlier question about her background and how she came to work for Sandy. She hadn't wanted to discuss it with Frank present. "Sylvia, you may think I'm foolish, but I don't talk about personal things in front of a man I don't know. Frank is your man, and I'm sure he is discreet, but I don't know him well enough yet."

"You will soon."

"Anyway, I feel comfortable enough to answer your questions now that we're alone. My mother came first to Nassau and then here to Abaco from Haiti. When she arrived, she spoke only Haitian Creole, but she did housekeeping work for English speaking people and learned enough of the language to get things done. I was born here and always spoke English. My father is a white fisherman, but they never got married. They're still good friends. I got to see many other islands when I helped him on his boat as a teenager."

"How did you meet Sandy and come to work for him?"

"I met a man at a bar, and I thought we clicked as a couple. His name was Rufus, and he turned out to be ruthless. He talked me into moving in with him, and then he thought he owned me. Every time I tried to go out alone, he would beat me and lock me in my room. He was kind to me when we were out together, but he was afraid I would abandon him if I went out alone. It didn't take more than a few beatings for me to decide that I had to get away from him."

"How did Sandy enter the picture?"

"One day Rufus took me with him to Weatherford & Rolle because he needed to get a new faucet for the kitchen sink. Sandy noticed me looking sad in the background. He had someone else show Rufus faucets, while he talked to me. As I said, I don't like to talk about personal things with men I don't know, but I was desperate, and Sandy has his charming way of making you feel comfortable. Anyway, I told him about the way Rufus treated me, and he took me to the faucet section, signaling a couple of other male employees to come with him."

"Did he fight with Rufus?"

"That was the strange part. Sandy rescued me without any violence. He simply told Rufus that I would be moving out and that the other employees would be accompanying me to be sure I did so safely. In exchange, Rufus could have any faucet he wanted without charge. Sandy told Rufus to stay away from me in the future and reminded him that he was a Rolle and that there were many people in the Rolle family network that took care of each other and their friends. Rufus got the message, and even stayed away from his home while I moved out. I never saw him again."

"Wow! I guess Sandy carries a lot of weight around here."

"Many people owe him favors. If he wanted a political career, he could be in government."

"Did you go to work for Sandy right after you moved out on Rufus?"

"Sandy first offered me a job to be sure I was safe, but I showed him that he made a good decision. I make it much easier for him to run the store."

"After hearing your story, Joyce, I'll guess that Sandy is single and that you're interested."

Joyce blushed. "I just want to help him succeed and have a good life."

Sylvia laughed. "Does he realize you love him?"

CHAPTER 36 – TODD AND SANDY

After they left Angler's Restaurant Todd suggested that they walk to the dock where *Sweeney's Queen* was moored so that Sandy could meet Steve Sweeney and discuss freight-free importing with him.

As they walked, Sandy said, "I have two questions for you, Todd. How much do you want to get involved in the business while you're here, and what is your real mission on this trip?"

"You're good at observations. Yes, I do have a mission, and it affects both of us. As far as day-to-day operation of the store, I'll leave that in your capable hands, but I'll give you assistance whenever you find it valuable."

"Thanks for your offer of assistance, but tell me about your mission so that I'll have a better feeling about whether you actually will have time for store work."

Todd described his marriage to Lori and its deterioration because of his meeting, seduction, and sexual adventures with Emma Read. He hesitated slightly before telling Sandy about his battle with Lori on Thanksgiving, but he knew that Sandy needed to see both his good and bad sides. Finally, Todd described his supplying Emma with DNA swabs and her announcement that she was pregnant with his child.

Sandy stopped walking toward the boat dock. "I'll see Steve and his boat later. We have to get back to my office. Your situation is more serious than I expected."

As they reversed course toward Sandy's car, Todd asked, "What do you mean?"

"You're playing with a serious crowd, and your mission could be a matter of life and death."

"Whose death?

"Yours, among others."

CHAPTER 37 – OFFICE

When Sandy and Todd returned to Weatherford & Rolle, they found Frank and Sylvia looking over Joyce's shoulder at her desk reading a newspaper. As the two men entered the office, Joyce said, "Congratulations, Todd! I didn't know you were about to get married."

"I'm not. Where did you get that story?"

"It's in the Nassau *Guardian.* I found it and showed it to Frank and Sylvia."

"Who am I supposed to be marrying?"

"It says that you're marrying Emma Read in Adelaide Village. That's at the southwest end of Nassau's island. It's scheduled for Saturday afternoon at St. James Anglican Church."

Sandy frowned. "We have a more immediate problem than I thought. Today is Wednesday. We'll have to make our plans and get over there in time to stop that ceremony."

Frank punched his left palm with his right fist. "I'm ready for some action, and I never did like the way Emma used Todd in Chicago."

Sylvia asked, "Who is she marrying if it's not you, Todd? Why do we have to stop the ceremony?"

"Emma's goal was to seduce me into getting her pregnant, so that her child would be attached to our family tree. At first, she wanted me to divorce Lori and marry her, but after she talked me into giving her a bunch of DNA swabs, she apparently decided she didn't need me anymore. She's marrying some cohort she'll pass off as me using my DNA swabs."

Joyce looked puzzled. "Why does she want to pass her husband off as Todd, and why do we need to stop that wedding?"

Sandy answered Joyce's questions while scanning all the group's faces to be sure everyone understood. "Emma Read plans to swindle Todd and his family out of the property this store is sitting on, plus the rest of their sixty acres. She'll pass the impostor husband off as Todd to handle the legal paperwork. She doesn't know that Todd is in the Bahamas, so he may be safe for now, but in order to make her future child the rightful heir to this property, she and her group will attempt to kill Todd's father, George Weatherford, and then Todd also. We have to stop that wedding and publicize the fact that the groom is an impostor."

Frank repeated his punch into his left palm. "This property must be awfully valuable."

Sandy agreed. "It was always a key property because of its central location in Marsh Harbour, but a few years ago, they upgraded our airport with a modern terminal building and renamed it Leonard M. Thompson International Airport. We're quite convenient to it. This would be an ideal location for a resort hotel complex."

"And Emma Read thinks she can strong-arm or even murder Todd and his father to get this land. Who does she think she is?"

"I know who she is, Frank, and she's following in her ancestor's footsteps. That's the problem." The others all stared at Sandy, waiting for him to explain further.

CHAPTER 38 – SANCTUARY

"Long before the Loyalists settled in the Bahamas following your Revolutionary War, these islands were a sanctuary for pirates. The islands had ideal climate, plus perfect location for intercepting shipments coming from or going to Cuba, Jamaica, Mexico, and other Spanish and British colonies in the Americas. Add to those advantages for pirates the fact that they had many different island sanctuaries when they were pursued by warships from various countries."

Sylvia asked, "When did all this take place?"

"The pirates operated out of these islands for many years, but for the most part, they were captured or driven away by about 1720. One of the last and most colorful of these villains was a character known as Calico Jack Rackham, so nicknamed because of his soft cotton shirts. Jack was quartermaster in Charles Vane's pirate crew on board the *Ranger*. When Captain Vane ordered his crew to avoid rather than engage a French man-o-war ship, his crew voted against him and accused him of cowardice. They gave Vane and a few loyal crew members a small sloop plus supplies and sent them away. Then they voted Calico Jack to be their new captain."

Todd said, "Pirates voted for their captains? I don't think of pirates and democracy as being compatible."

Sandy continued, slightly bothered by the interruption. "Apparently they did vote on their leaders, at least in this case. Anyway, Jack went on to become a pirate of some notoriety, inventing the pirate flag with white skull and crossed cutlasses on a black background. He scored his biggest prize when he captured an English merchant ship, the *Kingston*, just outside the harbor at Port Royal, Jamaica. The local merchants saw the battle, realized they were losing their purchased goods, and pursued Calico Jack in their ships. They caught up with him when he and his crew anchored off a small island near Cuba. Jack and his crew rowed ashore, looking for some rest and diversion. While the pirates were on the island, the pursuing merchants put crews on the *Ranger* and the *Kingston* and sailed away, marooning Jack and company."

Todd shrugged. "That must have put Calico Jack out of the pirate business, but what does it have to do with Emma?"

"That's in the next part of my story. Be patient."

CHAPTER 39 – PIRATES END

Sandy continued. "Bahamas Governor Woodes Rogers had a standing offer of amnesty for any pirate who requested it and promised to retire to honest living. In May of 1719, Jack Rackham went to Nassau and requested such a pardon. For about a year, Jack actually fulfilled his part of the bargain. Then, he took up with Anne Bonny, already married to a sailor named James Bonny, and got her pregnant. Jack sent her to Cuba to have her baby, but when she returned to Nassau afterwards, James Bonny threatened Anne and Jack with legal action that would result in public lashing."

Todd said, "I'll bet they didn't have many divorces in those days."

Sandy didn't react to Todd's comment. "Before James Bonny could act on his threat, Anne convinced Jack to avoid any problems with the Nassau authorities. Jack, Anne, and ten others simply walked to the docks, boarded a twelve ton sloop named the *William*, and sailed away before anyone realized that anything unusual had happened. Calico Jack Rackham was back in the pirate business."

Sylvia said, "I doubt that it took long for Anne to convince him to head back to sea. As a pirate, Jack was someone special. He must have hated being a nobody during his more-or-less honest life on land."

Sandy returned to his story. "Focus in folks. Here comes the key part of my tale. As Calico Jack

111

rebuilt his pirate legend by capturing fishing boats and two merchant ships, he noticed that one of his crew members was a great swordsman. Jack also saw that this individual spent many hours with Anne, and he grew jealous of their relationship. One day, Jack confronted the two of them in Anne's cabin.

"At last I've caught you in the act, Anne Bonny. Dallying with this lout will get you punished good and proper. You promised to be true to me."

Anne moved in front of her companion to act as a shield. "Jack, you need not worry. Since you and I have been together, I've had no other lover."

"I don't believe you. Let this roughneck speak for himself. What say you, villain?"

"I say I have no romantic intentions toward Anne. We are friends, and that is all."

"I've seen you coming and going with Anne before. This is not the first time you have been in her cabin. Tell the truth."

"Indeed it is true that I have been here before, but not for romance."

"If not for love, for what reason do you two seek each other's company?"

The visitor looked a question at Anne, and she nodded slightly. He then said, "I have had no romance with Anne because I am not a man. I am a woman like her. Because we are the only two women on board this ship, we find friendship easy and comforting."

Jack grasped the hilt of his sword. "I do not believe your story. You are too good a swordsman to be a woman. Reach for your sword."

"I will prove my truth without the need for swordplay. Watch as I remove my tunic."

Jack stared in disbelief as the sailor removed his tunic, revealing a chest tightly wrapped with cloth strips. He unwound the cloth to reveal breasts that Jack would never have guessed were there. The sailor stood bare-chested facing Jack. "Do you believe me now?"

"I do indeed. You are definitely a woman. What is your real name?"

"I am Mary Read. Now that I am revealed, I will fight in the future as a woman."

Anne said, "I will fight side by side with Mary, and we will battle better than most men on this ship."

Sandy continued, "After that, Mary and Anne, who also could handle a sword well, battled as women, even becoming more favored than Jack in the eyes of the crew.

"Worse for Jack than losing the popularity contest was the fact that he was being hunted by a larger ship commanded by Captain Jonathan Barnet for the theft of the *William*. Barnet caught up with Jack off Jamaica in a fog bank where, hearing noises, he shouted into the fog to discover whether there was another ship nearby and if so to identify it. The response to his "Who are you?" was "Jack Rackham." Captain Barnet fired a broadside into the *William* by aiming in the direction of Jack's hailing reply. The *William* lost its rudder and was easily boarded.

"After a quick trial, Calico Jack and most of his crew were hanged in November of 1720, one day after their conviction. Anne Bonny and Mary Read were spared from execution because they were both pregnant. Now you have Emma Read's pedigree. Be prepared for anything when we go after her."

CHAPTER 40 – CEREMONY

St. James Anglican Church rapidly filled with well-dressed attendees for the pending ceremony. Many of the guests were government officials rather than relatives, but those who fell into the latter category overwhelmingly occupied the bride's side of the aisle. As they sat waiting for the ceremony to start, many of the guests commented on the antique white carriage pulled by four white horses they had seen outside the church. Those who planned the wedding of Emma Read and Todd Weatherford intended to make a grand social statement.

The organist played prelude music that started softly and soared to a crescendo, successfully quieting the jabber of voices in the congregation. Then the music retreated to serene expectancy as the wedding party processed down the aisle, groomsmen paired with bridesmaids. Once everyone including the Maid of Honor, Best Man, and Groom were in position alongside the altar, Father Griffith walked between them, facing down the aisle. He nodded to cue the organist, and the congregation stood as the bride made her entrance to the strains of *Here Comes the Bride*. She wore a simple white gown of modern design without a train, and was escorted by her uncle who would give her away in the absence of her late father.

Once everyone was in position, Father Griffith began the service with the Welcome, followed that with the Preface, and then moved to the Declarations.

"First, I am required to ask anyone present who knows a reason why these persons may not lawfully marry, to declare it now."

Sandy Rolle stepped into the aisle at the rear of the church. "I have an objection."

The congregation and members of the wedding party all turned to look at him. The question had to be asked as a fundamental part of the ceremony, but it was highly unusual for someone to actually respond.

Father Griffith said, "Identify yourself and state your objection."

"I am Sandy Rolle, Managing Director of Weatherford & Rolle Home Improvement & Building Supplies. Todd Weatherford is my business partner. The bridegroom at this wedding is not Todd Weatherford."

Very quietly, a television news cameraman who had recorded Sandy's initial statement crept down the side aisle so that he was in position to record the faces and words of the priest and the wedding couple.

Father Griffith turned to the groom. "What is your name, and can you prove your identity?"

The bride said, "This interruption is frivolous and ridiculous. I'm Emma Read, and I confirm that the groom is Todd Weatherford."

Father Griffith said, "Church law says we cannot proceed until we investigate an objection."

He turned to the groom. "I repeat my question. Who are you?"

The groom removed folded papers from his inside jacket pocket. "I'm Todd Weatherford, and I have DNA evidence to prove it."

A second man stepped into the aisle at the rear of the church as another cameraman prepared to record him speaking. "What is ridiculous is that someone would carry DNA identification evidence to his wedding. He was prepared to have his identity questioned. I am Todd Weatherford, and I object to Emma Read fraudulently passing this man off as me. If you wish, we may take new DNA samples from both of us and delay the ceremony until the results are known, or this groom may marry Emma under his own name, but not while pretending to be me."

Many members of the congregation began murmuring and talking to each other.

Father Griffith whispered something to Emma. She nodded, grasped the hand of her groom, and the two of them walked forward to a small drapery-covered doorway behind and to the left of the altar.

After the couple disappeared through the doorway, Father Griffith said, "Our apologies to all the guests and other attendees. I will not be able to perform the wedding ceremony today. A serious question as to the identity of the groom has been raised, and it must be investigated. The church cannot be a party to fraud. The organist will now play recessional music. Please leave the building in an orderly manner."

As they left the church, guests watched as television and newspaper reporters gathered around Sandy Rolle and Todd Weatherford for interviews. Several well-dressed government officials joined those discussions.

A small article in the Nassau *Guardian* the following day described two people's accounts of witnessing an automobile accident in which an unidentified man had driven off a dock on the ocean side of Paradise Island. The vehicle and body had not yet been located.

CHAPTER 41 – PUBLICITY

Todd was pleased that he and Sandy had sabotaged the first stage of Emma's plan. It would be difficult for her to continue her efforts to take over his property without having to first answer many questions. Even the priest at St. James Anglican Church had voiced the word *fraud* in front of his congregation.

What Todd didn't expect was the way he had become an overnight celebrity on the islands. Television news reports had made his face and his successful interference in the counterfeit wedding ceremony familiar to all who enjoyed gossiping about recent items in the news. Weatherford & Rolle enjoyed increased business, and whenever Todd appeared in the store aisles, people approached him to ask about the terminated ceremony and his future plans.

One afternoon, Todd joined Frank and Sylvia in visiting Marsh Harbour Boatyard to look for a possible vessel for their future tour guide business. Most of the boats that were for sale had obvious problems that needed major work. There was one exception, a 1996 Fountaine Pajot Venezia 42 catamaran with twin diesel engines plus sails. The 42 foot craft was priced at about two hundred thousand American dollars, which was way beyond Frank and Sylvia's budget.

As they examined the boat, the boatyard manager, Edward Burley, came over to them. "Hello, Mr. Weatherford; I recognized you from the television news. Are you and your friends interested in this Venezia 42?"

Todd said, "Frank and Sylvia June, here, are the ones who might be interested, but it's far beyond their price range. They're interested in learning more about used boats for a possible future venture."

"Then you two are looking for a working boat rather than a yacht. How much experience do you have on the ocean and around the Out Islands?"

Frank said, "We're a couple of optimistic lunatics with no experience whatsoever. Should we have our heads examined, or is there a chance for us to become sailors?"

"You look young and healthy. I have some boats here that were abandoned after poor upkeep and hull damage. If you two would be willing to supply sweat equity to repair one of them, we might find something satisfactory that would fit your budget. If you fix up the boat and pay our negotiated price, I'll throw in sailing and navigation lessons for you. How does that sound?"

Sylvia nodded to Frank and said, "I have to tell you that we don't yet have Bahamas work permits, and we're here to help Todd with a project, so we may not be available to work on the boat every day."

"You won't need work permits. You're purchasing a boat with your hard work as part of the payment. That's not a job, and you can come and go whenever we're open. I won't require a particular schedule. What do you say? Are you interested?"

Frank extended his hand. "That sounds perfect if you have a boat that's suitable for sightseeing tours to the Out Islands and fishing."

Edward Burley shook hands with Frank. "Come back tomorrow morning, when I have more time, and I'll show you all the possible candidates. It's good to meet you Mr. Weatherford. I do a lot of shopping at your store."

"Call me Todd, Edward. Frank and Sylvia will be good students for you. Be sure the boat they fix up is seaworthy before you let them tackle the waves. They're good friends, and I wouldn't want to lose them."

As they walked away from the boatyard, Frank said, "Your new celebrity status opens a lot of doors for possible business deals."

Sylvia elbowed her husband hard.

"What was that for?"

"Celebrity also makes Todd an easy target."

CHAPTER 42 – RETALIATION

Sandy and Todd studied diagrams and charts on the conference table in an intensive tutoring session aimed at giving Todd insight into the dynamics of their business. The goal was for him to be comfortable running it when Sandy was on vacation or otherwise unavailable. After two hours of this effort, Todd began to feel that he could handle the business solo for a limited period of time. He suggested that Sandy should take a week of vacation to give him the ultimate test of his understanding of the business. As they flipped pages on the calendar to select a promising week for the test, Joyce entered the office.

"Todd, you have a call, and I suspect it's your dragon lady. Do you want to take it? I told her you were tied up in a meeting, so you don't have to talk with her."

"I'll take it. No sense hiding from a good battle."

Sandy said, "Joyce, stall her for a minute or two while I set up the recording equipment. Then, we'll have the conversation documented. I have a feeling that it might be valuable."

Sandy set up his equipment and then left the office, closing the door behind him. Todd would sound more natural if he talked without someone else in the room.

He raised the desk phone and prepared for almost anything. "Todd Weatherford speaking; may I help you?"

"Hello, Todd. It's Emma Read. You were a huge surprise at my wedding that never happened."

"I was pretty surprised myself to read in the newspaper that I was marrying you that day. You abandoned me in Chicago, and I thought you were gone forever."

"I had no idea that you were in the Bahamas. Is this your first visit?"

"It is, but I plan to stay for quite a while, perhaps permanently."

"I was in your store once. I wasn't impressed."

"We don't stock cutlasses and Jolly Roger flags except for Halloween costume use."

"So, you've learned a bit about my family history."

"I have, and I now realize that your goal is to recreate your family business. You're three hundred years too late for that."

"Be nice to me, Todd. I'm carrying your child. Perhaps we should revisit the idea of getting married. You are divorced and free of the bitch who almost killed you?"

"You won't earn any points with me by calling her that. I'm sure that I'd be safer with Lori at her angriest than I would ever be with you. Emma, for a while you had me believing you were someone special, but you were the sizzle of a poisoned steak. After listening to you, I almost killed Lori. The best thing you can do for me is to stay out of the rest of my life."

"I'm afraid I can't do that, Todd. You have some things that I intend to get, with or without your cooperation."

"Try pirating someone else's treasure. I'll resist you every inch of the way."

"You're an amateur at understanding how to manipulate the laws and powers that be in the Bahamas. Between that and your illness, you don't stand a chance. How is your lupus developing? You won't be able to keep up with my moves much longer."

"Emma, they should have hanged Mary Read with the other pirates in 1720 to keep you from being born. As for your glee over my lupus, you might as well forget it. I got a second opinion from Doctor Raskin when I was in the hospital after Lori stabbed me, and he said my problem was Lyme disease, which has similar symptoms. A tick bit me in the woods. It's curable, and I'm halfway through the process, so don't count on my being an easy target."

"That's too bad. Even if you're well, you can't be everywhere. I'd suggest you check what's happening at your old Kentucky home. Goodbye, Todd. You'll hear more from me soon."

Todd opened the office door and invited Sandy to review the recorded conversation with him. They sat in complete silence while it played. Then Sandy asked Joyce to bring in the papers they had discussed while Todd was on the telephone.

"Here they are, Sandy: the article from the newspaper and my notes from the call from the police detective."

Todd asked, "Why did a police detective call?"

Joyce said, "It's your *doppelganger* again, the guy who was using your identity to marry Emma Read. They found him dead in a car that drove off a dock on the ocean side of Paradise Island. The police called for confirmation that you were still alive. They haven't learned his true identity yet, but he had your DNA test results in his hip pocket. A police official who was at the sham wedding remembered his trying to use those papers for identification there."

"That proves how dangerous Emma Read is. I'll guarantee that the deceased bridegroom didn't volunteer to drive into the ocean. I'd better check whether everyone is safe in Kentucky, per Emma's threatening suggestion."

Joyce went for coffee while Todd phoned home. This time, Sandy stayed in the office.

Todd's mother answered the telephone.

"Mom, Todd calling; how is everything at home?"

"Are you calling from Abaco? I thought I recognized the store number on the display. We're fine. Did you think we had a problem?"

"I've had a few run-ins with Emma Read, and she made a threatening comment that I should watch out for possible trouble at home."

"No problems so far. Wait a minute. I have a call coming in on the other line. I'll take it and get right back with you."

Todd explained the situation to Sandy while he waited for his mother.

She came back on the phone. "Hello, Todd, we do or almost did have a problem. That woman must have put her agents to work before she talked with you. Your dad was on the other line. Someone tried to run him down while he was standing near the pumps in front of the gas station. He jumped out of the way and got the car's license number. The state cops are chasing that car right now. I told George you thought that Emma woman would be behind anything bad that happened. He's fine and will be home soon. He doesn't want me to be alone if bad guys are after us. I love the way he wants to protect me. I'll keep the shotgun loaded and ready in case of trouble."

"Just don't shoot Dad by mistake. Call me back at the store if the cops catch that guy and identify him."

Todd ended the call and told Sandy about the attempt to run his father down with a car.

Sandy said, "Emma Read has been doing her homework. She knows where everyone in the family is."

"I don't think she knows where my older brothers and sister are. They left home long before Emma Read came into my life. Carter, Hampton, and Amy have each moved several times because of job changes. They'd be hard for a stranger to locate. I'm your designated partner in the store, but I'm not even the oldest potential heir for the land. We'll have to be sure she never finds Carter, Hampton, and Amy."

Sandy left the office and went out into the store. A few minutes later the telephone rang. Joyce answered and yelled to Todd that it was his mother.

He took a deep breath and picked up the receiver. "Hi, Mom, what news do you have?"

"Both the good type and the bad. The state cops caught up with that guy, but he had a gun and tried to shoot his way out. The cops returned fire, hitting him in several places. He died on the way to the hospital."

"Did he have any identity papers?"

"They found papers, but one of the cops already knew about him. He's a local thug from the next county. He has a record of causing trouble to make himself feel important. I doubt that they'll be able to connect him to Emma Read and her cohorts."

"Even so, it's time for us to go on the offensive here."

Todd leaned back in his chair, wondering what Emma and her crew would do next to retaliate for the interrupted wedding. He heard a commotion in the store. When he stepped outside the office, he saw all the employees and a few customers running toward the warehouse section. He followed and arrived at the loading dock in time to see several employees using fire extinguishers on a pile of merchandise cartons. He saw Sandy through the open garage door standing on the pavement outside.

"Sandy, what happened?"

"Someone drove past the loading dock and threw two Molotov cocktails. One went inside and ignited those cartons. The other was aimed at lumber cutoffs stacked against the building. Luckily, that one bounced away from the lumber, so it had no fuel to start the building on fire. We escaped serious harm this time, but we'll have to be prepared for another possible attack in the future."

"Looks like someone we know is trying to get back at us for torpedoing her wedding. Back home, the cops shot the guy who tried to run down my dad. Did anyone get a license plate on the guy who tried to burn this place?"

"We didn't have video cameras, but we will by this time tomorrow. I'll put off that week of vacation you suggested."

CHAPTER 43 – RESEARCH

Todd examined the numerical table displayed on Joyce's screen. "I see how scanning the bar code on each item as it's sold reveals our remaining inventory, but do we automatically order replacements, or does a person make the reordering decision?"

"Some of each, Todd. We tag items in the inventory list as category A, B, or C. Items marked with an A are standard and are reordered automatically. Items marked with a B are monitored as to sales level. I reorder those that are selling well, and if they sell well for several periods, I may recode them with an A for automatic replacement. B items that rarely sell are eliminated at some point. The code C in the listing indicates an item that we special-ordered for a customer, and it is never replaced."

Sandy Rolle entered the office and waited for Joyce to complete her explanation before he spoke. "Todd, I checked with a few of my contacts, and learned a few things about Emma Read."

"Like what?"

"She owns a home in Adelaide Village, not far from St. James Anglican Church where they staged that wedding. She owns that home, but she rarely stays there. It's supposed to impress people, especially government contacts. Being at the southwest end of Nassau's island, it's convenient for meetings. Emma and some associates are trying to develop a resort on Lynyard Cay, which is a skinny island northeast of Bridges Cay, the small island that was part of Martin Weatherford's original land grants. Lynyard Cay is low and has no protection from ocean storms. It would be a risky place to invest in a development. Anyway, that's where she spends most of her time."

Todd examined the map of the Abaco Islands. "She's after something from me, and Lynyard Cay is close to Bridges Cay which is or was family property. That's too much of a coincidence. I need more information about Weatherford land holdings from Dad. I'll give him a call to see whether he has any suggestions."

He went into Sandy's private office and closed the door for privacy. Then he made a few notes on a scratch pad and keyed in his dad's mobile phone number. It rang three times before it connected. "Hi, Dad, it's Todd. Are you someplace where you can talk about serious things?"

George Weatherford said that he'd move to a quiet location in the corner of the coffee shop. "Go ahead, Son."

"Are you and Mom edgy or bothered after that guy tried to run you down?"

"Not bothered, but we're prepared for anything. They won't surprise us again."

"I'm positive that Emma Read was behind that attack on you. I have a recording of her on the telephone just before it happened, suggesting that I check to see if there were problems at home."

"That woman is a strange piece of work."

"Sandy gave us another history lesson. It turns out that Emma Read is descended from a well-known female pirate named Mary Read who escaped hanging in 1720 only because she was pregnant, and the court didn't want to kill her baby."

"The law does make mistakes."

"My feelings too in this case. I'm trying to figure out what she wants from me. She told me I have something she wants and is determined to get. I don't stand to inherit the land in Marsh Harbour. I'm your youngest child, not the oldest. My only thought is that she wants the store for some reason."

"I doubt that."

"We did find out that she's working on developing part of Lynyard Cay, which is near Bridges Cay; that's the small island that you said was one of Martin Weatherford's land grants. Could that have something to do with her aggression?"

"It might."

"What do you mean, Dad?"

"The family sold Bridges Cay about fifty years ago. The proceeds were split among several relatives in my generation. I used my share to buy some acreage on the Abaco coast north of Bridges Cay and south of Wilson City; that's an old lumber mill town that shut down a century ago. The land was cheap because it hadn't been developed, and I designated you to inherit it after I'm gone. The older kids would share the Marsh Harbour land except for the parcel the store is on."

"That has to be what she's after, Dad. That's why she had no interest in ambushing Carter, Hampton, and Amy."

"Why didn't she come to me and try to buy the land?"

"That pirate heritage. She'd rather trick me into having a child with her to inherit it so that she pays nothing. That plan also eliminates the problem of your possibly not wanting to sell it."

"I wouldn't have sold it. I consider it your birthright as part of the Weatherford family. She probably figured that out and decided to go after you as the long-term target. We now know what we're up against. Why is she so determined to get that land?"

CHAPTER 44 – BOATYARD

Frank and Sylvia June had practically disappeared for two weeks. They had quarters in a rooming house, while Todd had rented a small house to show that he intended to be active in the business for the foreseeable future. Todd felt sure he knew why he seldom saw them, but it was time to check his theory. He drove a company car to the Marsh Harbour Boatyard, parked, and waved to the manager at the entrance.

"Hello, Edward; I'm looking for Frank and Sylvia June. Are they here?"

"Hello, Mr. Weatherford – I mean Todd; they're almost always here nowadays. They took me up on my offer of using sweat equity as part of the price of an older damaged boat, and they've done a whole bunch of sweating so far."

"What type of boat are they working on, and where will I find it?"

"You'll see their project for yourself if you go all the way back to the far corner of the yard. We moved their selected boat there and put it up on cradles because they wanted privacy and because it will take a long time for them to finish working on it."

Todd shook hands with Edward Burley and walked the zig-zag paths through the array of old and damaged boats to the farthest corner of the boatyard. Some of the old boats he passed were beyond repair and could only have value for parts. When he reached his destination, he saw Frank attempting to bend a sheet of aluminum to conform to the hull shape of a boat that was much larger than Todd expected.

"I'll give you a hand with that, Frank. What type of craft is this?"

"Hi, Todd; good timing. I'm patching a damaged section of the hull, but I have to match the curve closely to avoid leakage. Aluminum is easy to bend, but I'm using trial-and-error bending to get the curvature right, and the material fatigues if it's bent too many times. I can use some help and a couple of extra hands."

As they worked on the bending, Todd asked, "What kind of boat is this? I haven't seen one before, and it's much larger than I expected. How can you afford it?"

Sylvia came around from behind the boat. She patted Frank on his shoulder. "My Special Operations warrior spotted it right away. It's an old 41 foot US Coast Guard utility boat. It got damaged on a reef while on some kind of coastal assignment. In addition to the hull damage, it had scratches and dents from other operations. It has a smallish cabin, so it sat in this boatyard for a long time without attracting any interest. Edward gave us a bargain as-is price to clear it out of here. Make that as-was. We've already made it a lot more seaworthy than its condition when we agreed on it."

Frank continued, sounding excited. "Todd, when fixed up, this vessel will do 20 knots steady and 25 knots in full throttle bursts. It also has towing capability plus radar, a depth finder, radio, and other electronics I haven't figured out yet."

Sylvia added, "More important for the immediate future, Edward is letting us sleep in the boat's cabin, eliminating our rooming house cost, in exchange for acting as night watchmen for the boatyard. That's why you haven't seen much of us. We're here almost all the time."

"Well, I'm certainly glad you two are doing well on your boat project. Let me know if and when you need cash outlays or materials from the Weatherford and Rolle store. We're learning a few things about Emma Read and her targets. I'll fill you in over lunch tomorrow if you're available."

Sylvia said, "We'll be available and hungry."

Frank wiped his hands on a rag. "Hopefully, we'll have our boat ready to act as your navy by the time you're ready to move out against that woman."

"Not to be unkind, but your boat looks as though it will take quite a while to finish. I may ask Sandy whether some of our employees couldn't assist you with tools and materials from the store if we photograph them working and use the pictures in advertising."

Sylvia gave Todd a hug. "You're an amazing friend."

Frank said, "Make sure those photos are close-ups. We won't want the dragon lady to know about this boat."

CHAPTER 45 – LUNCH MEETING

When Frank and Sylvia walked into Angler's Restaurant for their lunch meeting with Todd Weatherford, they were surprised to find Sandy Rolle and Joyce White there also.

Frank waved to the group. "Hi, all. Who's minding the store while you're over here?"

Sandy stood and shook hands with the newcomers. "Our team is flexible and trained at several levels to step in and run things when we're away. When I heard from Todd about your lunch plans, I decided that Joyce and I should join you. This group is the Board of Directors for Todd's project."

Concerned that someone might be overhearing them, Sylvia scanned the restaurant and realized that there were no other diners. Then she spotted the sign on the door, *Private Party Inside*, and noticed that all the tables under umbrellas outside were occupied. Sandy had strong connections with other business owners in Marsh Harbour. She and Frank sat down and waited to hear from the team leaders.

Todd announced that Sandy had arranged for lunch to be prepared buffet style, and encouraged everyone to visit the serving table for food and refill their plates later if they were still hungry.

When the group reseated themselves, trays in hand, Sylvia and Frank had by far the largest portions, but no one seemed to notice. The many seafood dishes had everyone enthusiastic. Todd nodded for them to start eating and indicated he would enjoy his lobster quesadillas, before making any comments.

When he finished eating, Todd said, "Friends, it's hard to believe the many changes in my life in the last couple of years. I've gone from being an apprentice country musician to being a happily married tour guide in Chicago, to getting seduced into ruining my marriage and almost ending my wife's life. Now I find myself in the Bahamas as a partner in a business with a long and vibrant history, trying to outmaneuver the woman who seduced me into getting her pregnant."

Sylvia nudged Frank. "That's the second time he mentioned that pregnancy."

Frank said, "It's the key to her attack on Todd and his family."

Todd continued. "Now that woman, Emma Read, the descendant of a pirate, wants to use that future child to swindle me out of some family real estate, after killing my father and me so that the baby becomes heir to the property. Why does she want that land, and how will we disrupt her plans? Sandy, please lead us into this discussion."

"Todd, you are my new business partner, and I must say that we work well together. I look forward to many years of this partnership and for you to remain active in the business, rather than being a silent partner as was your father. Having said that, I must state that your safety is our top priority. The first line of defense against Emma Read is for us to make sure that she and her cronies don't manage to kill you and your father. Both in Kentucky and here, we will provide the best security possible."

"Thanks, Sandy, I agree with you, but I won't hide out like a scared animal."

Frank waved his hand for attention. "I'm the guy with the military background in this group, so I have to suggest the one sure-fire tactic."

"What's that?"

"If Emma doesn't have her baby, she can't use the child as a weapon against you."

"Frank, if you're suggesting that someone eliminate her, I can't go along with that. My mother pointed out that the child is mine as well as hers, and I promised not to harm it."

Joyce said, "Before we reject Frank's thinking completely, let's consider a less drastic version of it. He's right in saying that Emma Read plans to use the child as a weapon against you. Instead of eliminating her, we could disarm her."

Todd looked skeptical. "What do you mean?"

"We could mount a smear campaign to prove that she is not qualified to raise the child and, as the other biological parent, you could petition the court to award the child to you."

Sandy said, "That couldn't be done until the child was actually born, but we could lay the groundwork for it as one possible approach. We already have several valid points against her. She is the descendant of a pirate, and I'm sure she hasn't followed the law in some of her past dealings. We could have someone check her record. We caught her in front of many witnesses and the press, trying to marry an impostor posing as Todd. It was no coincidence that the impostor died under suspicious circumstances the day after the fraudulent wedding. We also have her on tape suggesting that Todd check for problems in Kentucky just before someone tried to kill his father with a car. All of these, plus new things I'm sure we'll find, make a case for her not being qualified to raise the child."

Sylvia agreed. "That's good thinking. It should be one of our approaches, but I have the feeling that Emma Read has some officials on her payroll. We need a primary approach that will produce a criminal case against her."

Sandy said, "I hope you don't mind, Joyce, but I'd like you to spend some of your store time checking with the authorities to learn what permits she has applied for on Lynyard Cay. My guess is that whatever she is doing on that long and narrow island has something to do with her goal of grabbing Todd's land across the cut from it on Greater Abaco. It looks to me as though she wants to control the land on both sides of that channel between Greater Abaco and that Lynyard Cay. The question is why?"

"Will do, Sandy. I have some friends in the Ministry of Public Works and the Ministry of Environment and Housing. If they don't know what the Read woman is doing on Lynyard Cay, they should have contacts in other ministries that could find out."

Sandy continued, "That assumes she's following the rules. She may be trying to buy out existing land owners before she files any formal plan applications."

Todd nodded his affirmation. "Back in Chicago, Emma told me she was working on building a resort in a place that hadn't been developed. Is it possible that she was telling the truth? She'll try to buy existing properties cheaply before she files papers that reveal the nature of her project. She may even have thugs work to force non-sellers off their land."

Sylvia said, "If we can prove she's trying to scare property owners, it will help build our case that she's unfit to be a mother to her coming child. What do you think, Frank?"

"I think that Sandy and Todd should sign me up as a building supplies salesman for Weatherford and Rolle. Then I could visit property owners on Lynyard Cay to encourage them to do building and refurbishing projects on their homes and vacant land. That might get them to talk about someone trying to buy their land or force them out. Whatever I learn should help reveal Emma's plans. How about it, Sandy?"

"You're hired. If Frank does some door-to-door reconnaissance, and Joyce works her government connections, we have two active probes into Emma's plans. I'll add a third by using my contacts to learn the autopsy results for that guy who was going to marry Emma, posing as Todd. They may also have witness statements for how his car hurtled into the ocean."

Todd said, "We've accomplished more than I expected today. Now we'll have to wait for the results of these first three actions. Before we end this meeting, let me say that we've paid for all the food on the serving table. Feel free to take the rest of it home with you."

By the time the stampede to the serving table ended, only the decorative plastic fruit remained.

Loyalties

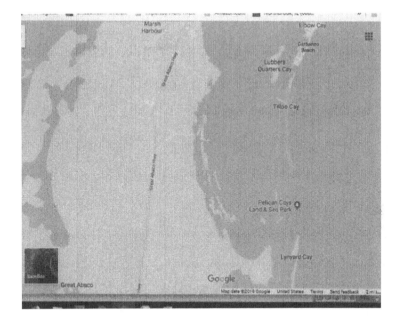

CHAPTER 46 – EMMA READ

Sometimes I think I'm an idiot. I was greedy when I walked out on Todd in Chicago after he got me pregnant. I figured I didn't need him anymore and wouldn't have to share future payoffs with him. I wanted it all for myself. Back then, he thought he was a simple country boy, and so did I. He didn't know anything about having property and a business in the Bahamas, and that made the seduction process easy. I don't know why his family didn't tell him he had more resources than his income from guiding tours, but his ignorance made life easier for me.

My problems started when I didn't think ahead. As soon as that puppy ran home with his tail between his legs, his parents told him everything. I should have taken care of Todd's father early in the game, perhaps his mother too. Now Todd Weatherford has developed into a different person. He's my enemy, confident and gathering new friends and resources every day.

That scene at my so-called wedding was embarrassing. Many powerful people saw me caught red-handed passing off Ike Trowbridge as Todd Weatherford. That's my fault too. I wanted the elite in Bahamas to consider me special for my own deeds and not just for Mary Read having been my ancestor. Naturally, they put my high society wedding plans in the newspaper, where Todd and his friends could see them. I had no reason to suspect he might be in the Bahamas. It was a shock when he suddenly appeared in the church.

This Sandy Rolle guy needs watching. He may need to be moved out of the way. In him Todd discovered a strong partner and a friend who knows the ways of the islands. Rolle could anticipate some of my moves. Most in that Rolle clan are agricultural people. This one is a sophisticated businessman with connections.

I suppose I shouldn't have assigned that Kentucky misfit to get Todd's father. I figured a local guy would do the hit and disappear into the background. I didn't have time to send someone from the islands. I need to develop a better crew and network.

My goal is to do big things while appearing to be nothing but a legitimate business owner. My name is both a blessing and a curse. The family history helps me attract associates, but it also makes me suspicious in the eyes of the law. Hopefully, my new venture will change that image.

And this baby growing inside me is a necessary part of my plans, but once it's here, I'll have someone else take care of it. I'm certainly not going to be a homebody. I have to manage all aspects of this venture very carefully.

CHAPTER 47 – IKE TROWBRIDGE

After the wedding that didn't quite happen, the bride and groom, Emma Read and Ike Trowbridge, avoided the press and distinguished guests by slipping out of the door behind the church's altar before any people in the congregation left their seats. They filtered out of the church through that small drapery-covered doorway in compliance with whispered advice from Father Griffith. For Emma, the disappearing act avoided embarrassment. For Ike, it was the beginning of the end.

Ike had been Emma's guardian angel since he was a teenager. His own parents weren't able to pay him a weekly allowance, but Emma's father gave him a generous sum each week for serving as his daughter's bodyguard at school and during the rest of the day, whenever Quentin Read's military assignments took him away from home. The result of Ike's paid devotion to Emma was that many in their age group considered them adopted brother and sister.

Thanks to Quentin's continuing generosity, Ike attended the same university as Emma with all of his fees and expenses fully covered. He continually reminded himself that Emma was his assignment and meal ticket, but not his girlfriend.

After Quentin's fatal airplane crash into that Guatemalan mountain, Ike assumed his guardian assignment had ended and started to study the classified ads for job openings. When he announced to Emma that he had received an offer to work at the local newspaper, she told him he couldn't take the job because she still needed him to be her bodyguard and assistant. She increased his pay level and took him along when she traveled.

Trowbridge accompanied Emma when she went to Chicago to seek out Todd Weatherford, and he was only mildly surprised during their flight back to the Bahamas when his employer announced that she was going to marry him as a stand-in for Todd.

Until the date of their wedding, Ike considered himself totally committed to Emma, and he expected that even though the ceremony had failed to occur, he would accompany her for many years to come.

That turned out to be a bad assumption.

After they left the church through that small draped portal, Emma announced that she would drive home by herself and that he should wait for a ride from her cousin Lydia after the guests dispersed.

Ike followed instructions and waited by Lydia's car. She was one of the first guests to emerge from the church after Father Griffith cancelled the ceremony. As she approached, he said, "I'm supposed to get a ride home with you. Emma wanted to go somewhere by herself. She was pretty upset."

"No problem. Throw your tuxedo jacket and tie in the back seat. After that fiasco, I need to stop for a drink or two. I certainly didn't think I'd be the one riding off into the sunset with the groom."

Lydia drove to a dilapidated pub named The Right Tern where she donned a sweatshirt over her dress and tucked a pair of blue jeans under her arm before entering. For his part, Ike discarded his dress shirt and untucked his undershirt to look more casual. Once inside, he headed for the bar while she went to the women's rest room to exchange her dress for the jeans.

Ike ordered a pint of Bass Ale and took it to the back end of the room where he joined half a dozen men watching a high stakes dart game. As he watched, Ike wondered if he could beat either one of the dart throwers. By the time the game ended he felt woozy. Was it due to the tensions from his wedding that hadn't happened or had someone doctored his drink? He reached for a chair and felt two men each grab him by an arm and shoulder and guide him toward the back door.

By the time Lydia returned to the bar area, Ike Trowbridge, was a missing person.

By the time she returned home after having a few drinks with pub regulars she knew, Ike was trying unsuccessfully to free himself from a submerged stolen car that had plunged off a wharf on Paradise Island.

CHAPTER 48 – FRANK

Frank June returned from his mission to Lynyard Cay to find Todd helping Sylvia refurbish their boat. Frank had to yell his greeting to them in order to be heard over the sanding machine that Todd was using on the boat's steel railings. Upon hearing the voice, Todd switched off the sander, making the boatyard seem unnaturally quiet.

"Hi, Frank; I didn't realize how loud this machine is. What a contrast when it's off. I've been using it with emery cloth on the railings, and they're getting to be smooth enough for repainting. How did you do on Lynyard Cay?"

"Pretty well. I learned more than I expected. The island is long and thin; I'd say it's about two miles long. The people who live on it are at the north end where the cay is a bit wider. Toward the south end, there are places where it would be barely wide enough for a road, but there isn't one there, just bordering beaches, rocks, and scrub plants."

Sylvia popped her head up from the boat's cabin. "Welcome back, Frank. I was working below to avoid some of the noise from Todd's machine. I did hear your description of Lynyard Cay. The image in my mind is a long pork chop."

"That's not a bad comparison, Syl, but think of a chop that's on the thin side. The north end of the island is wider, but it doesn't bulge that much."

Todd wiped his hands on a damp rag. "Enough of the food images. Did you talk with people who live there? What did they say?"

145

"Everyone I talked with had been approached by either Emma Read or a real estate agent with an offer to buy their property for a higher price than they paid for it. They compared notes, and even though several agents appeared to be competing against each other, everyone felt that a single buyer, probably Emma Read, was behind the sudden interest in their property."

"Why did these people want to settle on such a rugged cay in the first place? When storms come up on the Atlantic Ocean side, that place must be positively scary. It's just a few feet above sea level."

"That's true, Todd, but the folks living there are rugged outdoor types who want to be away from tourists and government people. They want to be alone and think they can survive anything without outside help. They even post signs on the beaches near their homes warning casual sailors to keep their boats and their selves away."

"I can understand that. This is one of the few places in the world where there are still remote uninhabited islands."

Sylvia welcomed Frank with a kiss. "So much for the macho hermits on Lynyard Cay. What did you learn about why Emma Read wants to buy them out?"

Before Frank could answer, Sandy Rolle emerged from the winding path through the array of damaged boats. "I have a few clues for that mystery and another one as well."

CHAPTER 49 – PUZZLE PIECES

Frank retrieved a stack of four nested five gallon paint buckets from under a canvas tarp covering the boat maintenance supplies. He inverted the empty buckets and arranged them as a circle within a small cleared area between two boats. "Our conference room is now open for business. What did you learn, Sandy?"

As they all sat on upside down buckets, Sandy said, "The first intriguing clue I have comes from Joyce's calls to administrative aides to government officials. She has a network of people whose names are not well known because they're assistants, but they're the people who do the day-to-day work that actually runs the government. Others discuss projects, but these people make them happen. One such person told Joyce that Emma Read inquired whether she could control boat traffic through a channel between an offshore cay and Greater Abaco Island if she owned the land on both sides of the channel."

Todd slapped the bucket he sat upon. "She has to be talking about the Channel between Lynyard Cay and our family property south of Wilson City on Abaco. Does she want to charge tolls for boats to pass through that channel, or does she want to exclude pleasure and fishing boats? What's your guess, Sandy?"

"Whatever she wants, the Bahamas government is having no part of it, at least so far. Joyce's contact said that unless Emma submits a complete proposal detailing every aspect of her proposed project, there will be no discussion of it. Even if she does come up with the details, it isn't likely to succeed. There are too many voting boaters who won't tolerate having to sail on the ocean side of Lynyard Cay in bad weather."

Todd shook his head. "I hope you're right, but I have to wonder. From her past comments to me, I have the feeling that she's planning to bribe officials to rule in her favor."

"That is the wild card in this game, Todd. In past years, government officials have been caught spending much more than they're paid. The Bahamas is young as an independent country, and in some ways it's like the American Wild West. They'll get it right eventually, but there are still growing pains."

Sylvia asked, "Did Joyce learn anything else about Emma Read's plans or about her pirating ways?"

"Nothing beyond rumors, but it's said that she makes frequent trips to Mexico and that she may know people involved in Mexican drug cartels."

Frank nodded. "That would fit with her pirate background and her way of manipulating people. I could easily see her involved in drug smuggling."

"I said that line of thought is based on nothing better than rumors. We can't trust them."

Frank disagreed. "Sandy, there are rumors that are hard to believe and others that make perfect sense. Your rumors about Emma fall into the latter group."

Todd said, "Before we dwell too much on rumors of smuggling, let's get to what Sandy learned about that dead bridegroom who was passing himself off as me."

"First, his name was Ike Trowbridge, and he was a longtime bodyguard or assistant for Emma Read. His face did resemble yours, Todd, but he was a bit taller than you."

"Let's not dwell on height. I've heard short jokes all my life."

"The Coroner ruled that Trowbridge died an unlawful death at the hands of unknown persons. That's no surprise. The police say that his tuxedo tie and jacket were not in the car. I was amused by the fact that Trowbridge died in a stolen car. Since the victim had no criminal record, having him drown in a stolen car screams that this was no accident. The killers were probably street thugs working for someone with more brains than they had."

Sylvia said, "I'll wager her initials were E.R., and I don't mean the Queen. Emma was angry about the wedding screw-up, and Trowbridge, her impostor bridegroom, would have been the handiest target for her rage."

Todd multi-thumped his paint bucket seat. "You're right, but I find it hard to believe that witchy, conniving Emma would put herself in the position of being the most likely killer. It's too obvious. I wonder whether someone else was behind that Trowbridge murder. Maybe that person considered getting rid of Ike a favor for Emma."

Sandy agreed. "That's an interesting theory, Todd; it's a definite possibility. Anyway, death was by drowning after first having been hit on the head with a blunt object. He could have bashed his head when the car crashed through the railing, but it's not likely, because nothing hard in the car lines up with the wound."

"If we hadn't objected to that wedding, Trowbridge would have been declared to be me, and he would be on his honeymoon instead of dead."

CHAPTER 50 – STEVE SWEENEY

When Todd and Sandy returned to Weatherford & Rolle, Joyce was on the telephone, but she handed Todd a note as he walked by. He saw that it was a telephone message requesting him to call Steve Sweeney.

He keyed the indicated number. "Hi, Steve – Todd Weatherford returning your call. What's happening?"

"First, I wanted to let you know that I've returned from Florida. Tell Sandy I have his shipment of radial arm saws ready for pickup at my usual slot at Harbour View Marina. They've cleared customs and the duties have been added to my invoice. He can give me another order for my next round trip when your driver picks up these machines, or he can wait a few days, because *Sweeney's Queen* and I will be here for a while. I'm taking a break from charters."

"That's good news on both the business and personal sides. I'll send our driver over for the saws, and then I'll visit your boat in a couple of hours to fill you in on our adventures in case you still want to get involved with our motley crew."

"That's a definite affirmative, Todd. I'm taking this break because I'm a bit bored. I need to get occupied with something different."

"I don't know what else I can promise you, but our mission will be different."

Todd spent the next hour and a half arranging for the merchandise pickup from Steve's boat, asking Joyce to prepare a schedule of orders for

Steve's future round trips to Florida, and helping Sandy with paperwork so that he would have time to come along on the visit to Steve's boat.

When Todd and Sandy arrived at Harbour View Marina, they saw Steve hosing down *Sweeney's Queen* to rinse off ocean salt on the hull, decks, and windows. He waved to them, and then turned off the water and coiled the hose.

"I hoped to have this finished before you arrived. There's a bench at the end of the dock where we can sit until the boat dries."

Todd said, "We can stand next to the boat. It'll be more private than the main dock. I brought Sandy along to meet you. I would have introduced you when I first arrived with you from Florida, but on that day, an emergency came up while we were walking over this way."

Sandy shook hands with Steve. "You have a first class vessel, Steve, and you obviously maintain it well. Todd's suggestion that we use your services to eliminate some freight costs simplifies our logistics on the items you bring. We'll talk further about ways to match your schedule to our supply needs, but I think Todd wants to discuss his personal mission today."

Todd summarized everything that happened since he last saw Steve, including the interrupted wedding, the bridegroom's murder, the attempt on Todd's father's life, the attempted arson at the store, and their research into what Emma Read's project might be.

When they finished, Steve responded with a long whistle. "I thought these islands were restful places to relax and enjoy life. Todd, you've had a lot happen since I brought you here. You didn't mention Frank and Sylvia June. Have they had a quieter time than you?"

"They've been helping us find out what Emma's up to, but they're spending most of their time building our navy."

"By that, I assume they found a used boat to work on. What kind is it?"

"I'll take you over to see for yourself after we finish discussions here."

"Great. I'll see what I can do to assist their efforts. In the meantime I can contribute a rumor that may or may not have something to do with this Emma Read."

Sandy said, "We're looking for whatever we can learn to understand her and her goals. I'm surprised that you heard something in Florida."

"That's where the rumor comes from. I remembered it when you said that she's descended from a pirate. There's a shipbuilding operation in Panama City, Florida called Eastern Shipbuilding Group. They build all sorts of specialized vessels, from tugboats to Coast Guard cutters. The rumor is that they're building a pair of ships that look like traditional wooden-hulled pirate sailing vessels, but they have hidden catamaran hulls and dual inboard engines. They're the size of the old sailing ships, which is smallish, but they're sturdy and fast when they use the engines. I don't know who the buyer is, but there aren't that many pirates in this area anymore."

"That may be a key piece of information, Steve. I could see her building a pirate-themed resort, but I'm sure Todd will agree there has to be something illegal involved."

"I do agree, Sandy. She thinks like a pirate. Ike Trowbridge's death, plunging off the dock, was a modern version of walking the plank. If those ships are hers, she'll use them to take something away from its rightful owner and to make illegal profits."

"That's not the only thing that bothers me."

"What else?"

"If those ships are hers, she has someone with unlimited funds backing her venture."

CHAPTER 51 – BOATYARD

As Steve Sweeney followed Todd Weatherford through the maze of used and battered boats, he said, "I hope Frank and Sylvia found something better than most of these. No offence intended to the boatyard manager, but most of these old boats are junk. I wouldn't trust any of them with my life, let alone risk customer lives by using one of these in a business."

Todd didn't say anything, but kept his eyes on the narrow path through the array of boats. When they cleared the final few before reaching Frank and Sylvia's work area, he stopped. "Now, what do you think?"

Steve scanned the freshly painted red and white boat in the back corner of the boatyard. He saw a few hull patches that he would like to examine more closely, but all-in-all, he was impressed. "Not a bad job for a couple of landlubbers and their assistants." He walked up to the boat and knocked on a section of the original hull and then on a patched area."

Frank and Sylvia scrambled out of the cabin and peered over the railing. Frank shaded his eyes while they adjusted from the dark of the cabin to bright sunlight. "Who's hitting our boat?" As his eyes focused, he saw Todd and Steve. "Hello, Captain Steve; what do you think of her?"

"For the most part, you've done a great job. It's a U.S. Coast Guard utility boat, right? She's built for function rather than form, which means you'll get a lot of bang for your buck."

Frank climbed down the ladder from the cradle-mounted boat. He shook hands with Steve. "Great to see you again. What did you mean by 'for the most part' when you commented on our work?"

"I only meant that your striking paint job may be premature. I knocked on the original hull and your patched sections to learn whether your patches are sturdy enough. They sound as though they're single layer sheet metal with nothing behind them. You get a lot of impact when ocean waves lift the boat and then surge forward, dropping the boat several feet onto the water surface behind the wave crest. I think you're going to need at least a couple of additional layers of aluminum over your patched areas. You can overlap the sheets and put sealing compound between them so that, after conforming to the curve of your boat, they function as a single thicker plate. I'm not sure what you have here, but you should be using alloy 5086 aluminum which is weldable. This boatyard should have the proper welding equipment. You'll have extra work, but you need to do it to make your boat safer. You'll also want multiple coats of paint over the aluminum patches."

"Ouch! That'll be a ton of extra work. I guess we'll have to chalk that up to being rookies at boat repair."

"I have time to give you some help, Frank. You'll work your way up the learning curve pretty quickly. Have you had any seamanship and navigation lessons yet?"

"The boatyard manager, Ed Burley, said he'd work with us after we finished our boat repairs, but obviously, we haven't reached that point yet."

"Don't worry. I'll start training you and Sylvia on *Sweeney's Queen*. Todd, feel free to join us."

"That sounds great, Steve. I'll take you up on that offer. Even though their boat isn't seaworthy yet, Sylvia and Frank should get some credit for selecting this craft."

Steve agreed. "Definitely. This utility boat was built to military specifications for heavy duty work. Nothing else I've seen in this boatyard comes close to the potential for this craft. Have you decided on a name for it?"

Sylvia said, "We wanted *June Bug*, but when I searched online, I found two each of *June Bug* and *Junebug*, so we may have to settle for *June Moon*."

"That should work, or you could use the possessive trick, calling it *June's Bug*. With your family name, it fits."

"That's a perfect solution, Steve. Frank and I thank you for all your nautical wisdom."

Frank didn't say anything but noted that they had moved to the next phase of marriage, when the wife speaks for the husband as well as herself in making decisions.

CHAPTER 52 – TACTICS

The property that George Weatherford had purchase and earmarked for Todd to inherit was covered with trees. It had much earlier been intended for harvesting by the Wilson City lumbering enterprise north of it that went bankrupt. Wilson City began operations at the beginning of the twentieth century but lasted only a few years. The forest had thickened with the passage of time, but the individual trees were not top quality because of deficiencies in the island's soil.

Because the terrain was undeveloped and was surrounded by forest, Sandy and Todd drove over pathways and old logging roads in the company Jeep on their way to inspect Todd's land. Their route had many turns due to unexpected boulders, path narrowing, and fallen trees, but they eventually reached their destination overlooking the channel between Abaco and Lynyard Cay.

Todd climbed out of the Jeep and looked back at their tire tracks emerging from the trees. "That was a struggle to reach this point. We had so many turns and forks in the paths we took getting here that we may have trouble finding our way back again. We should have marked our trail."

"Don't sweat it, Todd. We have a compass and my amazing sense of direction to guide us back."

"I'm glad you have confidence. What if you take a wrong turn at a fork?"

"Then I have my ace in the hole."

"What do you mean?"

"We're not as remote as you think here. North of us is the old lumbering complex known as Wilson City. West of us and bearing the same name is the Wilson City Power Station. It's Bahamas Power & Light's main power plant on Abaco. BPL is unpopular now because their equipment periodically breaks down, sometimes for lengthy periods, making Abaconians survive with backup generators. Anyway, the Wilson City Power Station is located on the Great Abaco Highway. If we should take a wrong turn on our way out of here, all we have to do is drive west from that point until we cross the highway. We won't have a problem."

"That's good news. Without looking for the boundary markers that define this piece of property, I can see that it has a panoramic view of Lynyard Cay and the ocean beyond it. We're far enough above sea level to avoid flooding during a hurricane."

"You have a valuable piece of property, Todd. It probably includes the beach below this land. Now we have to find out why Emma Read wants it so much."

"I think I know how to do that."

"How?"

"The easy way, Sandy. I'll ask her. I have her phone number on your Caller ID screen from when she called me at the office. I can call her and say that I'm willing to lease a portion of my land to her if she will guarantee that it won't be used for illegal purposes."

"I get it. She'd have to tell you what she would do with this land before you would agree to lease it."

"Right, and if that satisfied her, I wouldn't have to worry about her trying to lay claim to our family land."

"I'll only give you a maybe answer to that one. She may agree to rent the property but still keep the ultimate goal of taking it away from you. Remember, she's carrying your baby for the predicted purpose of laying claim to your family property."

"I'll worry about the baby after he or she is born. I may still follow up on our earlier discussion and petition the court for custody of the baby because Emma is unfit to be a mother."

"Be careful; under Bahamas law, as long as Emma has control of the baby, she can demand that you make reasonable financial provision for the child, even if you file a will excluding Emma and the child from any benefits. You could battle in the courts for months or years to determine what you should pay as reasonable financial provision."

"In other words, I could lease this land to her and then have to return her payments as support for the child. That would give her the property for free, just as she wanted."

"That's one possibility."

"What if I sold this property to someone other than Emma? The baby would no longer give her leverage, although I would still have to provide some child support."

"It's one of the finest undeveloped land parcels on Abaco. Would you sell it just to spite Emma?"

"Not to spite her, but to rid myself of any threat she poses."

"It's not that simple, Todd. If you sell this land to someone else, that person is likely to sell it to Emma for a big profit. You'll lose the land; you'll lose that potential profit; and you'll still have Emma with her future baby coming after you for something else, like the store or the land it's on. As long as she can use that baby as a weapon against you, she will."

"In that case, I'll have to try Plan B. Let's take a few pictures of this property, and then head back to Weatherford & Rolle, so that I can get started."

CHAPTER 53 – PLAN B

When they entered the store's private office, Todd closed the door for privacy and sat next to the telephone to organize his thoughts. Sandy looked through his mail, expecting Todd to start a new conversation. When that didn't happen, Sandy took the initiative. "I need to know. What is Plan B?"

"Plan B is the same as Plan A, with a few variations and a ticking deadline clock."

"What's the deadline?"

"Emma can't spring her legal tricks on me until the baby is born. That's the deadline. Until that time I'm free to take any steps I want with little or no interference from her."

"What steps?"

"Emma Read wants to be a pirate like her ancestor. In this part of the world with sophisticated police and government agencies, the old type of piracy is difficult if not impossible. I'm going to offer her a lease on part of the family land to see how she responds. I need to learn her plans, and I'll speed up negotiations by telling her I have to go home in the near future and that I need a quick decision. I think I'll be able to force some kind of action from her."

"You're more optimistic than I am, but go ahead. You'll have privacy here to talk with her. I have to get back to solving a few store problems. I'll have Joyce take messages on any calls for you other than an Emma Read call-back."

Sandy left the office, shutting the door behind him. Todd wrote a few notes on a sheet of paper, asked Joyce to check her call log to find the telephone number he needed, and then called Emma. He had no idea how she would respond.

"This is Emma Read. Who's calling?"

"It's Todd. I decided that we should talk things out. We do have a common interest in your coming baby. How are you healthwise, by the way?"

"Thanks for your concern, genuine or not. I'm a healthy pregnant woman, well but not comfortable. Speaking of medical conditions, I'll admit I wasn't thrilled when you told me you were in better shape than your earlier lupus verdict indicated."

"Sorry to disappoint you by getting a better diagnosis. Your earlier expressions of love for me turned out to be far from true. Were any of your statements about your resort project true? You want to get your hands on my family's land, but you haven't told me why."

Emma paused before speaking to organize her thoughts. "If I tell you my plans, will you discuss the needs of my project in a businesslike manner?"

"I'm no longer a tour guide. I'm a partner in a successful business. That gives me a different viewpoint. Tell me what you're up to, and I'll do my best to respond in a reasonable manner. It won't be like opening the newspaper and discovering that I'm about to get married."

"That must have been a shock for you. I thought you were still in Chicago and would never see it."

"It was only after you disappeared on me that I discovered my Bahamas connections and business. It hadn't been part of my Kentucky upbringing."

"I suspected that. You didn't react at all when I talked about the West Indies."

"Flash forward from then to now. We're talking like two normal people. Please tell me about your project and why you want to steal our family land."

"You'd never make it as a diplomat; you're too direct with your questions. When we were in Chicago, I told you a portion of the truth, but not all of it."

"Spoken like a good negotiator; go on."

"I'm involved with others in a venture. A residential resort may be part of it later, but it will primarily be a theme park."

"On or near Lynyard Cay?"

"You have a good intelligence network. I'm impressed. You're correct, of course. We're going to develop a pirate themed park and run vessels that look like the old pirate ships up the channel between Lynyard Cay and Abaco. We may extend the voyage a little further north and sail into the Pelican Cays Land and Sea Park."

"Would you be taking passengers?"

"That's the whole point, a pirate themed destination for tourists, complete with a voyage on an old-fashioned sailing ship."

"That sounds like an honest enterprise so far. Why do you want or need our family land?"

"You still suspect me of doing something illegal. I'm not really a pirate. I'm just taking advantage of my family history to make an honest living."

"Ike Trowbridge might not agree with that 'honest living' statement."

Emma hesitated while gathering her thoughts. "Poor Ike; he was my watchdog for a very long time. I was sorry to hear about his accident."

Todd laughed silently. It was good she couldn't see his face during their telephone conversation. "I'm feeling charitable today, so I won't pursue your involvement in Ike's sad departure. Just remember that I've seen both of the faces you wear."

"Let's steer this discussion back toward business. My development group wants your land across from Lynyard Cay for our theme park welcome center and departure point for the longboats we'll use to row tourists out to the ships."

"When do you expect this project to happen?"

"I can't give you details, but some parts of the effort are already in progress. Are you willing to sell your land?"

"I'll consider leasing you part but not all of it."

"I want ownership, not a lease."

"A lease will get you started without a legal battle that could delay your project for years. It also gives you limited liability if your theme park fails to be a long term success."

"Todd, you know that I can attack your ownership in the courts once our child is born."

"This started as a civil conversation. That child would have no rights to family property as long as my father and I are alive, and you'd better not try again to change our status like you did in Kentucky when that driver attempted to run my father down."

"You're right. We should try to settle this peacefully if we can. I'll take your lease offer to my partners. If they agree, we can discuss the cost, terms, and percentage of your land that would be involved."

"I'll need a guarantee that my property won't be used for anything illegal. You'll also want to get a prompt decision on proceeding with negotiations. I have business that will take me back to the United States soon."

"I'll get right on it. I underestimated you. You're no longer the easygoing tour guide I knew."

Richard Davidson

"That old me is gone forever, thanks to your scheming."

CHAPTER 54 – ASSIGNMENT

The four men sat on the deck of *Sweeney's Queen* discussing Todd's conversation with Emma Read and the next steps they should take.

Sandy finished his Kalik beer and added his bottle to the box of empties. "Todd, thanks for telling us what Emma said, but how much of it do you believe? You made her sound almost civil."

"I have the feeling that she revealed the portion of her project that will be public information, but nothing more. She said she and her partners are building a theme park that offers tourists local rides on pirate ships. There may be some business sense in that, but I question that there would be enough profit to satisfy Emma Read and her partners."

Frank threw his empty bottle in with the others with enough impact that he walked over to the box to check for broken glass. There was none. He returned to his seat. "Who are these partners you keep mentioning? Their identities may tell us whether this is simply a tourist operation or something more devious."

Sandy said, "I'll come down on the side of devious for two reasons. First, Joyce learned from several of her sources that Emma Read has made frequent trips to Mexico in recent months. If she has Mexican associates with money to invest, they are likely to be connected to one of the drug cartels there. Second, I question how long her theme park could be profitable."

Steve Sweeney reacted to Sandy's comments. "Your first reason suggests that you remember what the Medellin Cartel did on Norman's Cay. I'm not sure why you think a pirate-themed park wouldn't be profitable."

"In a word, their problem would be competition. The Walt Disney people are asserting themselves. Disney already owns Castaway Cay on the west side of Abaco. That's less than thirty miles by air from Lynyard Cay. They use Castaway Cay as their private cruise port. They've also received preliminary government approval to build a second cruise port operation at the south end of Eleuthera Island, southeast of Nassau. The Walt Disney Company is focusing on the Bahamas. Other cruise lines are also developing private islands. Local tourist attractions will have trouble competing with them."

Frank asked, "Steve, what did you mean when you mentioned the Medellin Cartel and Norman's Cay?"

"In the late seventies, the co-founder of the Colombian Medellin Cartel, Carlos Lehder, was looking for a new way to smuggle drugs into the United States. He bribed Bahamas government officials to look the other way while he took over Norman's Cay, one of the small islands in the Exuma island chain, south of Eleuthera. According to a later television documentary, Lehder bought some land on Norman's Cay and then took over the rest of the island through extortion and murder. The cartel built a long runway on the island, installed radar, and then used armed guards and vicious dogs to keep outsiders away. For about six years, Lehder and his cronies used that island as a refueling stop for transshipping Colombian drugs into the United States. They used a fleet of small planes flying to a large number of tiny U.S. airstrips to transport drugs in much greater quantities than individual travelers or small boats could carry. They also used Norman's Cay as a party port to reward cartel workers. For years, it was a private kingdom for Lehder and the cartel. The operation finally got closed down in 1982 after U.S. government pressure and television exposes forced the Bahamas government to take action against Lehder and his people."

Frank said, "I've wondered whether someone could turn a small cay into a private country. There are so many cays, and most aren't inhabited."

Frank's comment got Todd's attention. "That sounds as though you've started to do some boating."

"Steve has already taught Syl and me quite a bit about the islands and about navigating a boat under varying conditions. We still have a lot to learn, but we're making good progress. Anyway, getting back to the Norman's Cay story, I think I hear Sandy suggesting that Emma's Mexican partners are looking for a new variation on the private island for drug shipping."

Sandy nodded. "Something along those lines, but I haven't figured out how they plan to do it. Drug smuggling is likely to be the key to Emma Read's operation. It brings in a lot of profit quickly."

Todd disagreed. "The profitability angle is right, but it's not the same situation for the Mexican cartels as it was for the Colombians. The Medellin people used Norman's Cay to get more drugs into the United States from Colombia faster than by other means. The Mexicans don't have that problem. They share a long border with the United

States, and they can hide drugs in tractor-trailers or their cargoes. Some shipments will get stopped, but most will get through border processing. I think the Mexicans will either be working with Emma Read on something else, or will be funneling drugs through the Bahamas to end up someplace other than the United States."

Steve Sweeney said, "I'm the outsider in this group, so I may be getting this discussion differently from the rest of you, but my impression is that you're not at all sure what she's up to, but you expect it to be lucrative and bad. I think it's time to stop talking and decide what to do next. My time is limited, if I'm to help you."

Sandy looked at Todd. "This is your mission, but I feel almost equally involved. If you don't mind, I'll suggest the next step."

"Go to it, Sandy. I trust your judgment."

"Steve told us about the rumored pirate ships they're building in Florida. They're the centerpiece of what Emma is doing. They're also where her investors' money is going. I suggest that we should commission Steve to visit that shipyard in Florida and find out all he can about those vessels. Their design features and cost may give us much more accurate information about her project than a whole day of speculating."

Steve nodded his agreement.

Frank said, "I'd like to go with Steve. I need some action, and I also need to learn more about shipbuilding and repair, even though our *June's Bug* refurbishing is almost complete. Is that all right with you, Todd?"

"Sounds great to me. Tell Sylvia to see me if she needs any assistance while you're gone. I have a feeling that those pirate ships are more than just tourist rides."

CHAPTER 55 – SHAKEDOWN CRUISE

While Steve Sweeney and Frank June were away investigating the shipbuilder, Sylvia decided it was time to test *June's Bug* for seaworthiness. She approached the boatyard manager, Edward Burley, on the dock as he waved to a departing refueling customer.

"Edward, how does your schedule look today?"

"Just the usual busy work. What do you have in mind?"

"I think it's time to put *June's Bug* into the water. I'm pretty sure she won't sink."

"You folks have made her look pretty enough. I think you're right. It's time to see if she's shipshape. I'll get the guys to clear a path through the array of smaller rehab and spare parts boats. They'll put a hoist rig on your boat and ease it into the water. It's heavier than most boats its size, because of all the Coast Guard requirements. We should have it in the water in about three hours. Then I'll join you to give her a good test in the harbor and out where the water gets rough."

Sylvia returned in three hours after doing some shopping in town. She hadn't wanted to be in the way or to second guess Edward's expertise while his crew maneuvered *June's Bug* through the field of damaged boats and other obstacles. When she reached the boatyard harbor area, Sylvia found her boat serenely sitting alongside a dock as though it had been moored there for days. She marveled at how different it looked when viewed from above as compared to looking up at it on dry-dock cradles. It looked smaller and sleeker because of the portion concealed beneath the water. All-in-all it commanded a powerful image with its red cabin topping a white hull, and its white deck surrounded by silver-painted safety railings.

Sylvia didn't notice Edward Burley coming up behind her.

"*June's Bug* passes the still picture test with flying colors. She looks great and floats. We fueled her up. Are you ready to see whether she can perform?"

They boarded the boat, and before starting it up, Edward looked at papers on Frank's clipboard. "I see your husband has prepared lists and tables showing the boat's specifications. Some of these are unexpected. I should have charged you more for this craft."

"What do you mean?"

"Don't worry; I'll stick with the original price, but the engines are more powerful than I thought. According to Frank's notes you have twin John Deere 6081 diesel marine engines putting out 375 horsepower each. Even allowing for deterioration with age and an amateur doing the tune-up, this vessel has potent power. It's listed as cruising at 21 knots and a maximum speed of 25 knots. We'll have to check actual performance against those numbers."

Edward started the engines and fed them enough fuel for a throaty idle. "They sound pretty good. Put on your life vest and we'll take her out slowly."

Edward eased *June's Bug* out of Marsh Harbour Boatyards through the narrow entrance channel, turned it left toward the Abaco Beach Resort, and then held the wheel until she transited a complete circle. Then he turned the wheel to complete a circle in the opposite direction. "She steers well. Let's take her across the bay to Elbow Cay. I'll give her a bit more throttle."

June's Bug surged forward smoothly in response to Edward's experienced touch on the throttle. They soon reached Elbow Cay, where Edward switched places with Sylvia. "Give her just a little fuel until you have a feel for her responsiveness. This boat is powered for speed, so you have to develop a touch for low throttle operations. Take her along the shore to Hope town Lighthouse. Then bring her about and head back toward Marsh Harbour."

Sylvia tried to look confident as she took over the controls for the first time, but her results were less than perfect. She held the wheel and increased the throttle to what she considered a low level. *June's Bug* shot forward at an alarming speed. Sylvia shut down the throttle, and the boat came to a bobbing rest. "Edward, I thought I gave her a tiny amount of fuel. Obviously, it was too much. How do you manage to control fuel flow for slow operations?"

"It does take a lot of practice. Don't worry. You'll develop a feel for it before Frank returns. Then you'll be able to reassure him when he gets the same result you did. Head back toward Marsh Harbour, and when you're in the middle of the channel, I'll take over for a performance test."

Sylvia eased the throttle open ever so slightly, and the boat responded with just a tiny leap forward before cruising at a steady speed. She steered per Edward's hand signals and then switched positions with him after receiving his thumbs up approval gesture."

As he took the wheel, Edward looked at Sylvia, standing with her feet widely separated for balance. "You'd better get a good grip on the railing. It's time to see what this baby will do."

Under Edward's practiced hand on the throttle, *June's Bug* seemed to lean forward, trying to always exceed the requested speed. The craft accelerated smoothly southward through the minimal chop of the cay-protected waters of the Sea of Abaco. Edward increased the speed until the diesel engines began to labor, and then pushed through that point, causing some unexpected vibrations in the boat's structure. He eased the throttle back and took a wide turn to port before reaching Pelican Cays Land & Sea Park. "That was fun. She needs a tune-up. Top cruising speed and maximum speed are about three knots below the specs. I'll have my guys try to figure out where that vibration comes from. She has a shallow draft, so we cleared the sandbars without a problem. Are you ready for the acid test?"

"What do you mean by that?"

I'm going to take her out into the open ocean beyond the barrier cays. It's time to see whether she leaks when slammed down after going through waves. Before we go, check below deck for any leaks up to this point."

Sylvia opened hatches and used her flashlight to look for water below the deck. "Looks dry so far."

"Good. Brace yourself. We're headed for the Atlantic Ocean."

As they passed the south end of long and skinny Tilloo Cay, the wind from the east picked up, and slightly choppy water became rolling waves.

Edward increased engine speed to fight the headwind, and the boat rose and fell as it cut through the persistent waves. Each time it passed a wave crest *June's Bug* slammed down into the following trough, shaking her structure and her passengers. Sylvia tightened her grip on the railing and bent her knees so they would flex to soften the impacts. After fighting the waves and headwind for ten minutes, Edward reversed course and headed back toward the Sea of Abaco's protected waters, now pushed by the wind and riding the waves, so that the boat accelerated. The transition to calmer waters as the boat passed the southern tip of Tilloo Cay was sudden and a welcome relief.

Edward reduced the motor speed to an idle. "Open the hatches and check for water leaks."

Sylvia's flashlight scanned every visible area below decks. When she stood aft6er completing her inspection, there was a smile on her face. "We're shipshape. No water below and I did expect to find some after that beating we took."

Edward nodded back at her. "*June's Bug* passed her first test, but don't congratulate yourself too much. The ocean is relatively calm today. Someday, you may have to venture out in a squall. Try to avoid ocean storms whenever possible."

CHAPTER 56 – PIRATE SHIPS

Steve Sweeney and Frank June flew from Marsh Harbour to Palm Beach, Florida on Bahamasair and rented a Buick Enclave for the remainder of their trip to Panama City in the Florida panhandle, the home of Eastern Shipbuilding Group. By the time they arrived at the shipbuilding facility, they had developed a plan.

Steve and Frank entered the lobby of the office building and asked to speak with someone about developing a customized vessel. After a short wait, a man and a woman came out to greet them. The man introduced himself as Peter Garrison, the Marketing Manager. The woman, Karen Quill, said she was Project Engineer for custom designs. Steve described his charter boat service operating between Florida and the Bahamas and said that he planned to expand his business in partnership with Frank to include exploration tours of many of the more remote Bahamas cays and islands. Steve indicated that he was looking to build a craft that would carry twenty passengers, have a low draft for operations in shallow waters around small islands, but still be seaworthy enough for open ocean travel.

Peter Garrison expressed interest. "You have an intriguing set of requirements. You require a vessel with shallow draft for close-in coastal work but it also must be stable enough for foul weather ocean travel. That sounds like a catamaran split hull design to me. What do you think, Karen?"

"It could be a catamaran with two parallel narrow hulls, or even a trimaran. Several designers are suggesting a third center hull that protrudes farther forward than the other side hulls to cut through the water with less drag while still having the stability of a catamaran."

"That would be a good idea, sleek and stable too. They'd need to carry a boat for beach landings, possibly an inflatable. Those are on the market as stock items. Karen, do you think Steve and Frank would benefit from seeing those two unusual catamarans we're building?"

"Good idea, Peter; they'll see that a catamaran design doesn't have to be super wide for stability. You take them on the tour while I put together a few sample pictures and sketches to discuss after you return."

As they turned to leave, Frank said, "Karen, I have a reconditioned Coast Guard utility boat. Would you have any manuals or design data on those?"

"We do build vessels for the Coast Guard and have pretty complete files on their fleet. That would be the 41-footer that's been retired from service?"

"That's it."

"Go on your tour. I'll see what I can find for you. I'll put what I discover on a flash drive for your computer."

Peter Garrison led Steve and Frank to a mud-spattered pickup truck in the parking lot. "We'll take this weathered beauty. It gets pretty dirty in the shipbuilding areas. I won't drive my car out there."

They drove down Nelson Street and through a gate into a work area where activity and industrial sounds surrounded them. The back end of a partially constructed freighter loomed over the waterfront area, with a tall red crane poised above it. Beyond that, they passed areas allocated to specialized tugboats and barges. As they continued down the unpaved service road, they bounced through muddy potholes and over steel plates covering deeper holes until they came to a remote section of the shipyard where two apparently identical craft were under construction. Peter Garrison parked the truck and led Steve and Frank toward the skeletal ship structures.

"These two ships will be almost but not quite identical. Final design work will make it easy for observers to tell them apart. They have a modern catamaran split hull, but they will have an external design that makes them appear to be wooden sailing ships of the old pirate variety. They will have masts and sails."

Frank said, "They're bigger than I expected. Will they be able to operate and handle as sailing ships, with normal responses to wind direction and speed changes?"

"In theory, yes. That's one of the design goals, but it's the first time we've built modern powered vessels that are supposed to act like sailing ships. The engines won't just provide auxiliary drive when wind is lacking. They'll be powerful enough to achieve a peak design speed of 18 knots. When operated at that speed it will be obvious that they're more than they appear to be. We're a little concerned about the extra drag of the external wooden shell that makes this look like a sailing ship and the maneuvering differences between a traditional hull and the concealed catamaran structure."

Steve asked, "Will you have wooden masts, and will they be strong enough to take the stress of a full spread of sails in a brisk wind?"

"The old wooden masts held up well, but we won't be taking any chances. This design will have a single mast, but the external wood will surround a metal composite core, to avoid any possible problems. The two ships will be sloop rigged with a bowsprit protruding forward from the bow to which the jib will be rigged, a forward staysail, a square topsail, and a larger gaff mainsail on a boom behind the mast."

"Has your customer given names to these ships, or will that come later?"

"The names are on the drawings, Steve. They'll be *Mary Read* and *Anne Bonny*."

Frank almost laughed because Todd and Sandy had predicted those names during their last discussion before this trip. Remembering their cover story about the boat they wanted to build, he said, "These ships are really unusual. Is there anything other than the pirate ship appearance and sails that wouldn't apply to the boat we want to build?"

Garrison looked at his notes. "I don't think so. Let's return to the office and talk more about design approaches for your project."

CHAPTER 57 – LYNYARD CAY

The civil engineer stood facing Emma Read at the southern tip of Lynyard Cay. He could hardly believe the nature and scope of the job she wanted him to quote. "You want me to build a road extending the whole length of Lynyard Cay?"

"The cay is roughly two miles long, so that's what I want."

"Do you own the whole cay? There are houses at the north end."

"We're in negotiations to purchase those properties."

"Who is 'we'?"

"'We' refers to my business group, and you don't need to know any more than that. We have the capital, and if we accept your proposal, you'll receive a letter from Central Bank of the Bahamas guaranteeing payment upon acceptance of the work."

"Even if you own this entire cay, the work you're requesting may be both impossible and illegal. Why do you want the road anyway?"

"Why I want it is no business of yours. What's impossible and illegal about it?"

"This is a very narrow cay. The road you've requested is two automobile lanes wide. Near the midpoint and at this southern end of the island there are places where the road would be wider than the land. It wouldn't be practical to fill new land on the ocean side of the cay because of the rough surf. If we added landfill on the calmer water side facing Abaco, the cost would be unreasonably high. There's also the question of the amount of loading the basic coral structure of the island will take. There's a legal question because the government has pledged to preserve natural environments and encourage ecotourism. Your road would eliminate Lynyard Cay's unspoiled nature."

"Are you saying that you don't want to bid on my project?"

"No, I'll bid, but the price will be high, and I'll include disclaimers as to the road's guaranteed durability if we don't do extensive testing first."

"That's fine. The road won't be carrying major loads anyway. Despite environmentalist protests, the government is letting Disney develop a new port of call for its cruise ships at the south end of Eleuthera. I don't see them holding up this project. Take your photos and surveys. Then put together a proposal for me. I'll expect it within three weeks."

That's not all she's expecting. That baby will be coming sooner than she thinks. She's also conning me about a road that has to be straight and won't carry major loads. She's hiding the fact that she's building a runway, and a long one at that.

CHAPTER 58 – FATHER AND SON

George Weatherford stared at his phone, not quite believing what his son had said. "Todd, if I understood you correctly, you want me to approve Emma Read's leasing our property across from Lynyard Cay. Why on earth would you do that? She's dangerous, and she wants to take that property away from us."

"I won't lease the entire property, only part of it. I'm taking this approach because it's the only way I can get her to talk about her project. I know she's not telling me everything, but I know much more now than I did before we started negotiating."

"You have to think like a lawyer with her. If she gets her hands on that land, she won't give it up at the end of the lease period. She'll use every legal trick in the book to hold onto it."

"And maybe a few illegal tricks too."

"Now you're getting the picture, Todd. You've talked with her about leasing the land, and you say you've learned some things about her project. How much more will you learn by leasing the land?"

"I'll learn about her construction plans and layout for the property."

"Is that enough added information to take a chance on losing the land forever?"

"I guess not, but I feel we have to do something to reduce her desire to threaten us before the baby comes, or she'll try to eliminate the two of us and claim that land in the baby's name."

"In other words, you're worried about my safety. Don't let that fear guide your actions. I've taken steps for self-protection if she tries to get me again. Tell Emma that you wanted to lease the land, but right now, that's my property, and I refused to lease it."

"That's taking a risk, Dad. They'll try to kill you and then put pressure on me."

"I'm willing to take that chance. The boys and I haven't had much adventure lately."

"Who do you mean by 'the boys'?"

"I can't tell you now, but let's just say we're prepared for anything. I officially refuse to lease that land to Emma Read. We'll learn more from seeing how she reacts to rejection than we will by agreeing to that lease."

"I hope you know what you're doing, Dad. I'll follow your lead and cut off the negotiations with Emma."

CHAPTER 59 – CONFRONTATION

When Todd called Emma, she said she would discuss her project further, but not over the telephone. She insisted that they talk face-to-face, and said that because of her advanced pregnancy, they would have to meet in Nassau, at her cottage in Adelaide Village. Todd agreed and scheduled their meeting two days later.

Sandy expressed uneasiness with the idea of Todd going alone to Emma Read's house. He suggested that they should have backup nearby in case the meeting turned out to be some kind of a trap. Todd had no guarantee that Emma wouldn't have henchmen waiting out of sight to ambush him. To satisfy Sandy's misgivings, Todd agreed to take Steve Sweeney and Frank June with him. They would fly to Nassau and then rent a car to drive to Adelaide Village. Frank and Steve would watch the front and back entrances to the cottage while Todd was inside. In case extra support was needed, Sandy would give them contact phone numbers for the local detectives who called him earlier while investigating the death of Ike Trowbridge.

Knowing the others were in position, Todd rang the doorbell of Emma's so-called cottage, which had enough wings and additions to be better described as a beachfront mansion. White with red roofing, only the road separated the house from the beach and the ocean beyond it.

Emma answered the doorbell with her left hand resting on the small of her back. Her future child

185

was getting heavier. "Come on in, Todd. You look different from when I last saw you ... tanned and more mature. I set us up to talk at the kitchen table. That will keep an informal mood. I have hot and cold drinks plus pastry."

Todd followed her to the kitchen, poured coffee from her carafe and sat down. "I'd like to keep this visit and discussion civil. You know that I don't trust you, but we can still have candid discussions."

"When we were in Chicago, you were naïve and trusting. Now, you're more of a poker player who reveals only a tiny glimpse of his thoughts." She poured a glass of orange juice and sat across the table from him.

Todd scanned the kitchen and the open-plan areas beyond it. "This is quite a house. I expected something much smaller when you called it a cottage."

"It started out as a cottage when the first owner built it, but it's had several additions since then. I sometimes rent it to tourists when I'm out of town."

Todd didn't want the exchanges of niceties to reduce his alertness, so he cut directly to the matter at hand. "I have bad news for you. I discussed the proposed lease of our land with my father, and he doesn't want to take that step. He's the legal owner, so I have to go along with his wishes."

"What would you say if I told you your father's decision doesn't bother me?"

Todd didn't know how to interpret her words. "I hope you're not implying that your goons might attack my dad to get me in control of our land."

"Not in the slightest. We can eliminate tension between us. My project partners don't mind spending money. They didn't like leasing, so they purchased land north of your tract in the old Wilson City lumbering complex. We don't need your land anymore."

"So, you're no longer going to threaten my land or my family. If true, that's a good development. Your partners' unlimited cash was probably illegally gained, but that's not my concern. I'm wondering why they need you at all. They can't expect to make huge profits from your theme park. They could make more by investing in established businesses."

Emma's smile was genuine. "Todd, you're actually anxious about my welfare. Don't worry; I know what I'm doing. I have something they want very much, so I won't be in danger."

"Will you tell me what your protective Holy Grail is?"

"Not at this time, but perhaps someday." She shifted the way she was sitting, looking for a more comfortable position. "Why can't men be the ones who get pregnant? This child is causing me a lot more discomfort and pain than I expected."

"You were the one who said I had to get you pregnant, back in Chicago. Have you had the baby's gender tested?"

"No, and now that I don't need your land, I won't. I'll put the child up for adoption as soon as it's born. I'm not about to spend two decades taking care of it."

Her unexpected words hammered Todd's moral compass. "You can't do that! I have a stake in the child too. If you won't take responsibility for him or her, I'll have to step in and be a parent. Is your rejection of the baby the real reason you wanted to meet with me here?"

"It had crossed my mind, but I mostly wanted to see you again. Please believe me; I'm no threat to you. My partners have obtained the land we need. Our theme park will be an honest business enterprise."

"I question your last statement, but we'll wait and see. Keep me informed about your health status and the coming of the baby."

Todd stood and prepared to leave. He couldn't help staring at Emma's pregnancy bulge. It contained a major portion of his future.

CHAPTER 60 – REPORTS

Sandy Rolle listened impassively to Todd Weatherford's summary of what happened during his visit to Emma's cottage. When he finished, Sandy said, "I hope you realize that she has more power over you now than she did when she was trying to get your land. You never considered the possibility of ending up with the child. Now, you're preparing yourself to be a parent, and she can push you into doing favors for her by simply threatening to raise that infant herself or put it up for adoption."

"I'll agree with that argument, but I can't think of anything other than the land she might want from me."

"What if she demands that you marry her?

"That I wouldn't do under any circumstances. It would be a complete disaster, and it would remind me every day of how I almost killed my wife Lori."

"That sounds as though you still have feelings for Lori."

"Of course I do, but there's no going back. I yielded to Emma Read's temptation, and I'll forever feel guilty about it."

Sandy closed the door to the office. "Changing the subject slightly, do you think Emma's pirate theme park will be an honest business venture?"

Todd shook his head. "She'll at least cut corners to keep it from being honest, but the big question I have concerns her investor partners. They're putting a lot of money into a risky business. They have a motive that we haven't seen yet. It may involve something else they're doing with those imitation pirate ships. Let's get Steve and Frank in here to discuss their shipbuilder visit. We didn't get into that when they were bodyguarding me at Emma's cottage mansion."

Sandy reached for his phone. "Good idea; I'll call them and ask them to come here after lunch. In the meantime I'll take you to the Jib Room. We haven't eaten there yet."

When Sandy and Todd returned to the office an hour later, Steve Sweeney and Frank June were already by Joyce's desk exchanging fishing and sailing stories with her.

Todd greeted them both and then addressed Frank. "I should apologize for all the time I've kept you away from Sylvia. You're still newlyweds, and I'm sure you want as much time together as possible."

"Don't worry about Syl being alone. Now that *June's Bug* has been judged seaworthy and is registered, She's designing brochures for our tour business and visiting local bars and restaurants to ask them to display them. She's using her organizing skills and enjoying the process."

"Are you all set regarding work permits and other technicalities?"

"Thanks to Joyce knowing how to work the system, we're in very good shape."

Joyce smiled at the overheard comment on her abilities. Then she suggested that the four men take coffee from her pot before going into Sandy's office for discussions.

Once they were settled inside the closed office, Todd asked, "Did you learn anything during your visit to the shipbuilder that tells us Emma Read is doing something illegal with her theme park project?"

Steve said, "It's too early for that question. The first thing we learned is that those pseudo pirate ships are indeed being manufactured for Emma Read's group. Remember that prior to our field trip, the connection of those ships to Emma Read was only a speculation based on a rumor. Frank learned a great deal by using a misdirection approach. While I was discussing a possible custom-built vessel with the marketing manager, Frank spent time with the project engineer. Tell them how it went, Frank."

"It was more luck than tactics. I figured I'd get some personal benefit from the trip by asking Karen Quill, the project engineer, to give me any files she had on my Coast Guard utility boat. While we discussed that data, I led her into mentioning some of the challenges she had faced with recent custom designs. That's when she told me that she had been required to match the mounting specifications for the blank-charge-firing cannons on the make-believe pirate ships to that of the Mk38 Maritime Machine Cannon that's used on US Coast Guard and Navy ships. The shipbuilders wouldn't be supplying any such weapons, but they would have to provide both the mounting configuration and the platform rigidity to allow any show-time cannon to later be replaced by a Mk38 weapon. Karen didn't treat these requirements as anything unusual. They deal with quirky specifications on custom vessels on a regular basis."

Sandy reacted by standing and staring out the window. "I consider that development very significant. The owners of these pretend pirate ships could turn them into real ones by converting any pretend cannon into a real modern weapon with major firepower. Those 25mm shells will do major damage."

Todd said, "Even if they wanted to do that, where would they get the weapons? You can't get them in a hardware store or from the U.S. government."

"Up to this point, we've been assuming that Emma's partners are Mexican, because of her many trips to Mexico and the fact that drug cartels there have unlimited funds. The US sells weapons to many countries, including Mexico. I could easily believe that cartel people have the influence and the money to misdirect a few government weapons for their own purposes."

Todd looked at Steve. "Did you or Frank learn anything at the shipbuilding company that would confirm or deny the Mexican connection?"

"The marketing manager showed me his notebook full of specifications, and I saw a couple of Spanish names in there. I didn't see anything that specifically tied the buyers to Mexico, though. Did you see a connection, Frank?"

"I'll have to go in a different direction. I saw a business card on Karen Quill's desk that belonged to someone named Montez, but instead of Mexico, it said that his home base was St. Kitts and Nevis. I'm not even sure where that is or if they're two different places. Are you familiar with that place, Sandy?"

"St. Kitts and Nevis is a small country containing two islands located southeast of Puerto Rico. It's a British Commonwealth country, same as the Bahamas. Culturally, it's not Spanish, but at different times in history, most of the islands had, French, Spanish, and British settlers. I don't know whether the address on that business card is important, but it's interesting. St. Kitts and Nevis is the smallest country in the Caribbean."

CHAPTER 61 – ENTERPRISE

It was a case of the blind leading the blind, but the first few groups of tourists who paid for voyages with Aquatian Tours enjoyed themselves thoroughly, thanks to the personalities and guiding talents of Frank and Sylvia June. The initial short trips headed to established destinations like Elbow Cay with its Hope Town Lighthouse, Man-O-War Cay, and Great Guana Cay, all easily reached going eastward and northward from Marsh Harbour, but staying within the calm waters of the Sea of Abaco. Ample supplies of liquid and solid refreshments increased passenger appreciation of Frank's philosophy of nature monologues.

When they didn't have passengers on any of their three weekdays designated for tours, Sylvia and Frank headed out to less frequented cays to learn about their characteristics in preparation for future additions to their guided outings list. Sylvia and Frank were having fun and making money too. They could already see a shortened timeline to the final payment on *June's Bug*. They shared one such private outing with Steve Sweeney, both for enjoyment and to explore ways of working together.

Steve took a turn at the wheel and then relinquished it with a smile. "You two did very well for yourselves in reclaiming this boat from the scrapheap. *June's Bug* will outperform everything around here except for fancy yachts. She's fine for your touring purposes, but I wouldn't suggest converting her for deep sea fishing charters. That would require adding superstructure equipment that would slow her down. She's fine as-is for fishing in waters protected by barrier reefs and cays."

Sylvia took a beer from the cooler. "It's probably due to our backgrounds as city tour guides, but I feel more comfortable with keeping the boat moving and showing landmarks to passengers than I would being quiet and patient while others fished. I don't mind doing my own fishing, though. I'd rather be active than passive out here."

Frank looked up from the radar display. "I was just checking for other traffic in the area. We appear to be alone. I'm a military guy, and I like to be prepared for anything. If Sylvia doesn't object, I'm going to dream up a few extra gadgets for this craft that will give it some extra capabilities in case they're needed to support Todd's mission. Are you all right with that, Syl?"

"That's fine with me, but I'm not sure I know what Todd's mission is at the moment. Emma Read claims she's no longer interested in his land, and that she's no threat to the Weatherford and Rolle store. I don't see Todd trying to keep her from opening her pirate theme park, so what are we aiming to do?"

Frank looked at the distant shoreline. "Todd and Sandy both think Emma's involved in something bad. Just like that island in the distance, I can't quite identify it, but I know it's there. People are pouring big money into her project, and they expect something special in return. At this point, Todd's mission is to find out what they're trying to do so that somebody can stop them, whether it's us or some appropriate agency."

Steve said, "That sounds pretty open-ended to me. They could be doing something too big for us to sabotage it."

"You're absolutely right. That's why I want to be prepared for anything and make some friendships with members of official forces. I found some of the original designation and communication channel data for this boat. If I get a chance, I'm going to make some informal contacts with US Coast Guard people, and cultivate some relationships there. We could later be put in a position of needing to call in some support."

Steve finished his beer and took a new bottle. "And here I thought we were relaxing and dreaming up new business options. Count me in for the long run anyway."

CHAPTER 62 – PUBLICITY

Life went on in normal fashion for residents and tourists in Abaco and its barrier cays until one day when unexpected vessels appeared in the Sea of Abaco, sailing in from the north. For the first time in three hundred years, two old-fashioned pirate ships openly skirted Marsh Harbour with a crew dressed in appropriate period costumes. Amused and excited crowds gathered along the shoreline, not knowing what to expect. Their questions were partially answered when the lead ship fired a blank charge cannon broadside that made witnesses nervously scan the air above them for cannon balls. As the ships passed, young people dressed in pirate costumes circulated among the onlookers, distributing brochures for Calico Jack's Pirate Adventure Park that would be opening soon. Having been alerted to the schedule for the arrival of the two ships, a television crew, positioned on a boat well offshore, videotaped the ships with the cheering crowd in the background. All in all, it was the most festive event in Marsh Harbour for quite some time.

As the *Mary Read* and *Anne Bonny* sailed by the town, workmen scrambled to finish preparing the designated docks for the two ships on the inner coast of Lynyard Cay. Jeeps and golf cart vehicles involved in various supporting activities rolled up and down the new road that ran the length of that island. Large signs displaying a pirate flag with crossed cutlasses and the words *Calico Jack's* embellished the new docks and the opposite coastline slightly south of the old Wilson City lumbering site. Two large tents behind the *Calico Jack's* sign would serve as temporary museum and gateway facilities for arriving visitors.

It was a triumphant day for Emma Read, but she couldn't enjoy it due to intense labor pains as she rode in a siren-blaring ambulance toward Marsh Harbour Healthcare Centre, impeded by the cheering crowds she had instigated. Her baby and her theme park would be born on the same day.

Three hours later, Todd received a phone call.

"Mr. Weatherford?" The female voice was unfamiliar.

The unexpected call didn't immediately register as important. "Yes."

"This is Selma Swift at Marsh Harbor Healthcare. We'd like you to come here to sign some legal papers."

"What kind of papers?"

"The ones that give you full custody of your newborn son."

He almost fell off his chair. "Are you saying that Emma Read had her baby and that it's a boy?"

"That's exactly what I'm saying. She told us that you are the father and that you were taking responsibility for raising the child. You'll have to take a DNA test to confirm your biological parenthood, but the rest of the process will be straightforward. Please bring your insurance card. The baby's mother said that you had agreed to pay all medical expenses."

Todd silently gave thanks that Joyce White had added him to the store's medical and life insurance plans. "How are the baby and Emma?"

"They're both doing well. How soon will you get here?"

"I'll be there in ten minutes."

Todd yelled the news to Sandy and Joyce as he ran out of the office, "I'm a father. I have a son, and I'm off to the hospital!"

When he arrived in the lobby, Selma Swift was waiting for him.

"Thank you for coming so promptly. I'll take you in to see Emma and the baby. Then you will sign the papers and give us your insurance information."

"I'd like to see the baby first."

"You can view him through the nursery window. After you sign the papers and change into a surgical gown, you'll be allowed to hold him. He is a good size, eight pounds, so you'll be able to take him home soon."

The impact of her words 'take him home' was huge. Up to this point, the baby had been an abstract concept. One glance through the nursery window at a round-faced, infant with an amazing amount of blond hair, wrapped in a striped blanket made him very real indeed. Todd stood looking at him through the glass for a full three minutes before Selma tugged on his sleeve.

"Time to see Ms. Read now. You'll have plenty of time with your son."

When they arrived at Emma's room, Todd was surprised to see her dressed and sitting on a cushioned chair. Selma left them alone but said she would be waiting in the hallway.

"Shouldn't you be lying down or something? You just delivered a baby."

"Correction – I just delivered our baby. He'll always be that, even though I'm sticking to our agreement for you to raise him. I'd be a lousy parent."

"Selma Swift says the paperwork will be simple."

"It's lengthy, but simple. I've already signed my portion of it."

"Should I expect any surprises?"

"She'll explain everything to you."

"That didn't answer my question. Will there be any surprises?"

"Maybe one, but you'll work it out. I have one requirement I didn't mention."

"What's that?

"As compensation for my giving you the child, you have to kiss me one last time."

Without comment, he approached her, leaned over her chair, and prepared to kiss her on the cheek. As he leaned down, Emma pushed his head toward her lips and gave him a long sensuous kiss.

"That hurt like hell when I pulled you toward me, but it was worth it – almost like the old days."

"Almost, but not quite. I promise to give the boy a good home."

"I know you will. You're that type of guy. Now it's time for you to do the paperwork while I get someone to take me to the celebration for my soon-to-open theme park. Goodbye, Todd."

He left the room and followed Selma to the front office, where she laid a pile of papers on the table for him to sign and complete as required. Todd was halfway through a first scan of the forms when he found Emma's surprise and laughed.

Selma walked over to see if there was a problem. "What's wrong? Is there a mistake?"

"Just a small correction needed. You have the boy's name as Cal Jack Weatherford. That's his nickname. His complete official name is John Sandy Weatherford."

CHAPTER 63 – JOHN SANDY WEATHERFORD

By the time Todd returned to Weatherford and Rolle the offices were in the early stages of a full-fledged party. The Junes and Steve Sweeney had joined Sandy and Joyce. Even though the outer office door was closed, passing customers stared at it, wondering about the noises they heard beyond it. Todd opened the door quietly, trying to look nonchalant but not even coming close to succeeding. A cheer went up, and everyone started talking and shouting at the same time.

Todd raised his hand, requesting attention. "I see that my news has spread. If there is something around to drink, give everyone a glass. I want to raise a toast."

Joyce gave Todd a glass filled to two finger height with his favorite Kentucky bourbon. Sandy distributed rum and gin to the others as individually preferred. Then they stopped talking and faced Todd.

"Today, my life has changed. I'm father to a very handsome child. Please raise your glasses with me to toast newly arrived John Sandy Weatherford."

Everyone cheered, but turned to look for the source of a sudden loud thump. Sandy had sat on the edge of Joyce's desk, knocking the telephone onto the floor. He looked shocked.

"You named him after me! I'm amazed and honored."

"His first name is John, after the only Weatherford who was an American patriot, but his second name recognizes my partner in many ways. Raise your glasses again to Sandy."

Those who had only empty glasses rushed to fill them. Todd said nothing about Emma manipulating him into naming the baby John to replace her teasing suggestion of Calico Jack. Todd and Sandy converted their handshake into a hug.

After Sandy's third drink he said, "Now we know the identity of one partner in this business for the next generation. Someday, I'll have to think about the other one."

Sylvia pushed Joyce forward until she faced Sandy. He looked at her, blushed, and rushed out of the office mumbling, "I need a bathroom."

The party continued until one hour after the store closed.

During a relatively quiet point in the festivities, Todd entered Sandy's office and closed the door. He called home and held his breath, wondering which parent would answer the phone. When he heard his mother's voice, he responded with as calm a tone as he could muster. "Hi, Mom; I have some news for you. You may want to sit down before I give it to you."

"It's happened! Is it a boy or a girl?"

"How did you know what I was calling about?"

"I can count months. I had a red question mark on the calendar for a week from Wednesday. I repeat, is the child a boy or a girl?"

"He's a good-looking boy with a lot of his mother's blond hair. He weighs eight pounds, but I didn't get the data on how long he is. There's one other thing you might want to know about your grandson."

"What's that?"

"He's all mine. Emma Read no longer needed him to swindle me out of family land, so she signed away her rights and gave him to me."

"That's hard to believe. I thought she'd keep the boy away from you just to show how mean she is."

"Maybe she remembered what a terrible child she was, and wanted no part of having that responsibility."

"What's our grandson's name?"

"He's John Sandy Weatherford, named after our ancestor who fought on the American side in the Revolutionary War and my business partner."

George Weatherford had picked up the extension phone. "Good choice of names, Todd; I'm sure he'll be a great addition to the family. Judy, what do you think of his name?"

Judy ignored her husband's question. "Todd, you know absolutely nothing about caring for a baby. We'll be there tomorrow. Congratulations! We love you. Now hang up, so we can get packing. I'll email our flight information."

Just before he disconnected, Todd heard his mother yell, "George, pack enough for a long stay in Abaco!"

CHAPTER 64 – FAMILY

Todd met the Bahamasair flight at the Marsh Harbour airport, officially known as Leonard M. Thompson International Airport. He didn't expect the excitement level he felt when he saw his parents, but he realized it was a combination of relief that they were no longer threatened by Emma and her group trying to get family land and even more relief that he now had support in learning how to raise a baby.

His mother ran to hug him. "Todd, you've changed since we last saw you. You're tanned and stronger, but are you eating enough? How's the baby, I should say John? That should be an easy name for a Weatherford to remember; we've had so many Johns throughout our history. Is John home yet?"

George Weatherford put his hand on his wife's shoulder. "Judy, just say hello for now. Todd will answer all your questions while we pick up our luggage and head for his place. – Hi, Son; it's good to see you again."

As they walked toward the baggage area, Todd did most of the talking. "It's great that you're here. I definitely need someone who knows what to do for a baby. John is still in the hospital nursery. I'm still a little shell-shocked about having a son to talk about. We have another day to prepare before they'll release him. I wasn't even sure Emma would follow through with her promise to give me custody, so I didn't buy any supplies or set aside an area for him in the house. Speaking of the house, I have only one bedroom, so you two will sleep there, while I sleep on the couch in the front room. We can get a crib and put it near the couch, or anywhere else you suggest. We'll have to do some shopping. How long will you stay?"

George said, "Slow down, Todd; plenty of time to answer all your questions and concerns. We're here for as long as you want us, and maybe even longer."

"That's fine with me, Dad. I'll need all the help I can get."

After they claimed the luggage and packed it into Todd's company Jeep, Judy broke her silence. "I've listened long enough to you men being matter of fact about the baby. Now drive directly to the hospital so that I can meet my adorable grandson. When we get there take lots of pictures. I'll bet you didn't even think of using your phone's camera, Todd. We can worry about baby supplies and accommodations at the house later."

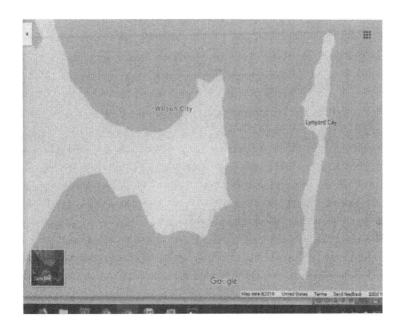

CHAPTER 65 – THEME PARK

The first few weeks at Calico Jack's Pirate Adventure Park were disorganized but bustling. The local newspaper and radio station reported that both tourists and local residents were flocking to the park to get a taste of the old pirate days in the Bahamas and to get rides on the pirate ships. While the media showed enthusiasm for the new attraction, they devoted most of their coverage to the fact that at least thirty local residents had new jobs at Calico Jack's and that more jobs were scheduled to open up within the next few months as park business increased. Most of the new hires were ticket sellers, food handlers, museum guides, groundskeepers, and boat dock personnel, but a few individuals with technical backgrounds had prize assignments maintaining the pirate ships.

One such maintenance worker, Ken Birch, had spent the last three years working at the contractor service desk at Weatherford & Rolle, although he didn't reveal that information on his application for a theme park job. Instead, he listed his part-time work at Marsh Harbour Boatyards. Ken didn't mention that his efforts in the boatyards involved rehabbing a boat that would later be called *June's Bug* or that he had been assigned there by Sandy Rolle. Ken would be humble and efficient as he worked on the pirate ships, but he would keep his eyes and ears open for anything unusual, and he would relay his observations to Sandy and Todd. Ken enjoyed the fact that he was being paid by two organizations and that he was doing intelligence work. He pictured himself with a vodka martini, introducing himself to a swimsuit model as *Birch, Ken Birch.*

For the first month of working at Calico Jack's, Ken had little to do, except look efficient. The two pirate ships were brand new and needed minimal maintenance attention. His main task was to reload the cannons with blank charges between sailings. He did observe that there was a warehouse near the docks on Lynyard Cay that was locked and off limits to employees. He photographed it and sent pictures of that building and other facilities near the docks to Sandy. There were a few other small buildings halfway down the island to the south, one of which contained the blank explosive charges that his supervisor brought to him before each ship departed.

Ken kept his eyes open for Emma Read and management types who might be Mexican, but during his first few weeks on the job he struck out on both counts. He did identify one of the pirate crew as possibly Mexican when he heard him between cruises talking on his phone in Spanish. Ken asked a Bahamian crewmate about him and learned that the suspected Mexican was a Cuban-American actor from Miami. Ken arranged to be doing work near that crewman's station just before one of the tourist cruises.

Ken looked up from tightening bolts as the sailor drew near. "Hi, amigo, have you been in the islands long? I'm Ken Birch."

"How come you called me amigo? I'm not your friend, and you're not Hispanic."

"Maybe I'd like to be friends, but there's no way I'd make it as a Spanish speaker. What's your name?"

"You can call me Diego, and as to time in the islands, I was born in Cuba, so I'm not a rookie to island living."

"Cuba's a bit bigger than the Bahamas islands, but it's good to meet you, Diego. I thought you were Mexican when I first heard you speaking Spanish."

"Cuban Spanish and Mexican Spanish are almost two different languages, but there are some Mexicans working at Calico Jack's. They don't show themselves much because they're part of management. I saw a bunch of them on one of the early demonstration cruises."

Ken packed up his tools as the ship's bell signaled that departure was imminent. "Do the Mexicans hang out in one of the tents on the Abaco shore?"

"They come and go, usually individually not as a group. Speaking of that, it's time for my show, so you'd better go ashore. I'll look you up later, and we can talk some more."

"I'd like that. Bon voyage."

Ken went down the gangplank to the dock as tourists were climbing out of the longboats that ferried them to Lynyard Cay from the museum and park on Abaco. Their pirate guides directed them to board the *Mary Read*, which was about to depart.

From the shadow of a shed, Ken studied the current group of passengers. He observed that a surprising number of them appeared to be Mexican.

CHAPTER 66 – ANTONIO MONTEZ

Antonio Montez preferred to be called Tony in informal settings because it made him feel like an old-time Mafia boss. He liked to control projects and people, and to do so in a way that kept his associates from recognizing his manipulations. As he watched a group of Mexican nationals board the pseudo pirate ship *Mary Read*, he congratulated himself on getting his master plan rolling. His partner in Calico Jack's, Emma Read, thought the pirate theme park was their ultimate goal, and Tony encouraged that belief. After all, there was nothing wrong with a successful business venture that appeared to be completely honest. It gave him a touch of status, but it was only a step along the path to his final objective. Let Emma revel in the way she had recreated her pirate ancestry. It would harm no one.

Emma Read had been quite useful during the course of negotiating permits and favorable arrangements for Calico Jack's Pirate Adventure Park. She had introduced him to major Bahamas government officials, and he had done enough minor favors for them that they would remember him with a sense of obligation when he needed their support in the future.

Emma lived in the past because her family's pirate background was so important to her, but Tony focused his thoughts on the present and future, both of which appeared to be increasing in brightness. Hopefully, he would be able to avoid a major battle over the difference between their viewpoints. At heart, Tony was a peaceful man, so long as everyone did things his way.

From an unobtrusive vantage point, Tony watched Emma Read in pirate costume welcoming park visitors. He smiled. *Let Emma glory in her heritage. My descendants will feel the same way about me if my plans succeed. As for this park, I'll be the silent partner, not interfering with day-to-day operations, but manipulating long term goals.*

CHAPTER 67 – BABY CARE

Judy Weatherford watched Todd change baby John's diapers and then sit on the couch while not looking at the child he was holding. "Look at your son's sweet smile, Todd. You need to pay more attention to him and make him feel loved and safe with you."

"Mom, I'm learning how to care for him, but it bothers me that I didn't expect to even see him after he was born. I don't feel that close to him yet."

"You're lucky that you have him all to yourself."

"That's just it. Emma manipulated me into getting her pregnant. She wanted to use this baby as a tool against me. When she no longer needed him or our family land, she dumped John and ran. I wasn't supposed to end up with a baby, being a single parent."

Judy laughed. "I applaud your realizing how a woman feels when a casual date on a one night stand gets her pregnant and makes her a single parent. It happens every day, but usually not to a man."

"It's not funny, Mom. I'm the youngest of your kids. I never helped you with babies. I don't know whether I'll be a good father to John while he's small and unable to do things for himself."

"Don't worry, Todd. He'll learn rapidly once he gets past being fully dependent on us. Your dad and I expect to be here long enough to teach you how to cope with fatherhood."

"Where is Dad?"

"He went over to visit with Sandy at the store. They're probably sharing stories of their time together as partners. Why don't you join them? I'll take care of John for now. Before long, I'll get you a baby carrier so that you'll be able to take him with you."

Todd scowled. "There's something to look forward to. I'd probably do something wrong and hurt him."

"Don't worry. Babies have managed to survive untalented parents for a very long time."

CHAPTER 68 – STORE TALK

Todd walked into the Weatherford and Rolle office area and found his father alone in Sandy's inner office. Both Sandy and his administrator, Joyce, were elsewhere.

"Hi, Dad, did you fire Sandy and Joyce and decide to run everything yourself?"

"I'm just reminding myself of the old days when I was Sandy's father's partner. That was before we moved into this modern building. We had a smaller place on this property. When we tore it down, we recycled some of its materials into fixtures and used inventory for this store. In the old days, there weren't many cars on Abaco, so we sold most items within the local neighborhood plus lightweight products that people could carry on a bicycle or a motor scooter."

"That must have been a quieter time."

"It was peaceful, but more folks were out of work. Most businesses were small scale, so the bulk of jobs were in tourism, boating, and fishing. We had some customers who traded us garden vegetables, chickens or used lumber for their purchases."

"Speaking of peaceful, do you think we have anything more to fear from Emma Read?"

As Todd asked that question, Joyce White and Sandy Rolle came back into the office.

Joyce moved a bowl of fruit from her desk to Sandy's to encourage everyone to take something. She said, "We had a small victory. We negotiated a reduced price for merchandise on a truck that arrived a full week ahead of schedule."

Sandy continued. "We have to keep tight controls on supplier scheduling so that we don't spend money long before we can sell their goods. Our suppliers need cash, so they try to get us to take their products early. Just-in-time inventory is a new concept to small business people around here. Todd, I heard your question about Emma Read. I look at her as a snake that still has its fangs, but is busy elsewhere. She won't be a threat so long as her pirate park is doing well, but she'll always be a potential threat. She tried to kill your dad back in Kentucky, and I'm sure she was behind the death of Ike Trowbridge."

George left Sandy's chair and approached his son. "Don't forget how she got you to attack Lori, split up your marriage, and tried to cheat us out of our family land. Speaking of her expected legal attack, how is her supposed-to-be secret weapon, my new grandson?"

"John is fine but a bit cranky. I'm cranky too, because I can't get used to the idea of being a single parent. I'm not good at caring for a baby, and I don't see myself getting much better."

Joyce winked at Sandy. "There's a simple cure for that. Find yourself a mate, with or without a marriage."

"Maybe sometime in the future, but I haven't even had a date since I came to Abaco. I suppose I'll have to start thinking along those lines. Mom and Dad won't be here forever."

George Weatherford cleared his throat to get attention. "Todd, the topic didn't come up before, so I didn't push it, but your mother wants us to retire here. We have the land near the store plus the

216

parcel across from Lynyard Cay that I plan to leave you later. Her suggestion took me by surprise, but it makes good sense. You may not have to rush into some female's arms just to get help with your son."

Joyce looked disappointed, but she said nothing. Matchmaking might have to wait a while.

Todd's relief was obvious. "That's good news, Dad. I need some independent time to learn what Emma's hidden investors are planning. I guarantee they want more than mock pirate ship excursions."

CHAPTER 69 – KEN BIRCH

During the first few weeks of working on the pirate ships, Ken loaded the cannons with blank charges that his supervisor delivered to him before each scheduled departure. As time passed, that manager got bored with his setup duties and gave Ken the keys to the park's Jeep and the padlock for the munitions shed. Ken accepted his additional responsibilities without any outward sign of emotion, but inside, he celebrated. He now had both the means and authorization to travel around Lynyard Cay and discover any unknown secrets.

On his first solo trip to pick up cannon charges, Ken examined the munitions shed. He saw that the explosives were stored neatly with adequate separation and protective dividers to ensure that an accidental spark wouldn't explode everything. Caution and Danger signs outside and inside the shed commanded that employees handle munitions with respect and listed specific procedures. Ken concluded that the person who developed those procedures had military experience with explosives. He photographed the contents of the shed and its instructional signs with his telephone and sent the pictures to Sandy's phone. Because he was on a tight schedule, Ken headed back to the docks without exploring the other storage buildings or their surroundings. The frequent ship sailings would require that he check the remaining facilities in short segments on each munitions resupply trip.

At the dock where the *Anne Bonny* was being prepped for its next sailing, Ken loaded his explosive charges on a two-wheel cart and walked toward the boarding gangplank.

Suddenly, he heard someone shout, "Hey, Birch!"

Ken turned to see one of the top managers waving at him. "Is anything wrong?" He worried that someone might have seen him looking around beyond the munitions shed.

"No problem. I just need the Jeep for an errand. Throw me the keys. When I'm done, I'll leave them for you at the ticket booth."

Ken complied and then slowed his walk up the gangplank to see where the manager was going. The Jeep passed beyond the munitions shed and appeared to be heading for the other end of Lynyard Cay. Ken made a mental note to take that route when he next drove for munitions restocking.

Once aboard the *Anne Bonny*, Ken reloaded the cannons, appreciating the way crew members and others stayed well away from him for fear of an accidental explosion. He would take advantage of their cautious respect for his duties by claiming he was carrying explosives whenever he went to check out other parts of the island.

CHAPTER 70 – SANDY AND TODD

When Todd walked into Sandy's office one morning, he saw his partner doodling a series of geometric patterns on a pad of paper while drinking his coffee. Todd approached the desk and saw that the doodles surrounded two words, *Mexican tourists.*

"I see your artwork. Is there something unusual about Mexicans coming to the Bahamas?"

"We don't usually see many Mexican tourists at all, but we've been flooded with them since Calico Jack's Pirate Theme Park opened. Is that because Mexicans love pirates, or because the Mexican backers of that park have some kind of criminal operation going?"

"There could be a planned operation without it being criminal, Sandy."

"I suppose I'm just suspicious because of the drug cartels in Mexico."

"Why don't we check up on some of those tourists' airline flights and travel plans? We could even follow some of them to see whether separate individuals and families gather together before they leave the Bahamas."

"Thanks, Todd; you just put your finger on what was bothering me. Ken Birch, my undercover man at the theme park remarked that the Mexican tourists are all adults. They're not coming here as families with children. Wouldn't children be the most likely to want to visit a park like Calico Jack's?"

"You're right. I'd expect there to be at least a reasonable percentage of people with kids. I can see only one reason for those tourists all being adults. They're on a mission of some type. We definitely should check up on the next batch of Mexican visitors."

"Ken Birch has a Cuban-American friend in the crew who could give him some feedback on their Spanish conversations. I'll ask Joyce to see what she can find out about their airline ticketing when Ken next spots a group of Mexican adults."

"Let's take it further than that. Frank June is our Special Forces military man. He and Sylvia could follow the group after they leave Cactus Jack's."

"I don't know about that suggestion, Todd. Following them could put the Junes in danger, especially Sylvia."

"Don't underestimate her. She handled some pretty obnoxious people when she was a tour guide in Chicago, and Frank taught her self-defense skills. The people we want to track will be less suspicious of a newlywed couple in their midst than a single muscular veteran."

Sandy sat quietly considering Todd's plan. "I'll go along with sending the Junes on the tracking operation, but in the meantime, you should watch your nemesis, Emma Read, to determine whether she's involved in the Mexican scheme."

CHAPTER 71 – LYNYARD EXPLORATIONS

Ken Birch decided to use his spare time to explore Lynyard Cay while he waited for the next group of Mexican tourists to arrive. So far he had seen Mexican tourist groups every couple of weeks, so he expected to have at least a few free days before the next batch arrived. His use of the Jeep to get munitions and other ship supplies had become routine, so he felt confident that no one would pay much attention to him if he widened his itinerary.

Ken's first deviation from his normal route was to follow the road southward past the munitions shed to the southern tip of the two mile long island. He passed an area marked by caution signs because the road sat on freshly filled land that widened the narrow island at that point. When he reached the end of the road, he saw a slight pavement widening to allow vehicles to turn around, and a small shed. When he got out of the Jeep, Ken saw that what little land there was on the ocean side of the road was rough and rocky. He was sure that in a storm the ocean surf would completely cover this end of the island.

Ken approached the small shed and saw that it was padlocked. On a whim, he tried his key for the munitions shed in the padlock. Surprisingly, it fit. He wondered why management would have keyed any lock to match the munitions shed because of the danger of unauthorized people having access to explosives. Upon opening the shed door, Ken found that it contained a few shelves with a rolled-up canvas assembly and small boxes. A large electrical switch box was mounted on one wall. He threw the switch to the ON position. Nothing happened inside the shed. He went outside and saw bright lights bordering the road at ground level on both sides. The road also served as a runway for incoming planes. Ken realized that the canvas device was a wind sock that would hang on a post near the shed to alert incoming pilots to the wind direction.

Ken photographed the road in its runway configuration with the lights on and then repeated the same shots with the lights turned off. Unless you looked very carefully, you wouldn't see the turned-off lights even in bright daylight. Ken locked the small shed and drove northward toward the ship docks. He was curious about the garage-size building near the docks, but it had a combination lock. He had never seen anyone go into that oversized shed. People passed it as though it wasn't there, but Ken knew it was significant. He'd have to wait before attempting to break into it.

CHAPTER 72 – SHADOWS

Frank and Sylvia June, dressed as tourists with dark sunglasses and straw hats, descended the gangplank from the *Mary Read* after taking a pirate ship cruise accompanied by mostly Mexican passengers. Their attire was aimed at keeping an accidentally encountered Emma Read from remembering them from their favorite Chicago tavern. Frank's short hair and lack of a beard would make him look different to Emma if they did meet. Frank was impressed by the improvements made to the ship since he first saw it under construction at the Florida boatyard. It did appear to be constructed entirely of wood. During the excursion, he had barely noticed the engine noise and vibration as crew members climbed the rigging and deployed the sails, pretending that the ship was propelled solely by wind against canvas.

During the cruise, Sylvia paid less attention to the performance characteristics of the ship than she did to details about her fellow passengers. They appeared to be mostly but not exclusively Mexican. She estimated the Mexican contingent to be about eighty percent male, and in keeping with Ken Birch's earlier report, there were no children in that group. Sylvia observed one surprising thing. The Mexicans behaved as though almost all of them were strangers to each other. Sylvia saw very few engaged in long conversations. They simply reacted as individuals to highlights of the cruise such as course change maneuvers, crewmen climbing the rigging, and cannon firings.

When they returned to the dock, Frank and Sylvia used a trip to the nearest souvenir stand to cover the extra time they spent watching their fellow passengers. When they saw several of the Mexicans purchase bus tickets, Frank and Sylvia did the same while clutching Jolly Roger pirate flags and licking ice cream cones. Sylvia approached an English speaking Mexican woman she met on the ship.

"Did you enjoy that ride?"

"It was fun, but I always worry about getting seasick. I live in the mountains and rarely get on a boat."

"Where do you go from here?"

"I'll be on the bus with you to Marsh Harbour. Then I have to take another boat to Nassau. At least after that, my tour goes by airplane. I'm not sure where the next stop is, but our guide will meet us in Nassau and tell us."

"Are all the Mexican tourists traveling together?"

"No, no, my tour is a very small group. There are several different travel groups from my country here. I have to go now, I hear them calling me."

Sylvia watched the woman hurry away and then walked over to Frank. "The Mexican tourists are either traveling in many different groups, or they're doing a good job of pretending they are."

"You seemed to be having a good conversation with that woman, but she left you abruptly. Any idea why?"

"She may have been bothered by the number of questions I asked. I'll have to remember to tone down the questioning. She may have thought I was connected with the police."

"Anyway, the buses are boarding. Let's be sure we take a different bus from her so that she doesn't think we're following her."

"Which, of course, we will be, but from a distance. I didn't hear many Mexicans speaking English on the pirate ship. I'll try to find another English speaking woman. I can be more casual with another woman than with a man."

"I don't know about that, Syl. I bet that if we sit separately on the bus and I stay in the background, you'll have several men wanting to speak with you,"

As they boarded their bus, Frank lagged behind Sylvia and acted as though he didn't know her. She sat about four rows back from the front door, while he took a seat on the aisle in the rear of the bus. He would be able to watch her and spring into action if necessary.

As Frank anticipated, an English speaking Mexican man sat next to Sylvia. As soon as the bus departed, he began to chat with her. She acted as though she didn't want to talk to a stranger, but bowed to his persistence after several minutes. He introduced himself as Jose Garcia.

"I see from your ring that you are married. Do you often travel without your husband?"

"This is the first time. I have a sick uncle in Nassau, and I want to visit him before I return to the United States."

"You're being wise. Do your fun vacationing first, before you get involved with family problems. I am traveling without my wife and children, but it is for a different reason."

"And what is that?"

"I am looking at a possible new home for us on one of the islands."

"One of the islands in the Bahamas?"

226

"No, it is a different smaller country, but they didn't tell us the name. I won a free vacation trip to the Bahamas if I would visit this other country and consider moving there. I don't turn down free vacations, so I will listen to what they have to say at this other place. It is not always safe in Mexico, so I will see if this is a better place to raise my children."

"What is your business? Will you have trouble finding a job in a new island country?"

"I don't think so. I am a cook in a restaurant in Mexico City. People have to eat everywhere. If they don't have a restaurant there that needs me, I can open up my own place."

"There appear to be many Mexicans traveling with us today. Are you all together?"

"I don't know any of the others except for casual comments. They may have won vacation trips also. I didn't ask them. The people who interviewed me said that all their candidates for moving to this island had to speak English because that is the language there. I learned English during my restaurant work, so I had no problem. If we all end up with a home on that island, I will open up a restaurant serving Mexican food to keep the others from getting homesick. They're supposed to tell us where the island is when we fly out of Nassau."

The bus pulled up to the Marsh Harbour dock where the Bahamas Ferry boat was loading. After getting off the bus, Sylvia found a shady spot under a tree and waited for Frank. As he left the bus she waved to him.

"Frank, I think I understand what's happening, but I don't know why."

"Who are these people? Are they with one of the cartels?"

"They're ordinary citizens with some business skills. It's like the old Florida land development scheme in the States. They would fly you to Florida for a free vacation if you agreed to consider their pitch to sell you a new house there. In this case, someone is recruiting Mexicans for a free Bahamas vacation if they'll consider moving to a smaller island country. These folks don't yet know which island it is, but they'll be told when they board their plane in Nassau. What interested me is that one of the qualifications for this junket is that the Mexicans had to speak English. Most are speaking Spanish to each other now because it's easier for them, but they were tested for English capability before they came to the Bahamas."

Frank thought about Sylvia's comment for a few seconds. "That English requirement tells me that the people behind this project have done their homework. They realize that large numbers of Spanish speakers going to live in an English-speaking country might not be accepted by the other residents. Having the newcomers speak English increases the likelihood that they'll be welcomed."

"I think you just put your finger on what bothers me about this business of transplanting Mexicans to an island. My gut tells me this is an illegal scheme, but so far, everything we've discovered makes it look like a well-designed business promotion."

CHAPTER 73 – BREADCRUMB TRAIL

Sylvia and Frank watched the ferry's boarding process while considering their next step.

Frank finished checking schedules on his smart phone and frowned. "I don't think we should take the ferry with them. It leaves soon, at 1:00 PM, but it doesn't arrive in Nassau until 2:00 AM tomorrow morning. Let's check with Sandy and Joyce to see if we can learn about the Mexicans' itinerary by telephone or computer searching. If that's not practical, we can still fly to Nassau and arrive before the ferry gets there."

"I like your thinking. That thirteen hour boat ride doesn't excite me."

When they arrived at Weatherford & Rolle, Frank and Sylvia entered the office and found that Joyce was the only one there, and she was on the telephone. She gestured for them to take some coffee while she finished resolving a shipping problem. Ten minutes later she gave up on expediting the shipment and told the vendor to cancel the order.

Sylvia brought Joyce a cup of coffee. "Here, I think you need this after all that arguing."

"Thanks, Syl. Sometimes our vendors think they can drag their heels on deliveries because we're on an island and don't have multiple sources for the products they supply. They don't realize that I keep rating sheets on each supplier. If they get too many low ratings, I'll find a competitor, even if it costs us more. Service is more important than price."

Frank asked, "Is this dispute over a large item?"

"Not really; we need a new source for nails, screws, and small hardware parts. They're heavy but compact items."

"Steve Sweeney went back to Florida for more charter work. Contact him. I'm sure he'll be able to find another supplier and then deliver your shipment on *Sweeney's Queen*. It may not be a long term solution, but it will send a message to your problem vendor that you have other ways of solving your supply problems."

"Thanks, Frank; I'll do that. Do you two have any problems today?"

Sandy entered the office as Joyce asked that question. "I'll bet they don't have any problems at all. They're here to give us answers to our questions. What did you learn about those Mexican tourists at the pirate park?"

Frank nodded for Sylvia to respond. "I learned a lot more than I expected because I spoke with two of them. Surprisingly, they can all speak English. It's a requirement for why they're here." She continued with the rest of the free vacation and possible resettlement story. "Right now, they're on a thirteen hour ferry boat ride to Nassau. We came here to see whether we could find out more about their project and ultimate destination through a computer search or some key telephone calls. If that approach doesn't work, we'll still have time to fly to Nassau and meet their ferry when it arrives."

Frank said, "By the way, where's Todd. He should be in on our tracking fun."

Sandy shook his head. "Not this time. He's on a different assignment, keeping an eye on Emma Read and figuring out how or if she's involved with the Mexican project."

Frank removed his phone from his shirt pocket. "We'll have to text or call him to bring him up to date on what we've learned so far. Syl, give Joyce the name of the Mexican man you rode with. She may be able to check his background story or determine his destination."

"My new friend is Jose Garcia, and he said that he's a cook in a Mexico City restaurant."

Joyce went into a new private office they had partitioned off for Todd to do her research work while Frank texted their current information to Todd's mobile phone.

At Calico Jack's Pirate Adventure Park, Todd located a bench next to a souvenir stand where he could sit and watch the stream of visitors and employees without being noticed. It was deliberately inconspicuous so that employees could use it for rest breaks without being noticed by many of the tourists. When he felt his phone vibrate, Todd folded his newspaper and opened the text message. After reading it, he returned his phone to his pocket and mentally congratulated Sylvia and Frank for their good detective work. He now had a better feeling for what was going on, but how would that information affect his surveillance of Emma's activities?

Todd felt a tap on his shoulder and turned around to see Emma Read dressed in a pirate costume.

"What are you up to, Todd? Are you here for the festivities, or are you trying to decide whether I made a good investment?"

"Actually, I'm waiting for my dad. He took one of your pirate ship cruises."

"Didn't you want to go along?"

"I'm not much of a sailor. I also didn't want to draw your attention to him. You had someone try to kill him once."

"I'll never admit to that, and things are totally different now. You have no reason to fear me. I have a partner with deep pockets, so I pledge to leave you, your family, and our son alone. Where is little Cal Jack by the way? Have you abandoned him?"

"John Sandy Weatherford is enjoying the loving care of my mother. He'll always have someone nearby to love and protect him."

"I'm hurt. You still don't trust me."

Todd scanned her outfit. "You're most comfortable when you're dressed that way. You enjoy copying your pirate ancestor. Didn't you have any law-abiding ancestors to serve as your role model?"

"I loved and admired my father."

"Your father was an undercover flying pirate for at least one intelligence service and perhaps more."

"Thank you, Todd, that's the nicest compliment you've ever given me."

"I guess you're unredeemable, but be careful when you play in the sandbox with people much tougher than you. I don't trust your Mexican partners."

"There's just one main partner, and Tony's easier to control than you were. He's also better in bed ... sorry about that."

"You'd better go back to your Mistress of Ceremony duties, and I do mean *mistress*."

"Enjoy your stay at the park."

As Emma walked away, Todd smiled. During her gloating, she had revealed that she had only one partner; he was indeed Mexican; and his name was Tony, probably short for Antonio. Not a bad day's work. He left the park without waiting for the return of the cruise ship that didn't have his father on board.

CHAPTER 74 – JOYCE

Joyce White began her quest for information on the Mexican tourists by calling the major airlines at Nassau's Lynden Pindling International Airport. She told each contact that she was trying to find the airline that had a passenger named Jose Garcia because he had visited Weatherford & Rolle in Marsh Harbour and had left his wallet and telephone when he arranged for shipment of his merchandise back to Mexico. Joyce said she was sure he would need these items during the remainder of his vacation trip, so would the airline representative please check the passenger manifests to determine Mr. Garcia's flight and destination? The representatives were quite willing to check their records for Joyce, but none of the major scheduled airlines showed a listing for Jose Garcia.

After contacting the major carriers, Joyce called Bahamasair and again asked for a check of passenger manifests. This time, the representative, Willa Porter, after making an initial scan of her pending flights, asked Joyce to hold the line while she checked something else.

When Willa returned to the telephone, she sounded excited. "We have your Mr. Jose Garcia. He wasn't booked on a scheduled flight, but rather a charter. He and his group will be departing Nassau at 11:00 AM tomorrow. If your private pilot arrives in Nassau before that time, have him or her contact me at the Bahamasair counter. If I'm not on duty, I'll leave instructions for the other agents."

Joyce made a few quick notes and prepared to add more. "We'll try to meet your schedule, but if we can't get there and we have to ship Mr. Garcia's belongings, what is the destination of that charter flight?"

"It's going to the country of St. Kitts and Nevis, landing at Vance W. Amory International Airport on Nevis. Bahamasair doesn't have scheduled flights to Nevis, but we do have an office at that airport. If we don't receive your package before the charter flight departs, I'll notify our Nevis office to watch for your shipment. Address it to Jose Garcia, c/o Bahamasair, Vance W. Amory International Airport, St. Kitts and Nevis."

Joyce thanked Willa, ended the phone call, and ran to Sandy's office, where Todd was summarizing his encounter with Emma Read at the pirate park to Sandy, Sylvia, and Frank.

"...and in the course of her teasing me about how she was so successful while I was worrying about baby diapers, she revealed that she has only one partner, that he is Mexican, and that his name is Tony. I assume that would make him formally Antonio."

Frank jumped up. "Hold it! That was the name on that business card I saw at the boatyard in Florida. The pirate ships were ordered by Antonio Montez of St. Kitts and Nevis."

"Double hold it!"

Everyone turned to face Joyce standing in the doorway.

"I've just learned that Jose Garcia and the other Mexican tourists will be flying on a Bahamasair charter tomorrow to St. Kitts and Nevis, arriving at the Nevis airport."

Sylvia joined the conversation. "Jose told me the individuals coming from Mexico were being asked to consider moving to an Island country. That has to be St. Kitts and Nevis."

Sandy pulled a map out of his desk drawer. "Let's take this discussion one step further. Nevis is the smaller of the two islands that make up that country. The larger airport is on St. Kitts. If the charter flight is landing at the Nevis airport, then that's exactly where they want these people to settle. Antonio Montez is engineering an effort to resettle a large number of English speaking Mexicans on the island of Nevis. The question is why?"

Loyalties

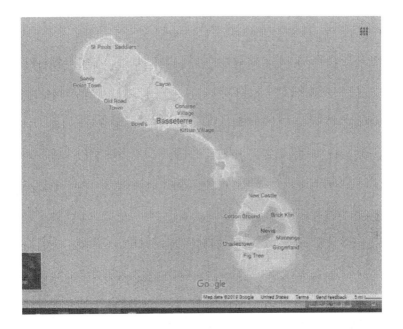

CHAPTER 75 – RESEARCH

Sandy and Todd were beginning a computer search for Nevis information when Joyce knocked on the doorpost to get their attention. "I have a contribution for your research." Joyce gestured with her hand at a blond woman wearing a colorful blouse and jeans standing next to her. "Meet Barbara Filkins. She's a travel agent, and she knows a lot about St. Kitts and Nevis."

Todd greeted Barbara while estimating her age at about twenty-seven and her height as just slightly more than his. *Is Joyce contributing a resource to our study of Nevis or being a matchmaker per her past hints?*

Sandy invited Barbara and Joyce to join them at his conference table. Barbara sat down, but Joyce said she had to deal with a couple of store problems but would bring in a carafe of coffee for them.

As they waited for the coffee, Barbara said, "Joyce gave me a little background for your study goals. I hope I'll be able to contribute something useful. Before we get started, I'll ask you to call me Barb; I think Barbara is too formal among friends. Just don't call me Barbie; I get too many Barbie Doll jokes."

Joyce delivered the coffee along with a telephone message for Sandy. He took the note, nodded, and put it on his desk.

Todd started the discussion. "We know that St. Kitts and Nevis is a federation of the two islands, with Nevis being the smaller of the two. We also know that Nevis has a volcano in the center of the island. What else can you tell us, Barb?"

"You're American, so I'll start with the trivia bit that Alexander Hamilton was born on Nevis. At the time when your states were still British colonies, Nevis was the biggest sugar cane source for the world. It has fresh water springs and undrinkable hot springs, and beaches with different types of sand. What else would you like to know about the island?"

"Tell us about its political setup. It's a little unusual to have a country made up of two small islands."

"St. Kitts and Nevis is the smallest country in the Caribbean. That's why most people have never heard of it. St. Kitts is the larger island. Its original name was St. Christopher, but they shortened it for everyday use. Nevis at one time was a separate British colony, while St. Kitts was under French control, and the French attacked the British on Nevis. The combined country of St. Kitts and Nevis became independent but part of the British Commonwealth in 1983. Nevis has its own government administration and has the right to secede if it holds a referendum and two thirds of the voters approve secession."

"That's interesting stuff, Barb. Do the people on Nevis want to secede?"

Sandy said, "I'll answer that one. About twenty years ago, they held a secession referendum and it barely lost. It was in the newspapers and on television news here."

Barb added, "The vote was only a few percent short of the two-thirds needed for secession, so the majority of the people on Nevis would like to be independent of St. Kitts. Their economy has budget surpluses, but under the present setup, most of the money goes to the central treasury on St. Kitts."

Sandy stood. "Thanks for your input, Barb. I have to take care of a problem with some defective products. That was what Joyce's note was about. You two feel free to continue here in my office."

After Sandy left, Todd said, "Thanks for your input on Nevis, Barb. If you have a little more time, how about taking a ride north of Marsh Harbour. I haven't spent much time up that way. We might find an unusual place to have lunch."

"That sounds good to me. I'd like to learn more about why you're so interested in Nevis. Joyce hinted that it ties in with some mission of yours."

"If you want to go into all that, this will be a long drive and lunch."

CHAPTER 76 – BARB FILKINS

As they walked out of Weatherford & Rolle, Barb stopped. "If you don't mind, Todd, I'll drive. It's the red Mini over there. I'll put you in the sightseeing seat so that you'll be free to appreciate areas you haven't visited before."

"That sounds great to me. I'm almost embarrassed that I haven't taken the time to explore all of Abaco and the surrounding cays. I worked as a tour guide in Chicago."

"Joyce mentioned that. We have something in common. We've both worked with tourists and know they make unexpected requests."

They drove through Marsh Harbour and up the S. C. Bootle Highway, the main road northward.

Todd enjoyed Barb's precise control of the compact car. "Tell me more about yourself. Have you always lived in the Bahamas?"

"No. I was born in Canada, but I've lost any accent that would reveal that fact to strangers. I went to school in the U.S. at Wellesley, and then decided to take a year off before looking for a job. I couldn't think of a better place to spend that extra year than in the Bahamas, so I came here and decided to stay. Large numbers of Canadians and Americans vacation here, so it was natural to work as a travel agent."

"Wouldn't you have more customers where the tours originate, in the U.S. or Canada?"

"I'd have local customers there, but there are fewer agencies on this end, so I can represent many different companies from mainland North America and elsewhere. My primary job is to make sure nothing goes wrong for the vacationers when they get here."

"That could be a really big job."

"I have some assistants, so I don't have to be everywhere at once. Joyce told me that way back when, your ancestors were Loyalists who settled in the Bahamas after the Revolutionary War."

"That's true, but I didn't know about them until recently. I grew up in Kentucky, in a branch of the family that didn't reveal its Loyalist background."

"I know that feeling. My ancestors were Loyalists who fled north to Canada from Boston. When I went back to Massachusetts for college at Wellesley, I didn't reveal that I was from a Loyalist family."

"If your family had supported the other side, you would have been an American. Too bad the two groups couldn't get along together after that war."

"True, but would you be in the Bahamas without that scattering of your family?"

"I doubt it. Joyce apparently primed you with some of my background information."

"She's a natural matchmaker, but don't worry, I'm just here to help with your project. Would you like to tell me about it?"

"It's a long and embarrassing story. For now, let's say that I and my family were threatened by a woman named Emma Read who is descended from the pirate, Mary Read. She and a hidden partner developed Calico Jack's Pirate Adventure Park. Emma has been behind at least one murder and several attempts at murder in the past, and I believe that she and her partner are still scheming something major. My friends and I want to unravel their plot and keep them from succeeding."

Barb turned her head toward Todd as she drove so that she could see his reaction. "What about the baby?"

Todd's face reddened. "I didn't know how much Joyce told you, so I skipped that part of the story. Back in Chicago, Emma Read seduced me, asked me to get her pregnant, and in the process broke up my marriage with almost lethal results. She was planning to use the resulting baby to swindle me out of land on Abaco that I didn't know I would inherit someday. Once she hooked up with her wealthy partner, she didn't need my land or the baby anymore, so she gave me the child after he was born and signed away her rights to him. His name, by the way, is John Sandy Weatherford."

"When Joyce told me you had a baby involved in your story, she said you had named him after Sandy."

"He's a great friend and partner, and it's obvious how much Joyce cares for him."

"It's clear to you, but does Sandy know that?"

"I think he does, but he'll pick his own time to show his response to her feelings."

Barb increased the Mini's speed. "I know enough now to feel I'm a tiny part of your project, or should I say mission? I hope it turns out well. Now let's get back to touring and stop for something to eat and drink. The nice part about driving on an island is that it doesn't take very long to get to your destination."

"Where are you taking me?"

"I thought we'd cross over onto Little Abaco Island and stop to eat at Da Valley Restaurant and Bar. It's almost at the end of the road and is about as far north as we can drive."

"That not only sounds like a good destination; it sounds like a Chicago place. They joke about their football team as Da Bears. I'll feel right at home."

"That's a good point. Where is your home now – Kentucky, Chicago, or Abaco in the Bahamas?"

"I guess I've become an Islander."

CHAPTER 77 – MEETING WITH KEN

Ken Birch called Sandy to check on recent developments during his break between pirate ship cruises. "Hi, Sandy, I'm free for a while if you have any new information for me or want to have me work an extra task into my schedule."

"Thanks for the contact, Ken. Will you have a block of free time in the near future?"

"The first ship sails each day at ten o'clock in the morning, and I only need a half hour to get it ready. That means that I'm available in Marsh Harbour until nine o'clock each morning."

Sandy exchanged a few words with someone else in his office. "Sorry for the side-chatter there, Ken. Can you come to the store at eight o'clock tomorrow morning? I have someone who wants to talk with you, but I won't give any more details over the telephone."

"I'll be there, Sandy. I need a break from my routine anyway."

Ken arrived promptly at eight o'clock at Weatherford & Rolle the next morning. He entered the office and found Sandy Rolle and Frank June waiting for him with doughnuts and coffee.

Sandy extended his hand. "Ken, thanks for all the undercover work you've been handling for us. You're helping us to understand the secrets of that pirate theme park."

Ken picked up a cinnamon doughnut and took a bite. "There's definitely more to that place than meets the eye. The road that's actually a runway for instance."

"You worked with Frank June on his boat. He asked for this meeting to do a little strategic planning."

"Sure; what are you thinking, Frank?"

"You probably know that I have some military background. One of the things we learn is to anticipate the enemy's moves. Your reports keep mentioning that locked storage building near the ship docks. I think I know what it contains."

"What?"

"When those ships were still under construction, I visited the project engineer, and she mentioned that the mounting specification for the blank-firing show cannon matches that for the Mk38 Maritime Machine Cannon that's used on US Coast Guard and Navy ships. I believe the locked building contains the Mk38 weapons and their 25mm ammunition. At some point in this saga, your bosses are going to ask you to switch the pretend artillery pieces for the real things. It may be soon, but it's more likely to be months or even a year from now."

"When that time comes, do you want me to refuse to cooperate?"

"No, you may want to hesitate a bit for show before carrying out their instructions, but go along with them. You'll be prepared with a kit of special supplies that we'll ask Joyce to order today. She already has my request for some other unusual items. Here's what I want you to do ..."

CHAPTER 78 – BREAKFAST

Todd woke up when his telephone started to vibrate next to him on the couch. He answered quickly so that it wouldn't wake baby John.

"Hello?"

"Good morning, Todd; it's Barb. How about breakfast this morning?"

"That sounds good to me, but I might be dragging my tail a bit. I was up half the night with John. Mom has him all day, so I get night duty. I'll try to get out of here without waking the baby or my parents. Where do you want to meet?"

"My place. I'll text the address so that you won't get it wrong due to wooziness. I'm not too far from Central Abaco Primary School. How do you like your eggs?"

"If I have my druthers, I like them basted, but I'll take them any way you prepare them."

"Come on over as soon as you can. I won't cook the eggs until you arrive."

"Is there a reason for this breakfast date, outside of my irresistible charm?"

"That's a factor too, but I do have another reason. No hints until you get here."

Barb's house was easy to spot when Todd found her block. It was bright yellow with a gray roof and the tag *Journey's End* in black letters over the door. Todd parked the Jeep behind her Mini in the unpaved driveway, climbed two steps to the front door, and rang the doorbell.

When Barb answered the door, Todd asked, "How many strangers and castaways do you attract with that *Journey's End* sign?"

"Just you, so far. Come on in."

Todd walked in and saw that the inside walls mimicked the outside by being bright colors, each room having one wall a common color with the room next to it. The kitchen was green with one blue wall that continued into the dining room, which was primarily blue with one orange wall that continued into the next room. "Your house copies your taste for brightly colored blouses."

"Bright colors help me to stay cheerful."

"I've definitely seen your sunny disposition so far. My house is decorated exactly the way it was when I moved into it."

"You're occupying it, rather than making it yours. If you'd like, after I get to know your personality better, I'll give you some decorating suggestions to reflect what I see in you."

"That would be different. No one ever suggested that to me before."

"Forget home décor, and let's eat. I made eggs, bacon, blueberry muffins, and grits for a Kentucky boy."

"The food smells great. I usually have only toast and coffee. While we eat, will you tell me that other reason for inviting me that you mentioned?"

Barb pretended to pout. "Eat and appreciate my food, and then we'll talk about that. You have to learn to relax."

Todd started by sampling everything. Then he buttered his muffin and his grits and added salt and pepper to the latter. "Wow, it's been a long time since I had real butter in a home setting. My habit is to buy margarine because it's cheaper."

"Maybe you should break that habit and eat to appreciate food rather than merely to consume it."

"Thanks, Barb; I haven't enjoyed a breakfast like this for quite a while. You must enjoy the whole process of planning a menu and then cooking it."

"I do, in part because I don't work in a product-based business. Cooking is my creative outlet."

They finished their meal, and Todd volunteered to wash the dishes. Barb dried and put them away. Then Barb took Todd's hand and led him to her den where she had an inverted clipboard on her desk.

"You've been very patient during the meal, so I'll give you a choice. You can sit on the couch with me for a while, or I'll give you some new information for your project right away."

Without saying a word, Todd led her to the couch. They sat close together and then Todd put his arm around her shoulders. She kicked off her shoes and pivoted to stretch out on the couch with her head on his lap. He looked down at her and touched her hair.

"You came into my life as an expert who might contribute to my mission. Would you like to contribute to other aspects of my life?"

Barb raised her head toward Todd's. He lowered his and they kissed for the first time. Then they shifted into more comfortable positions and got to know each other better. When they came up for air much later, Barb pushed her hair back and said, "Now, you're beginning to relax."

It took a while for Todd's thoughts to focus on anything other than Barb, but after a half hour of occasional cuddling and a cup of black coffee, he said, "I don't want to be a killjoy, but what about that information you have on your clipboard?"

"Right – back to that other world." She poured more coffee for both of them and then brought the clipboard into the kitchen. "I stayed up late last night and did some more research on the island of Nevis."

"You're very dedicated once you get interested in something."

"Or someone – anyway, I followed up on Sandy's input about the secession vote in 1998."

"So, he was right about that timing."

"Don't interrupt. I have some interesting stuff for you. The secession referendum failed by just a few percent of the votes. It needed sixty-seven percent to pass and sixty-two percent voted to secede."

"So?"

"There you go again. The population of Nevis is about eleven thousand people, not all of whom are voters. If we assume that extra-large eleven thousand voter figure, the secession vote failed by only five hundred and fifty votes. If someone wanted to win a new secession vote, he'd have to convince at least six hundred more of the current voters to choose secession, or increase the voting population of Nevis by fewer than one thousand people, assuming they could be relied upon to choose independence from St. Kitts."

"I see where you're going with this exercise in logic, but the added people would have to be citizens in order to vote."

"They have a program for purchasing citizenship. It costs $100,000 for an individual and $195,000 for a family of four."

"You're thinking that Mexican drug money might be available to buy Mexican nationals citizenships in Nevis."

"You'd be talking about less than one hundred million dollars. That's a reasonable amount for the drug cartels."

"Why would they do it?"

"You tell me, Todd. If you were a drug lord and you controlled a country, what would you do?"

"I'd pass a no-extradition law, and then I'd move there."

"Bingo! That's what I think too."

"But why would you give that plan any probability of working?"

"Two reasons. First, Nevis already has a financial secrecy law that allows people to stash money in Nevis banks and be confident that their home countries won't know about it."

"What's the second reason?"

"The name of the out-of-power opposition party leader in Nevis is Antonio Montez."

"He's Emma Read's deep-pockets partner. You're a hell of a researcher, Barb." Todd gave her a passionate kiss.

"And don't you forget that. You'll want to keep me on your side."

CHAPTER 79 – DEVIATION

Todd moved more rapidly than usual when he entered the store the following morning. He waved to several employees in the sales area without talking to them and rushed into the offices. Joyce looked up from her computer as Todd walked directly to Sandy's office. He knocked on the closed door.

Joyce watched him with some surprise. "He's not here, Todd, and by the way, good morning. You're full of energy. May I help you in Sandy's absence?"

"Sorry, Joyce, I was so focused on talking with Sandy that I forgot to greet you. Will he be back soon?"

"I don't think so. He came in early and left me a note suggesting that I refer any major problems to you. Fortunately, everything in the store is normal so far. Feel free to stay in the office or spend some time on the sales floor if you want to wait for Sandy. Otherwise, I'll call you when he returns."

"I'll take the call option. It'll give me a chance to spend time with my son."

Joyce watched Todd in the parking lot on the new security TV monitor. At the end of the store driveway, he should have turned right to visit his parents and his son, but Todd turned left instead.

It was a last-second decision, but Todd felt the need to check up on the Pirate Park and Emma Read once more. Was it because of a hunch, or because he still didn't feel comfortable being alone with his own son? He promised himself to face his fatherhood responsibilities and to rely less on his parents' willingness to fill in for him.

When he drove into the lot at the theme park, the attendant directed him to the end of the last row of cars next to the woods. Todd complied, parked, turned off the ignition, and climbed out of the Jeep. As he tugged on the door handle to be sure he had locked it, someone grabbed him from behind and dragged him into the woods. He heard a gruff voice say, "Stop snooping around here; you're not welcome." Then something hard hit the back of his head, and he collapsed. When he awoke, his head ached, and he could feel a not-quite-solid scab forming where he had been struck. He opened his eyes, expecting to see the parking lot and his car beyond the trees, but instead he saw water all around him. He was on a tiny rocky island.

Todd decided that his attack had been a warning but not an attempt to kill him when he discovered that his pockets hadn't been emptied. He reached for his telephone, and it vibrated as he pulled it out of his pocket. He answered and heard Joyce's voice.

"Todd, Sandy's back and in his office. You can see him now."

His hoarse voice surprised him. "Can't come. Need help. Marooned on island."

Joyce yelled for Sandy, and he came on the phone. "What happened, Todd? Where are you? Are you hurt?"

"Ambushed while parking at Pirate Park. Slugged with something hard. Just woke up on tiny island. Head hurts. Feeling woozy."

"Stay on the phone. Joyce will call the police on the other line, and they'll track your phone's location."

"Good. Don't know what happened to your Jeep. If I'm on island, Jeep could be anywhere."

"That's good, Todd. You're starting to think better. Keep talking. How big is the island, and can you see any other land?"

"Not big. Not much above water. Lots of little islands even smaller. Bigger land in distance away from sun direction."

"Good thinking. The sun's high in the Western sky now, so the land is to your east. If there are other tiny islands around you, you're probably off the west coast of Central Abaco. I'll get someone with a boat on a trailer to launch and search that side of Abaco. The deep water docks are on the east coast, and it would take time to go around Abaco to get to you."

Sandy held the phone against his chest while he yelled. "Joyce, call Edward at the boatyard and see if he has a power boat on a trailer available. Maybe Frank June could launch it on the west coast."

"Todd, are you still there? Keep talking to me."

"Want to talk but getting dizzy and tired ..."

CHAPTER 80 – RECONNECTING

Todd woke up in a hospital the next morning. It looked like the same one where John Sandy Weatherford had been born. *Why didn't I go home to my son instead of sticking my nose into trouble without anyone knowing about it? I'm going to be a lousy father.*

He heard a knock on the door. A nurse came in carrying a vase of flowers. "You have a visitor waiting to see you, but I want to check your stitches and your ability to balance first." She examined the back of his head with a flashlight and the tips of her gloved fingers. "So far, so good. You took a good wallop with something hard and round. You'll have an indentation in your head for a long time, if not forever. Now, put your legs over the side of the bed and stand. I want to see whether you can balance without holding onto anything."

Todd stood, a little wobbly at first, but then surprisingly well. Then he took a few steps, to the bottom end of his bed and back, being ready to grab the bed for support if needed.

"You're doing very well, Mr. Weatherford, but don't do anything extra, like walking across the room, until I tell you to. I'll be back in an hour to test you on walking around our hallway course. If you handle that well, we'll release you by the end of the day. You'll have detailed instructions for continuing to treat your concussion at home."

"May I sit in the chair instead of going back to bed? I'll feel more normal that way."

The nurse agreed, helped him into the chair and covered his lap with a folded blanket. "Pull that up higher if you feel cold. I'll send your visitor in now."

She left, closing the door. A minute later he heard another knock, and the door opened.

Barb entered and smiled. "You're going to have to take better care of yourself. I want you around me in one piece."

"Thanks for coming. The nurse said they'd let me go home by the end of the day if I pass my walking test. Will you be available to drive me home? I seem to have lost my car."

"When she called me to tell me what happened, Joyce said they found your Jeep in the airport parking lot. That probably means that the men who attacked you are no longer on the island. Of course, I'll drive you home. You'll have to rest and recuperate for a good while."

"And why did Joyce call you? I didn't tell anyone about my visit with you yesterday."

"I could say that news travels fast on Abaco, but I'll admit to calling Joyce and thanking her for inserting me into your life." She leaned over his chair and kissed him.

"When we get home, I'll introduce you to my folks and little John. We're living in close quarters over there. I might have to request that some of my rest and recuperation takes place at your house."

"I'm sure we'll be able to arrange something."

At five o'clock, Barb drove her Mini to the hospital entrance, and an orderly helped her move Todd from a wheelchair into the car.

He belted himself in. "I always get a kick out of hospitals releasing patients in a wheelchair, but I guess the lawyers insist on it so no one falls on the way out the door. I called home, so Mom and Dad will be expecting us."

"Thanks for the anxiety. I'll have to try to make a good impression on them."

They drove to Todd's house and parked on the street. Barb walked around and started to help Todd out of the car. George Weatherford came out of the front door, jumped the stairs, and trotted over to the car. "Hi. Let me help you with him."

Todd said, "Dad, meet Barb. Barb, meet my dad, otherwise known as George."

They shook hands and then maneuvered Todd out of the Mini. Then he walked to the front door with only a few balancing assists on the two steps. Once inside, Todd repeated the introduction process with his mom, Judy, and sat down on the couch.

She said, "Welcome to our home, Barb. This little fellow in the bounce chair is John. Would you like to hold him? If you do, I suggest you put a burp towel over your shoulder. I wouldn't want him to soil your pretty blouse."

Barb hoisted John and rocked him in her arms.

Todd waved his hand for attention. "Pardon me if I don't get up. I'm a little dizzy. Anyway, I suddenly realized how little I know about you, Barb. Do you have any brothers and sisters? You look as though you've handled babies before."

"I have, both as the oldest of three sisters and as a babysitter. My sister Jessica is twenty-three, and Janice is twenty-two. I'll admit to being twenty-seven. Shall we discuss your siblings, Todd?"

Judy reached out to Barb for the baby. "Let's save that part of the discussion until after supper.

Everything is hot and ready. I'll put John back in his bounce chair so he can watch us while we eat."

Dinner was fish chowder with Caesar salad and warm rolls, freshly baked.

"Barb, if you're used to a larger meal, I have an apple pie we can have for dessert. We usually save dessert for snack time, but we can easily change that timing."

"No thank you, Mrs. Weatherford, I minimize the desserts unless they're the whole meal which they sometimes are at my house. Where did you get the apples for the pie on this island?"

"Call me Judy. I'll confess that I used canned apple pie filling. This isn't Kentucky, but I still try to make a few Kentucky favorite dishes."

Todd said, "Mom & Dad, you don't have to worry about family skeletons coming up during our conversations with Barb. Her ancestors were Loyalists who moved from Boston to Canada."

George looked at Barb. "I don't know how conversations go when you're home in Canada, but we're more in tune with our one ancestor who fought for America against the British back in that famous war."

"We never talk about it at all. I'm the only one in the family who emphasizes the importance of history. The others don't talk about anything earlier than the twentieth century."

Judy moved the bouncing chair with her toe to please John. "Barb, Todd never talks much. How long have you two been going together?"

Todd almost choked.

Barb laughed. "Approximately two days."

"Oh, forgive me. You two are so comfortable with each other that I thought it was much longer. He's never brought a girlfriend home to meet us before. Even when he was married, we didn't meet her until after the wedding."

Todd glared. "Mom! I didn't bring Barb home to meet you. She brought me home from the hospital."

George said, "Todd, come outside with me. I need you to help me smoke my pipe."

CHAPTER 81 – PULLING STRINGS

With Todd forced to recuperate, Barb called Sandy and suggested that they should hold the next tactical meeting at her house, the patient's temporary quarters.

Sandy asked Joyce to attend with him and to invite Frank and Sylvia also.

Joyce said, "Frank and Sylvia are taking tourists to Green Turtle Cay and the Albert Lowe Museum. I'll be happy to go to a house party with you."

"This isn't a date, but you're right, we should go out for fun sometime. How did Todd get to be staying at Barb's house?"

"It didn't take them long to get close, and then she took charge of him after his time in the hospital. It's a better setup for a meeting than it would be at his house with his parents and infant son there."

When Sandy and Joyce arrived at Barb's house, they approached the front door. Barb opened it before they could knock or ring the bell, and put her finger to her lips.

"Todd's napping. Come on in and get settled before I wake him up. He had a bad night. His head pain comes and goes, but it kept him from sleeping through the night."

They entered Barb's den, a combination office and sitting room, and saw Todd, dressed for the meeting, but asleep sitting on the couch. Barb pointed to a fruit bowl alongside a carafe of coffee plus beer and soft drinks. "Help yourself while I wake him up."

Todd slowly responded to Barb's words and looked around, blinking. "Oh great, did I sleep right through the meeting? What did you decide?"

Sandy laughed. "I could feed you a straight-faced story about all the things that went on while you slept, but the truth is we just now arrived. You didn't miss anything."

"Good. Barb, if you don't mind, please take detailed notes during the discussion in case my fuzzy brain doesn't remember everything."

Joyce shook her head. "No, Barb, you handle the hostessing while I take notes. I want to feel useful."

"You'll be plenty useful, following up on leads based on what Todd and I discovered."

Todd gestured for attention. "Barb's being overly generous. We're here for this meeting because of information she researched. All I did was follow the logic of those findings."

Sandy raised his beer bottle in a toast. "To Barb, the newest member of our team, for her research that will guide our discussion. ... Now that we've assigned credit, let's hear what news you have for us."

Barb and Todd re-stated the right of Nevis to secede being guaranteed by the constitution of St. Kitts and Nevis. They described the closeness of the 1998 referendum for secession, and the small number of additional pro-independence votes that would be needed in a future referendum. They related the discovered effort to resettle Mexican business people in Nevis with the existing laws in that island country allowing the purchasing of citizenship and secrecy in banking. Finally, they revealed Barb's discovery that Antonio Montez, silent partner in Calico Jack's Pirate Adventure Park, was also the leader of the opposition party in Nevis.

Todd concluded, "It doesn't take a huge leap of logic to predict that Montez will press for a new secession referendum as soon as he has enough resettled Nevis voters loyal to him. We also predict that in an independent Nevis, the Mexican cartel leaders who put up the money to buy those new citizenships will arrange to have a law passed prohibiting extradition and will have Nevis bow out of any existing extradition treaties."

Joyce agreed. "I follow your thinking, and it sounds reasonable to me. What can we do about it?"

Sandy said, "I think you've stated the agenda for this meeting, Joyce. Time is on our side. It will take months or even years for all these predicted developments to be accomplished. As outsiders, we can't stop the resettlements or the other expected steps. The existing government of St. Kitts and Nevis will have to interfere with the cartel plans."

"What can they do?"

"All the government has to do is to tweak the rules so that it will be much harder for Nevis to secede. Our job is to alert them to what's happening so that they can act."

"How would we do that?"

"Joyce, you and I both have connections with the offices of key figures in the Bahamas government. They, in turn have key contacts in the government of St. Kitts and Nevis. If we can nudge their thinking with hints of this information, we may be able to develop a plan and make them think they thought of it without our help."

Todd's eyes had partially closed, but he opened them wide at Sandy's suggestion. "I may not have looked awake, but you have me interested. What can I do to help?"

"You can't do anything until you've finished your concussion rehab. After that, you and your Dad can try to make some direct contacts with people in the government of St. Kitts and Nevis. Your dad told me he wants to do something active while he's here."

Todd looked amused. "I think I understand. We would be visiting business people who are thinking about expanding Weatherford and Rolle with a new branch in St. Kitts and Nevis. Potential employers are a magnet for government officials."

"And someday we should expand, but probably within the Bahamas."

"I can see Dad drooling over the prospect. Retirement is a dirty word to him."

CHAPTER 82 – EMMA READ

Emma smiled at her cousin Lydia across the table in her office. "Everyone thinks that I'm the only pirate descendant who enjoys reliving those days, but you may be even better at it than I am."

"You prance around for the press and the tourists, but my people have the muscle and the right outlook to be real pirates."

"Let's just say that I have the brains, Lydia, and you have the brawn."

"You can say that all you want, Emma, but you know you need us to get your battles won. Who got rid of Ike Trowbridge after he lost his value to you, and who clobbered your ex-boyfriend?"

"You almost did too well on clobbering Todd. You could have killed him. I told you to give him chloroform or something like it. He's the father of my son, and when I eventually reclaim that boy after he grows up, I don't want him to reject me because I killed his father."

"We didn't have anesthetics, so we put him to sleep the old fashioned way. Don't worry; he survived. It'll be a while before he's as sharp as he was, but he'll get there someday."

"Anyway, you and your gang got good money for those jobs, but there's a much bigger, and richer, one ahead."

"What's the plan?"

"We're going to eliminate Mr. Smarty-pants Montez and his people."

"I'm not sure that's a good idea, Emma."

"Why?"

"Because he's close to people who run one of the Mexican drug cartels. It wouldn't be smart to get on the wrong side of them."

"It'll never come to that. Montez is also a politician in St. Kitts and Nevis. It's easy to smear a politician's reputation so that no one will follow him again."

"Emma, I thought you liked that guy and his money. He paid for this land and those ships."

"The Pirate Park isn't worth much without the ships. They're what people come here for. Montez put up a lot of cash for them, but they're mobile assets. They move, and I've heard rumors that he plans to sail them out of here and leave me with only the land base. The park will die if that's the only part that's left. Never trust a politician."

"But you expect him to trust a pirate?"

"Point made. Don't trust anyone."

"How did you find out that he's planning to take your ships?"

"I have a spy working on the ships, a fellow by the name of Ken Birch. He's the one who drives the Jeep around Lynyard Cay. He thinks Montez plans to take the ships away to his home island of Nevis, southeast of Puerto Rico, where he'll set up his own pirate theme park without me."

"Emma, what would you think about having some real pirates crew your ships? We could gradually replace your current crew members with my people. They'll be armed and ready for anything when Montez acts."

"That's a great idea, Lydia. I'll have to create some more land jobs to give assignments to the crew we replace. If we just fire them, they'll protest and get attention in the newspapers and television. Start filtering in a few deckhands next week."

CHAPTER 83 – CONTACTS

Joyce started up the call chain of friends in government agencies, giving most of them the impression that she was looking for official information, but at the same time planting rumors that she hoped would eventually propagate all the way to corresponding officials in St. Kitts and Nevis.

"Hello, Mandy; Joyce White calling from Weatherford and Rolle. Yes, I'm fine, and I hope you are too. I need some information on laws and customs in St. Kitts and Nevis. The bosses are looking into putting a new branch there. Would you know who they should contact in the government there? You don't, but you'll find out. Thank you so much. You are a friend indeed."

"Rupert. Hello to you my friend. This is Joyce White at Weatherford and Rolle. I'm calling to ask whether anyone in the Ministry of Foreign Affairs knows about large numbers of Mexican citizens looking to settle in St. Kitts and Nevis. Actually, they all seem to be looking to live in Nevis, not St. Kitts. Somebody is giving them financial aid to move there. It must be some big housing developer, I guess. Who knows, that island may change from English to Spanish speaking if enough Mexican people move there. We've had some in our store, and some friends at the Pirate Theme Park have talked with them as well. No, they're not peasants. Everyone I've heard about was a business person. Anyway, Nevis will change greatly if they all decide to settle there."

"Hello, Ruth, you're sounding much better. That cold was a big problem for you for a while. Did you hear about all the Mexican nationals who are coming through Abaco but heading to the island of Nevis for resettlement? You did hear about it? Who told you? Oh, you heard it from Freddy in the Ministry of Foreign Affairs. Then it must be true. What other developments have been passing through your office? Is that so? How reliable is your information. Thank you much. I'll check with them."

Joyce put down her telephone and went to Sandy's office. She waited while he completed a call to the Prime Minister's office. As soon as he put the phone down, she entered his office and sat down.

Sandy looked up and studied her face. "What is it, Joyce? You look bothered."

"The thing about a calling network is the information flows both ways. I have confirmation that our story about the Mexicans clicked with the Ministry of Foreign Affairs, which is good news. They're already spreading the story to other parts of the government. However, I also received chit-chat about Barb Filkins that is very disturbing."

"Why did someone say anything about Barb?"

"You can't restrict these phone networks. People talk all the time. Barb was seen at the hospital with Todd, and people immediately linked them together and started talking. One of my more reliable sources told me that Barb has an embarrassing past she tries to hide."

"We all have something to hide."

"My problem is that I pushed Barb at Todd, both because she is a good source for information about many places, and because he needs a female someone to help with his new son. Todd knows absolutely nothing about taking care of children."

"So, you like to play matchmaker. What's the problem?"

"The problem is that reliable sources say that Barb never graduated from Wellesley College. She was kicked out."

"Lots of people don't finish school. It's not a crime or something to be embarrassed about."

"It is when you're kicked out for being the madam in a call girl operation."

CHAPTER 84 – TODD AND BARB

The coffee shop was busy, but most of the customers were tourists, and they naturally gravitated to the tables with a view of the harbor and the boats moving inbound and outbound. When Todd and Barb entered, they headed in the opposite direction, toward an isolated booth in the rear of the room.

Todd propped the cane he carried as steadiness insurance against the far end of the bench seat and lowered himself onto the near end. "I'm ready to dispense with that stick. Nowadays, I carry it more than I lean on it."

Barb gracefully slipped into her side of the booth. "You're almost back to the way you were, but I wouldn't recommend sudden movements or gymnastics yet. You need to avoid abrupt shocks to your brain."

"You've been a good friend and nurse, Barb. Thanks for all your help."

Barb pouted. "I hope that I'm a bit more than that to you."

The waitress interrupted to take their orders and then left.

Todd put his menu back in its stand-up clip at the far end of the table. "What were you saying? My memory's still a little fuzzy."

Barb pounded the table with her fist. "You're not going to get off that easily, Mr. Weatherford. Am I more to you than a nurse or not?"

"I said you are a good friend as well as a nurse."

"You're completely well and pretending to have memory problems. Don't toy with me, Todd. We met because Joyce thought I had knowledge that would help your project. Then, I was in the right place to help you after your attack injuries. From now on, our relationship has to be due to more than fate. Tell me."

He held her hand. "Barb, I enjoy being with you, but I have to let things develop over time. I had a horrible breakup of my marriage because of a corrosive relationship with Emma Read. I've stayed away from romance since then. You're the first woman to awaken my feelings. It's been great, but we'll have to see how we grow together. Is that good enough for you?"

"Sure, Todd, but I have to be open with you too. I lied when I said I came to the Bahamas for a gap year after my graduation from Wellesley. I never finished college."

"That's not a problem for me. I never even started it. My wife, Lori, pushed me in that direction, but I refused to take that path."

"Now that you're back to being yourself, what's next on the agenda?"

"That's interesting wording, Barb. There actually is an agenda. I'll be away for a little while. Per our meeting at your house, I'll be flying with my dad to St. Kitts to talk with government officials about the possible opening of a store branch there. It'll be the first trip alone with my dad for a very long time."

CHAPTER 85 – ST. KITTS

When Todd and his father went to the Marsh Harbour airport, George Weatherford drove the store Jeep, bypassing any possible concentration problem that his son might still have from his injury. They parked near one of the hangars and George went inside to arrange for a rental aircraft. He came out twenty minutes later, smiling and carrying keys and a clipboard full of papers.

Todd climbed out of the Jeep. "Are we all set?"

"Yes, but climb back in. We'll have to drive to the plane. It's parked beyond the terminal building."

"What did you get? I hope it has two engines. I'd be a little nervous going so far in a single engine plane. Of course, I haven't flown in a small aircraft at all."

"That's right, son. I forgot that for a long time, you didn't know I was a pilot. This will be your first flight with me."

"Just so it's not my last – I'm kidding, Dad. What plane are we flying? Will we have to make a stop along the way? My map calculation says that it's over eleven hundred miles."

"Maybe a bit more. I filed a flight plan along the east side of the island chain so that we won't ever be very far from land in case of an emergency. We'll have a curved route instead of a straight line, so the distance will be a little longer. We have an aircraft that can make the trip from Marsh Harbour on Abaco to Basseterre on St. Kitts without stopping. It's a Cessna 421 Golden Eagle with two engines and a range of about seventeen hundred miles. They said it's all fueled and ready to go, but I'll go through the preflight checklist with the mechanic who's been paged to meet us at the plane."

"Have you flown this type of Cessna before, Dad?

"Not this one, but a similar earlier model."

The mechanic was waiting for them when they reached the aircraft, which was white with red trim. He introduced himself as Woody Brown.

"Hi, folks; let me walk you through the checklist and tell you a few things about this baby. Which one of you is the pilot?"

George waved his hand. "I'm your culprit. I left my white silk scarf at home."

"The silk scarves went out with the barnstormers. You're not that old. Of course, some of the air show stunt flyers still wear them. Do you fly aerobatics?"

"I was kidding, Woody. I'm a Kentucky flyboy, and I'm very conservative. I won't do any maneuver that might cause a problem for your plane."

Todd watched as Woody and his father went over the aircraft in great detail, inside and out. They appeared to be old friends by the time they finished. Per Woody's suggestion, George and Todd visited a construction site portable toilet nearby before they took off. Their flight would last about five hours if they didn't stop along the way.

George radioed the control tower with his identification information and flight plan. They were cleared for takeoff promptly, which made Todd chuckle, remembering his seemingly endless waits on the taxiway in planes flying out of O'Hare International in Chicago.

The takeoff went smoothly, but Todd found himself concentrating on every move his father made, both because it was their first flight together and because he wasn't quite sure how skilled a pilot his father was. As soon as they were airborne and in level flight, Todd relaxed, impressed by his dad's ease at handling the controls.

During the long journey, Todd monitored the islands on the horizon to his right, using his map to try to identify them and chart their progress. The two men spoke occasionally on the intercom, but the engine noise interfered with long conversations. As they neared their destination, Basseterre on the Island of St. Kitts, George told Todd that Sandy had contacted the government ministry that handled commercial ventures and that they might be met by somebody official at the airport.

After receiving clearance from the control tower, George brought the plane in for a smooth landing, and the ramp marshal used his orange batons to direct their taxiing plane to its assigned parking space. As George opened the pivoting drop-down staircase, a black limousine approached them and stopped nearby. A dark-skinned man wearing a dark blue suit and tie got out of the car and approached George and Todd as they descended the steps from the Cessna.

"Good afternoon, gentlemen. My name is Malcolm Harkney, and I represent the Minister of Tourism, International Trade, Industry and Commerce. Mr. Sandy Rolle of your home office alerted us that you were coming."

"Hello, Mr. Harkney; I'm George Weatherford, and this is my son Todd. We've come to investigate the merits of establishing a branch of Weatherford & Rolle, Home Improvement & Building Supplies in

St. Kitts. Thank you for taking time out of your busy schedule to meet us here."

"We've arranged for a conference room at the St. Kitts Marriott Resort with catering during our discussions. We have also arranged for a suite for you in that hotel. I hope this will be convenient."

Todd hadn't realized that a branch of their store would be considered important to the St. Kitts economy. "That will be fine, Mr. Harkney."

When the limousine arrived at the Marriott, the staff hustled to attend to their needs. Mr. Harkney was apparently well known and respected for all the business his government department brought to the hotel. George and Todd were ushered up to their suite while Malcolm Harkney went directly to the conference room to be sure everything was in order. George and Todd would join him there in thirty minutes.

The suite was impressive. It had a large living room plus two bedrooms, each with its own bathroom. The windows overlooked the bustling beach with its tents and colorful umbrellas and the ocean beyond it. The bellman extended his wishes that they would enjoy their stay and suggested that they might like to spend some time in the casino.

When George and Todd arrived at the conference room, they found everything set up for their meeting, including bowls of fruit, coffee and pastry. Malcolm Harkney had shed his jacket to show that he was ready to talk in an informal atmosphere.

"Welcome, gentlemen. I hope you found your accommodations acceptable. If you don't mind, we'll use first names during our discussions. St. Kitts is a relaxed and friendly place."

Todd sat in a soft chair away from the conference table. "I was going to suggest the same thing, Malcolm."

"Todd, George, Take some coffee, fruit or whatever else you like and sit back while I show you a brief PowerPoint presentation about our country."

Images of beautiful beaches, inland scenery, bustling street scenes in Basseterre, and business buildings filled the projection screen accompanied by narration and music by a local band. As the music faded at the end of the show, a hotel assistant returned the lighting to normal.

George took the lead in responding. "That was all very impressive, Malcolm. You have a beautiful country, and I can see that you want to pursue additional economic development."

"Indeed we do. I took the liberty of researching your company, and I see that you have been building the business of Weatherford & Rolle for a very long time in the Bahamas. What makes you interested in expanding to St. Kitts?"

Todd placed several pieces of fruit on the table in a seemingly haphazard manor. "These represent the islands of the Bahamas. They are spread over an extremely large area, and most of them have little population and few government offices. We like the idea of having a branch in a place where we can get prompt government attention to any business problems or legal matters that might arise. St. Kitts fits that description."

"Speaking for our department and our government, I assure you we would give immediate attention to matters in which we might help your store fit into our economy. I do have one question. Are you convinced you want to have your business on the island of St. Kitts, or would you be equally interested in a location on our other island, Nevis. We are trying to build the Nevis economic structure and might assist with land acquisition there."

Todd latched onto the mention of Nevis. "Malcolm, we had considered Nevis, but with all their new settlers from Mexico, we felt that we would do better here. Nevis may become bilingual in a few years."

"What are you referring to? I have not heard about people from Mexico coming to Nevis."

"We heard about it from our contacts in the Bahamas Ministry of Foreign Affairs. As we understand it, a property developer is encouraging Mexican business people to settle in Nevis. The company may even be assisting them in applying for citizenship there."

"Is this new population only in Nevis, or in St. Kitts also?"

"We heard that the new settlers were going to Nevis only, but we don't know for sure."

George interrupted the exchange between Malcolm and Todd. "Malcolm, do you have a list of properties that might be available for our store, if possible with indications of their locations on a map?"

Malcolm appeared distracted. "I have that information, George, but I just remembered that there is a matter I must attend to at the office. If you'll excuse me, I'll be back here in a few hours, and we can continue our discussions then. If I get tied up, the continuation of our meeting might have to wait until tomorrow. I'm sorry for the interruption. You may want to visit the casino or the beach in my absence." Malcolm gathered up his papers and carried his jacket as he rushed down to the car.

George turned to Todd. "Well done, son. I think we've accomplished our mission."

"This does look like a good place to have a branch store. Too bad it's eleven hundred miles from our headquarters. The logistics would be terrible."

"How about one in Freeport on Grand Bahama Island, Todd?"

"That would be a great retirement project location for you, Dad. It's halfway between the Marsh Harbour store and Florida."

"Let's discuss that after we get back to the Bahamas. I might be interested in that possibility. In the meantime, let's spend some time in the casino, without telling your mother about that portion of our trip."

CHAPTER 86 – DEVELOPMENTS

When Todd and George arrived back at the Marsh Harbour airport, they found a message waiting for them at the aircraft rental office. It said that they should go directly to Sandy's office at the store.

When they arrived at the office, Joyce looked nervous and Sandy looked unhappy.

Joyce said, "I'm sorry, Todd."

Sandy cut her off. "George, Todd, please come into my office and shut the door. We have a problem."

As soon as the door closed, Todd asked, "It's not the baby, is it?"

"No, nothing like that, although little John was slightly involved."

George put his hand on Todd's arm. "Let's not guess. Sandy will tell us in his own way."

Sandy paced as he talked. "Back when we called a bunch of our government contacts to plant the story of the Mexicans resettling on Nevis, we received some other gossip in return. It was chatter about Barb Filkins from people who knew you were dating her, Todd."

"What about Barb?"

"Joyce received word that Barb didn't graduate from college. She was kicked out."

Todd thought about Sandy's phrasing. "Barb already told me she didn't graduate. That's no big deal. What's this about being kicked out?"

"According to Joyce's source, Barb was forced to leave school when they caught her acting as a madam for a call girl operation that involved other students as well as outside women."

"I guess that's something I'll have to discuss with Barb privately. Why is it a problem for anyone other than Barb and me?"

"While you were away, your mother decided to bring little John here to see the store. Joyce and I were in my office discussing a bunch of things with the door halfway open. Your mother wheeled John into our outer office just as Joyce and I were debating whether the story received about Barb was true. She heard it all."

George asked, "How did Judy react?"

"She greeted us with a strange expression on her face once we realized she was in the outer office. She said very little and then decided that she had chores at home that needed doing. She didn't give us a chance to say much of anything."

George nodded. "You're right. It's a problem. I'll go home and talk with her before you get there, Todd. You may want to talk with Barb now or wait for later."

"I'd better do it now. Delays only spread more gossip and make it worse."

As they left the office, George and Todd saw Joyce at her desk. This time she was not quite sure whether to smile or not. "Guys, again, I'm sorry for accidentally spreading gossip. However, there is interesting news. Freddy, at the Ministry of Foreign Affairs called. He said that his minister had talked with his counterpart in St. Kitts and Nevis. They both concurred that the influx of Mexicans to Nevis was true and that it might lead to difficulties. The minister in St. Kitts said they were drafting legislation to head off any possible problems."

Todd smiled for the first time since coming back to the store. "Whatever they have in mind, it won't be good news for Antonio Montez. Joyce, don't beat yourself up over what my mother overheard. We'll straighten things out."

Barb was surprised to find Todd sitting on her steps when she returned from her office. "I thought you were out of the country."

"I was, but I got back a couple of hours ago. Flying in a small plane for a long distance is nothing like a jetliner. I'm tired."

"I'll have to give you a key. You're not supposed to get worn out after that concussion."

"Can we go inside? We have to talk."

"That sounds ominous. Come on in." She led the way and closed the door behind them. "May I get a couple of drinks before we start talking?"

"Sure; split a beer with me. I'm supposed to take it easy on drinking for a while."

Barb returned with two half glasses of beer. "I can't remember the last time I drank beer from a glass instead of a bottle or can. What's up, boss? Am I in trouble?"

"Word is out on why you didn't finish college at Wellesley. I've heard the gossip. Now, I want to hear the story from you."

"Right from the horse's mouth in other words. I won't kid about you calling me a horse. It's time to be serious. I don't know what you heard, but it's probably essentially true. I screwed up. A couple of my friends at school were talking about using their bodies to work their way through school, and I figured there might be others in that situation, so I organized them into a business. It wasn't smart or even ethical, but I did it, and after a while I got caught by one of the deans. I'm guilty as charged, but I did my best to never let the girls go out with anyone who looked at all weird or evil. I did online and social media pre-date research on the guys."

"Did any of your girls have bad experiences?"

"There may have been a few. None so bad that we had to call the cops. To answer the question you're thinking but not asking, I was the administrator, not a participant."

"How did you feel about it afterward?"

"I was sorry I got caught, and that I couldn't finish school. Beyond that, I said the appropriate contrite words, but I really didn't mean them. Those girls were going to turn their tricks anyway. I only added organization and safeguards."

"How did your family feel about what you were doing, getting caught by the faculty, and missing graduation?"

"By that time in my life, my parents had died and my sisters had their own problems to worry about. We had stopped being a family."

"You told me that your job now is to take care of tourists vacationing here and make sure they have a good time. Does any of that include providing men with women or any other types of dating escorts?"

"Not a chance. I learned my lesson. My turn to ask questions."

"Shoot."

"Will mistakes in my background make me ineligible to earn your love?"

"No, but they may cause family complications." Todd told Barb about his mother overhearing the conversation at the store office."

"Ouch! I like your mother."

"And she'll like you after she gets over the initial shock to her moral code. I have no idea how long that will take. Dad's at home trying to reason with her now. That'll be my next stop."

Barb leaned over and gave Todd a lengthy kiss.

"What was that for, not that I didn't appreciate it?"

"That was for just-in-case your mother won't let you see me again."

"She doesn't have veto power, and it won't come to that anyway. I'll see you later tonight. Keep a light in the window for me."

"Don't worry; the light won't be red."

When Todd unlocked the front door of his house and entered, he sensed immediately that his parents had been arguing. His father sat in a corner chair, reading a book and defiantly smoking his pipe inside the house. His mother was in the kitchen cleaning spilled flour off the counter. Baby John was screaming as loud as he could. Todd took the path of least resistance and went to console his son. When he returned carrying the infant, George said, "She wants to call Lori to come here and make up with you. I told her we shouldn't try to control your life. That was an hour ago."

Todd went into the kitchen and found his mother sobbing as she cleaned up the mess from the flour canister she had slammed onto the counter.

"Mom, please don't get all upset. You're scaring the baby. I have to live my life, and you have to allow me to make a few mistakes along the way if they do happen. Right now, I think Barb is far from being a mistake, no matter what she did in the past. I almost killed Lori back on that Thanksgiving

Day. That's far worse than what Barb did, and she's willing to take a chance on me."

"I was hoping that if Lori saw you in your new position here, she'd run to make up with you."

"Mom, one of the reasons we couldn't get along back then was that Lori thought too much about status and career positions. Even if we got by that one, Lori and I would always remember our battle and would worry that it could happen again. Lori is a wonderful woman, but she's part of my past. I have to worry about the present and future. Let's build on where we are and what we have today. One of the few quotes I remember from high school Shakespeare readings is 'the past is prologue.' We have to live that way."

Judy stepped out from behind the counter and gave her son and his baby a hug, covering them both with the flour she had been sweeping up.

Todd looked at the results on his and the baby's clothes. "Mom, I guess you're showing us that everything's all white now."

CHAPTER 87 – ANTONIO MONTEZ

The call from St. Kitts stunned Tony Montez. The National Assembly of St. Kitts and Nevis had taken advantage of his absence as the leader of the opposition in Nevis and had introduced new legislation regarding immigrants purchasing their way to citizenship. The primary proposed regulation required that all those who achieve citizenship through payments to the government treasury must live in Basseterre on St. Kitts for three years before they become free to move anywhere they wish in the country. The law claimed to be aimed at ensuring that new citizens become familiar with the government and social responsibilities before they disperse to areas outside of the capital. Tony knew that most people who live in one place for three years will want to stay there or move nearby because of the friends and habits they've developed during that period. The second proposed regulation was just as bad for Nevis secession. This resolution stated that immigrants purchasing their way into citizenship could not vote for five years. Tony thought he might be able to get that one overturned in the courts if it passed. It was obvious he would have to fly back to Nevis to organize resistance to this proposed legislation.

He didn't know how, but apparently the St. Kitts establishment knew about his plan for Nevis secession, and they had increased the difficulty of his achieving his goal. His financial backers from the cartels would not be pleased with this development. They might even come after him personally. He needed an alternate approach to implement immediately.

Could a government coup work? He had enough contacts in the St. Kitts and Nevis infantry and maritime forces to make that worth considering, especially if he armed the pirate ships and added them to the forces. The problem was that the country was a member of the Commonwealth of Nations, and he couldn't predict whether the British and other Commonwealth Caribbean countries would come to the aid of the existing government. The British response to Argentina's attempt to claim and occupy the Falkland Islands was a bad precedent for him.

Tony called a number in Mexico. Someone named Raoul answered it. "Hola, Tony. What's happening?"

"Slight change in plans. I'm flying back to Nevis for a government crisis. You'll lead the troops. Fly your people in here this evening. I'll arrange to have the landing lights on. Then take over the ships and arm them from the main shed. You have the combination for the lock. A local guy named Ken Birch is my munitions man. He'll cooperate in changing the guns. If the current crews on the ships resist your people get rid of them. Then sail the ships to Nevis to give me a show of force if we need it. You should get there within two days of continuous sailing."

"What about your pirate queen partner? Do we take her along?"

"Absolutely not. She's served her purpose and isn't part of my future plans."

"Good enough, Tony; you take care of the government stuff and we'll take care of the ships.

We'll run them with full sails plus the inboards. My guys are all experienced sailors. This will be fun."

"Enjoy yourselves, but no slip-ups. This is serious business."

Tony made one more call to Ken Birch. "Ken, you've always been trustworthy in the past. I have two special assignments for you that will earn you ten thousand American dollars. Can I rely on you?"

"Sure, Tony. Keep talking."

"Tonight at eight o'clock, turn on the runway lights at the south end of the road on Lynyard Cay. I'm sure you've figured out how they work by now. I've seen you drive the Jeep down there. Hang the wind sock on its post too."

"No problem. What else?"

"One of the people flying in, Raoul, is my right-hand man. He'll unlock the big shed you've always wondered about. It contains military machine cannon that fit on the same mounts as our antique blank-shooting guns. Your job is to swap the modern weapons for the show pieces. Your payment will be in an envelope with your name on it attached to the runway light circuit breaker. This is very important. I'm depending on you."

"I'll take care of it, Tony, and thanks. My family can use that money."

After ending the call from Tony, Ken made three calls of his own. One was to Frank June, one was to Sandy Rolle, and the third was to Emma Read.

CHAPTER 88 – BOARDING PARTIES

The *Mary Mead* and the *Anne Bonny* sat peacefully at their moorings as landing lights illuminated the southern end of the combination road and runway that ran the two mile length of Lynyard Cay. Two DC-3 two-engine propeller transport planes landed over the course of the next ten minutes and taxied close to the end of the island where the ships were moored. As they came to a stop, the landing lights went dark, and a Jeep drove northward from the switching building. The Jeep came to a stop next to the lead aircraft as both planes unloaded men, their personal weapons, and supporting supplies.

Ken Birch climbed out of the vehicle. "I'm looking for Raoul."

A swarthy six-foot man approached. "I'm Raoul. You must be Ken Birch."

They shook hands and walked over to the large shed, where Raoul opened the combination lock. Then he turned back to join his men. He motioned for them to go on board their assigned ships. He signaled the planes that they could turn around and return to their base.

As the planes took off, the men split into two crews that went up the gangplanks of their assigned pirate ships. When they were halfway up to the ship decks, shots rang out. Lydia's thugs had taken up positions on the ships while Ken was at the other end of the island controlling the landing lights. Ken dove into the unlocked shed, wondering if a building full of guns and ammunition was the best place to hide.

The Mexican crews grabbed their weapons and fired in the general direction of the ship decks while they scrambled to find cover from their exposed boarding positions. Somebody switched on the floodlights that normally illuminated the ships for promotional purposes during the nighttime hours. Now the fighters on both sides could see each other, and the intensity of gunfire increased.

Raoul urged his Mexican fighters on in both Spanish and English. Emma Read, on board the *Mary Read* commanded her troops while exchanging her pirate cutlass for an AK-47 assault rifle. It was obvious that both sides had trained fighters. The pirate group had the initial advantage, commanding the height and bulwarks of the ships, but Raoul's men were relentless, regardless of the number of casualties they suffered. The battle raged for about twenty minutes, and as the firing slowly eased, splashes echoed as the remaining pirate thugs jumped overboard and swam to the opposite shore. Emma covered their retreat with rapid fire, but fell with multiple fatal wounds as the last of her crew jumped into the water.

Raoul's side had won, but at the cost of half its manpower. They would be hard put to sail the two ships to Nevis on schedule. The victors laid out the dead and wounded from both sides on the dock for the next day's park personnel to handle. Raoul positioned Emma Read's body on a bench with her AK-47 next to her, in recognition of her valor.

Ken Birch crawled out of his hiding place and began removing the four cannons on each side of the two pirate ships. Several of Raoul's men assisted him with the heavy lifting. Fortunately, the shed contained hydraulic lift carts for both the antique and modern weapons. After the old cannons were removed, he proceeded to install the Mk38 Maritime Machine Cannons in their places. Raoul's men left the ships while he was doing the final installations so that they wouldn't distract him from his work. He completed the job as the sun rose. Raoul gave Ken a second fat envelope full of cash to use in treating the wounded and burying the dead.

As the ships sailed away from the docks, Ken called Frank June once more.

CHAPTER 89 – CAT AND MOUSE

Frank June and Sandy Rolle trailed the two pirate ships from a distance on Frank's *June's Bug*. They wore war surplus helmets and flak jackets. Frank had mounted steel armor plates to the railings on the Coast Guard utility boat to give them some protection if they were fired upon. He evaluated Sandy's appearance.

"You look pretty good in that outfit. Have you had any military experience?"

"Not a bit. I have to trust you to keep me from getting killed on this adventure."

"Don't worry about a thing. I'm calling a friend in the U.S. Coast Guard right now."

"Coast Guard, Puerto Rico, Lieutenant Daniels."

"Hi, Tommy; this is Frank June. We talked about my Coast Guard utility boat a while back."

"Hi, Frank. As I recall, you have a Special Forces background. What can we do for you?"

"I'm trailing two high-powered catamaran pirate ships from that theme park on Abaco in the Bahamas. Each one has been fitted out with eight stolen Mk38 Maritime Cannons, and they're on their way to St. Kitts and Nevis to interfere with that country's internal affairs. I'm sure the U.S. Coast Guard would like to find out where they got those weapons and prevent an invasion or coup."

"We would indeed, but we don't have a cutter close to your position. Our ETA would be about four hours. Is there any way you could slow them down?"

"As a matter of fact there is. Would I be authorized to do so?"

"Not officially, of course, but as long as no one gets killed on either side, it would be a help."

"I was hoping you'd say that. Keep tracking my GPS signal."

"We'll get a cutter on the way. Stay safe."

Frank signed off and turned to Sandy. "We're going to play a little cat and mouse with those pirate ships. The first step is to let them see us but to stay out of range of those Mk38's. They have an accurate range just under three thousand meters. That's about 1.8 miles. Let's see if we can get them to slow down and start firing at us."

Sandy fastened his helmet's chin strap. "I don't really feel good about this."

"Given the distance, they may not even realize we're not the Coast Guard. This boat fits their profile."

Frank pulled parallel to one of the ships at about two miles distance. As soon as he was sure they had been seen, he turned *June's Bug* so that it pointed at the pirate ship to be a smaller target. They crouched behind the armor plate sheets.

The pirate ship started firing. Almost all the shots were short, but one spent round plinked off the armor harmlessly. The second ship continued on its way and pulled far ahead of the one that stopped to fire. Frank repeated the maneuver, turning to be a larger target and then turning back again to minimize his boat's profile. The trailing pirate ship fired again. This time the 25mm shells were far short of their target. When Frank pulled almost within range of the Mk38 Machine Cannons on his third pass, nothing happened.

He slapped Sandy on his back. "It's working. Now all we have to do is go to their other side and repeat the process."

Sandy asked, "What's working?"

"That bank of guns is out of commission. They can't fire from this side of the ship. I had Ken Birch mount those cannons with nylon bolts instead of steel. The recoil of the cannons sheared the bolts. They now have loose heavy weapons they can't control. We'll get them to fire at us on the other side, and those guns will come loose too. Then we'll go after the other ship."

"That's smart, Frank, but we still haven't slowed them down much."

"The oracle says you must be patient and you will see."

Frank repeated the teasing process on the other side of the first ship, staying out of range, but drawing fire from the cannons three times. After that the pirate ship was quiet.

"Be prepared for anything now. We're going in closer. I don't know what small arms they're carrying, but they'll be shooting at us. Stay behind the armor."

Frank headed bow first toward the ship to present a small target. They heard gunfire, but nothing struck *June's Bug*. Frank opened a box and pulled out two flare guns. "I also had Ken Birch coat the sails with paraffin. They're very flammable."

Frank shot the first flare shell too high, and it flew completely over the ship. "These things have more power than I thought." His second shot hit the main sail and started a fire. They could hear shouts coming from the crew.

"Now it's time to go after the other ship. This one was the *Mary Read*. Time to tackle *Anne Bonny* before she gets away. Brace yourself. We're going high speed until we catch them."

When the U.S. Coast Guard cutter caught up with them later, the two pirate ships had only charred rigging where their sails had been, and due to other damage from the fires they were moving slowly along their original course. *June's Bug* trailed them at a safe distance, providing a GPS signal to guide the approaching cutter. The cutter dispatched armed Coast Guard boarding parties that took control of the pirate ships and their crews and put the vessels on a course for Puerto Rico.

Thirty minutes later, Frank June received a message from Lt. Tom Daniels of the U.S. Coast Guard congratulating him and his crew for delaying the *Mary Mead* and *Anne Bonny* and by doing so, helping to avoid an international incident.

CHAPTER 90 – NATIONAL ASSEMBLY

An assistant passed a note to the Speaker of the National Assembly of St. Kitts and Nevis as the proposed legislation for modification of the rules for purchased citizenships was being debated. The Speaker nodded, banged his gavel, and stood.

"Our debate will be interrupted for a short interval due to a matter of national security." He banged his gavel a second time.

Six soldiers wearing side arms entered the hall, led by a captain. The soldiers took positions behind the benches of the Nevis legislators.

The Speaker again banged his gavel. "The Chair recognizes Captain Lance Lawford."

Captain Lawford approached the podium, bowed slightly to the Speaker, and announced. "Information has been received from the United States Coast Guard that two armed warships have been intercepted headed for our shores with the mission of influencing the deliberations of this Assembly. These warships were funded by and operating under orders received by Antonio Montez, who is hereby placed under arrest for the crimes of treason and conspiracy to overthrow the elected government of St. Kitts and Nevis."

The soldiers surrounded Antonio Montez and raised him to his feet. Captain Lawford left the podium to join them.

The Speaker pounded his gavel once more. "Mr. Montez may say a few words of explanation before he is removed from this hall. He must do so from his present location."

Tony saw that he had lost completely. "I am a loyal son of Nevis. I was born on that island and I am proud to represent its people. Nevis was once a separate nation and will be once again. I only tried to accelerate the coming of that independence. I bow to the authority of the current government and the military." Tony turned and followed the soldiers out of the chamber.

The Speaker's assistant again approached him bearing a note. The Speaker nodded in the general direction of the Prime Minister's seat.

"The deliberations of this Assembly on the matters before us will be postponed for two weeks while legal charges against Mr. Montez are developed and pursued. This session is hereby adjourned."

In the back of the hall, Malcolm Harkney wiped his forehead with his handkerchief. *That was a close call for our country. Thank goodness those businessmen from the Bahamas gave us insight into what was happening. They probably didn't even know their words were significant.*

CHAPTER 91 – SANDY AND KEN

When Sandy Rolle walked into Weatherford & Rolle, the morning after the battle between Frank's boat and the pirate ships, he carried his helmet, intending to place it on an office shelf as a reminder of his brush with danger. When he reached the store offices, he found Joyce White talking with Ken Birch in somber tones.

Sandy put the helmet on a table and approached them. "It was a successful operation. Frank and I slowed down those ships thanks to your special cannon mountings and sail treatments, Ken. The U.S. Coast Guard arrived later and put them out of business."

Joyce said, "That's not the whole story, Sandy. During the night before your naval encounter, there was a close-combat battle between Tony Montez's Mexican sailors and the pirate thugs supplied by Emma Read's cousin Lydia. A lot of people were killed and wounded."

Ken shook Sandy's hand and then lowered his head. "I wasn't sure what to do, so when I called Frank to tell him that the ships were leaving their base on Lynyard Cay, I didn't mention the overnight battle. I wanted you to be alert and ready when you fought the Mexican crews. I was afraid that news of dead and wounded people would mess with your heads."

"So, how many died, and how many are in the hospital?"

Joyce checked her notes, "Some Mexicans with only minor wounds sailed on the two ships. As to the more serious casualties, there are thirteen dead and eighteen in the hospital, split pretty evenly between the two sides, but one of the dead was Emma Read. She led her pirate group with an assault rifle."

"Wow! She really did fight and die like a pirate. Her ancestor, Mary, was said to have been a vicious fighter."

Joyce leaned against her desk. "I'm worried about how Todd will react? She was his enemy, his lover, and the mother of his son."

"She was all that, so he'll probably have mixed emotions. Your words suggest he doesn't know yet."

"The Royal Bahamas Police are trying to keep the slaughter under wraps until they interview the wounded and Ken. They'll probably ask the U.S. Coast Guard to take statements from the sailors on the captured ships as well. In any case word will spread through all the gossip pipelines. The Pirate Park is closed and won't reopen. Lots of local folks are out of jobs, and they'll be talking about it too."

Ken showed Sandy two fat envelopes on Joyce's desk. "Two envelopes full of money. Tony left me one for working with Raoul, his crew's leader, and Raoul gave me the other to cover medical and funeral expenses for the fighters. I won't keep any of it because it's blood money. You can't make a profit on people getting killed and wounded."

"But you can get yourself a promotion to Floor Manager of our store. Thanks for all your help, Ken. You'll be in charge now when Joyce and I aren't available. Todd has enough on his hands with his infant son that he'll remain the less active partner in our enterprise."

Ken grinned and raised an eyebrow. "Thanks, Sandy, and are you suggesting that you and Joyce will be frequently away together in the future?"

Sandy looked at Joyce. She nodded. He said, "I might be suggesting just that."

CHAPTER 92 – REQUIEM FOR A PIRATE

Todd couldn't understand why the Royal Bahamas Police had left a message on his telephone that they wanted to talk with him at ten o'clock if possible, but he rearranged his schedule to meet the police request. At ten o'clock He entered the police station by the harbor and announced his presence to the officer at the front desk.

"Good morning; I'm Todd Weatherford, and I received a message that someone here wanted to speak with me at this time."

The officer nodded. "Thank you for coming, sir. Please go down the corridor to the second room on your left."

When he entered the designated room, Todd saw Emma Read's cousin Lydia sitting at a table, across from Ken Birch and a Royal Bahamas Police officer. The officer stood as Todd appeared and gestured him toward an empty seat on Lydia's side of the table.

"Thank you for coming, Mr. Weatherford. I'm Captain Ivory, and we're here to discuss the aftermath of a large battle that occurred two nights ago at the Pirate Theme Park docks. I'm sure you know Ken Birch, one of your store's employees, and I believe you know Emma Read's cousin Lydia."

Todd sat and said, "I know Ken, and I know Lydia from seeing her at a wedding ceremony, but I have no information about this battle you mentioned."

"That is because we have tried to restrict the spreading of that news until we have statements from all the concerned parties. The facts are that a battle using firearms of various types took place two nights ago over the control of the two well-known pirate ships from the park. Miss Lydia's associates were initially on board the ships, when a large group of Mexican fighters tried to drive them off. Mr. Ken Birch was an innocent witness who took cover so as not to be involved in the combat."

"It must have been a terribly violent battle, but why does it involve me?"

"The Mexicans won the battle, but many on both sides died and suffered wounds before the Mexican crews sailed away on the ships. Those ships were later seized by the United States Coast Guard and their crews were arrested. You are involved because one of those killed was the leader of the pirate crew side, Emma Read. She is the mother of your son. You and Lydia are, therefore, her closest relatives, and should have some say in her funeral arrangements."

Todd took a few moments before responding. "I assume the theme park is closed and will not reopen."

"I believe that is true."

"The theme park was Emma's dream, demonstrating to all that she was the descendant of a pirate. The battle was typical of old-time pirate actions. I suggest that the mainland portion of the theme park be turned into a cemetery for all those who died on both sides. Let it be called Calico Jack's Pirate Cemetery. Emma can have a central monument there, and some of the local people who lost their theme park jobs can maintain the grounds and act as tour guides for visitors who will want to come and learn about the pirate battle that happened three hundred years after the original pirates were put out of business. How does that sound to you, Lydia?"

"I like it. I was Emma's only blood relative, except for your son. I also lost many friends in that fight. Todd's approach will keep their memories alive and still be a tourist attraction for Abaco. Now we'll have to figure out how to pay for it."

Captain Ivory smiled. "That won't be a problem. We already have generous contributions from Ken Birch and from a man named Raoul, who was the leader of the Mexican fighters. Unless there is an objection from you, Miss Lydia, we will be burying the dead from both sides in this new cemetery."

"I won't object. People on both sides fought well. They all deserve to be properly buried and remembered."

Ken Birch relaxed for the first time. "Good. I feel that I've done my duty to them and that the money from Raoul and me will be well spent."

They started to get up from the table, but Todd gestured for them to remain seated.

"One more thing. We should all agree that Lynyard Cay should be returned to government ownership with the understanding that the authorities agree to make it a public park and rest area for boaters."

Captain Ivory said, "As the chair of this meeting, I ask that Todd's suggestion be made a formal motion. Will someone second the motion?"

Ken raised his hand.

"We have a motion on the table and it has been seconded. Are there any objections to converting Lynyard Cay to a government park as described by Todd Weatherford?"

Richard Davidson

Silence.

"No objections being heard, I declare that the motion has been approved, and I will take steps with the proper government departments to make the park a reality. Let us have a standing vote to adjourn. Thank you all for coming."

CHAPTER 93 – SANDY AND JOYCE

After work, as they walked to their cars, Joyce stopped and put her hand on Sandy's arm to restrain him.

He looked down at her hand. "What's up?"

"Sandy, we need to talk."

"We talk all the time."

"Not work talk, or Todd-related talk, but us talk."

"Go ahead."

"In the office, when Ken asked if we'd likely be away frequently, you said that we might."

"So?"

"So, we've never even had an actual date together. You take me for granted."

"Are you saying you're not interested in dating me?"

"Damn it, Sandy, you've known how I feel about you for a long time, but you never do anything about it. Why?"

"Because I'm too busy with the store."

"That's a bullshit answer. I work harder and harder to give you time and an incentive to act on your feelings. Maybe you don't know how to feel."

"Maybe I've been a loner for so long that I need someone to show me how to have a relationship where I can relax and be natural with other people. I'm always being responsible and playing a part."

"Fair enough, Sandy I'm calling your bluff. I've been your loyal assistant for a long time. It's time for you to let me lead. Leave your car here. We're going out tonight in my car."

"Where are we going?"

"You'll find out soon."

She drove into the Marsh Harbour business area and stopped at Kentucky Fried Chicken. "Sandy, you go in and buy a bucket of chicken plus some add-on side orders while I make a phone call."

As soon as he left the car, she called a number. "Hi, it's Joyce. I'm out with Sandy. Are you free and ready to go tonight?"

She nodded at the reply, even though no one could see her. "Good; I'll give you that extra twenty minutes. Thanks so much."

Sandy returned with two large paper bags. "All set Joyce."

"Load your packages in the back seat and hop in. We don't have far to go."

Joyce drove north to Bay Street and parked. "We walk from here. I'll take one of those delicious-smelling bags."

"I get it. We're going to eat on one of the docks and watch the boats. That's a good idea."

They walked eastward along Bay Street, past the Union Jack Public Dock toward the Harbour View Marina. When they reached that marina, they turned left and walked along the main dock with boats on both sides.

Sandy's fatigue showed when he asked, "How far do we have to go? All the way to the end?"

"No; stop here and turn left."

Sandy looked to his left and realized his destination as the lights on *Sweeney's Queen* lit up. Steve Sweeney stood on the deck waving at them.

"Hi, Sandy and Joyce. Welcome to an evening of fun and relaxation. You brought the food. I have beer and other drinks. It will be a moonlit starry evening, ideal for fishing, relaxing, or anything else you have in mind. I'll start our event as your host and friend, but anytime you choose to be alone, I'll become the invisible boatman. Give me your bags so that you'll have better balance, and then hop on board."

Steve assisted Sandy when his trailing foot slipped. "Now get comfortable with a drink. I'm going to take us over to Fowl Cay. It's long and thin and has a national park where everything is peaceful and natural. We'll eat offshore on the boat, and then you can decide whether you want to go fishing, exploring, star gazing, or whatever. If you decide to walk the shore of the island alone, I'll promise to have the boat ready when you want to return."

Dinner was fun for both Joyce and Sandy. They ate chicken with their fingers while Steve, after a quick snack, serenaded them with his guitar. Joyce was surprised at the quality of his voice as he urged them toward a romantic island mood with old Harry Belafonte songs. After they finished eating and drinking, Sandy and Joyce decided to walk the beach and tour the narrow island.

Steve eased the boat as close to shore as he could. "It's clear and shallow here. I'll shine my lights downward into the water. Roll up your jeans and carry your shoes."

Sandy lowered himself into the water first and then helped Joyce down. She leaned against him as her feet felt for the bottom. After they reached the shore, Sandy and Joyce dried their feet on a towel that Steve supplied. They decided to walk barefoot for a while before putting their shoes back on.

After the couple moved out of sight, Steve cast out a couple of fishing lines and prepared for some relaxing solitude. He rarely had the opportunity to fish quietly by himself. As he fished, Steve thought about the unpredictability of his schedule. He had expected to be Frank's crewmate when the showdown came with the pirate ships. When the time came, he had been on Grand Bahama Island, so Sandy saw the action instead. At least no harm had come to Frank's boat or its crew.

Steve's head nodded forward, and he fell asleep with his hands each resting on one of the fishing rods, securely latched into their sockets. An unknown time later, he was awakened by the throbbing of both rods. He slapped his cheeks to regain alertness and started to try to land two fish at once. It would be difficult.

Just as Steve was considering cutting one of the lines, Joyce and Sandy came out of the woods holding hands.

Steve glanced at them and then returned his attention to the fish. "Sandy, if you can get on board by yourself, I could use some help with one of two big fish on my lines."

"I'm not a fisherman, Steve."

"Joyce yelled, "But I am. I'll be right with you." She kicked off her shoes and told Sandy to bring them with him. Then she waded to the boat and vaulted over the side. "I'll take your left rod, Steve. You stay with the right."

While they battled the fish, Sandy climbed on board, not quite as gracefully as Joyce had. He sat with a bottle of beer and watched the fishing show.

Ten minutes later, Steve yelled for Sandy to grab the net, and together they brought a thirteen pound mutton snapper onto the deck. Steve secured his rod and forced the twisting fish into his fish locker. Five minutes later, Joyce yelled that she needed a net man. Sandy grabbed the net while

Steve helped her with the rod. Her mutton snapper dwarfed Steve's at twenty pounds. It took all three of them to wrestle it into the fish locker.

Steve beamed at the others. "At least from a fisherman's point of view this evening was a huge success."

Sandy smiled at Joyce. "It was from everyone's point of view. Many thanks, Steve."

Steve winked at them. "I'll clean these fish in the morning, and we can have a fish barbecue at noon in the store parking lot for all the employees and whatever customers are there. Tell Todd I found a great fishing spot, and I'll take him another time. You two come back for more outings too."

CHAPTER 94 – FISH BARBECUE

True to his word, Steve Sweeney had his barbecue set up in the parking lot of Weatherford & Rolle by eleven o'clock in the morning. Sandy had two of the floor sales people set up a tent and some benches for those who liked to eat in the shade. They attached strings of colorful pennants to posts to make the event look festive. In case the two mutton snappers wouldn't be enough to feed everyone, Joyce ordered salads to be delivered from Anglers Restaurant.

Earlier that morning, Joyce called Barb and Todd to reveal her romantic outing with Sandy, and to invite them to attend the fish barbecue. Barb said she had to work, but she would try to at least catch the end of the party. Todd said he had babysitting duty but would bring son John if his mother and father didn't get back before the barbecue started.

Sandy spent part of the morning thinking about Joyce's admonition that he had to learn to relax more, and reliving his completely unwound evening with Joyce the evening before. She had showed him how to have fun on a moment's notice. He hoped today's barbecue would continue that spirit.

At noon, Sandy flicked the switch to activate the store public address system. "Weatherford & Rolle will be closed from now until one o'clock for a special event in the parking lot. As a thank you to our employees and customers, everyone is invited to join us outside for a fish barbecue party. Fresh salads will also be available along with various beverages. Please join us. I'm Sandy Rolle, and Todd Weatherford will be here too. Feel free to introduce yourself to us." He switched off the P.A. and went outside.

Joyce was already there, standing behind the salad table, passing out plastic utensils and paper plates. Steve had finished barbecuing the smaller of the two mutton snappers, and Ken Birch was placing portions on plates while Steve wrestled the larger fish onto the hot grill. It wasn't long before the sound level rose so much that you had to lean toward your conversation partner to hear him or her.

Todd arrived shortly after the employees and customers came out of the store. His parents had not yet returned home, so he carried young John Sandy in a strapped-on baby carrier with a chest pouch. Periodically, Todd looked down at his baby's face, as if to memorize his features. He also studied the way originally straight blond hair was becoming curly.

Todd took a plate of fish with garnish from Ken and walked over to the edge of the crowd to eat it. He would socialize later, and he would definitely go with Steve Sweeney on that fishing trip he had offered. Todd found the mutton snapper to have been perfectly prepared. He was almost done eating it when someone tapped him on the shoulder from behind. He turned around and couldn't believe his eyes. He dropped his fish plate.

Standing in front of him was his ex-wife, Lori. She wore dark blue shorts, a matching top, a small backpack and an Aussie-style hat. She carried a professional camera with a long telephoto lens over her shoulder.

"Lori, what are you doing here? It can't be coincidence, so my mother must have called you." *(Even though I asked her not to.)*

"Your parents picked me up at the airport. You look different, and I don't mean just because you're carrying a baby. I assume he's yours with that bitch that broke up our marriage."

"Meet John Sandy Weatherford. He's my new pride and joy, and I'm doing my best to be a good dad."

On the other side of the event area, Joyce was on the telephone. "Barb, it's an emergency. Get over here faster than ASAP. Todd's parents brought his ex-wife here, and she's talking to him now. I'll try to interfere, but my stalling tactics aren't likely to succeed."

Lori asked, "May I hold the baby?"

Todd looked down. "Maybe later. He's gone to sleep, and I don't want to wake him. He had a bad night. How's teaching going?"

"It's not. After our violent fight, they fired me. No one wants an employee who stabbed her husband. My life has changed considerably too. I'm a freelance photographer now. I've learned how to do things on my own instead of depending on an employer and organization. It's a shock to see Weatherford on that sign; you're a partner here?"

"As was my father before me and his father before him. It's an old family business, but I didn't know about it when we were married. I'm not just a tour guide anymore."

"Touché. My prodding you to get qualified for a better job was a sore spot with you."

The tires on a bright red Mini squealed as the car entered the parking lot at high speed and turned into a parking space. The event guests all turned their heads to see what was happening and then returned to their conversations.

Steve Sweeney called out, "Barb, come over here. I saved a piece of fish for you."

She wasn't sure whether she should respond, but then realized Steve was giving her a subtle way to insert herself into Todd's conversation. She detoured toward the barbecue.

Steve whispered, "It tastes great. I have a second piece reserved for you in case you decide to throw this one in her face." He winked as he handed her the plate and a fork.

Barb walked over to the spot where Todd and Lori were talking. "Sorry I'm late, Todd. Busy day at the office. This fish is great. Did you catch it?"

"It is tasty, but Steve and Joyce landed the two mutton snappers. Barb, meet Lori. She was once my wife."

"Hi, Lori. That's a long lens on your camera. You must specialize in distance shots."

"Nature photography success depends on being able to sneak up on your prey without being detected. Actually, Todd gave me my first lessons in understanding nature."

Joyce grabbed Sandy's arm. "Come on. We have to be the cavalry. Todd's in trouble. He has his ex-wife and Barb fighting over him."

"How did his ex-wife get here?"

"Todd's mother defied her husband and her son to get her here. We have to remove the pressure so that Todd can make his own choice."

"Great fun, but how do we do that?"

"We'll run over there and have them focus on us. We can pretend we're going steady or something."

"Why pretend? Just say you'll marry me, and it will be the real thing."

"Sandy Rolle, you are the most perplexing man. I try to get you to give me one romantic glance for years and get nothing. Now that we've been on one real date, you want to marry me?"

"Yup; we've been working for years like a married couple anyway. So, what's your answer?"

"It's yes, of course. Let's spread the good news."

Joyce and Sandy ran over to Todd and the two women, positioning themselves so that when Todd looked at them, he faced away from Lori.

Joyce said, "I hardly believe this myself, but Sandy and I are engaged. He just now asked me to marry him. That fish I caught must be magic."

Todd laughed. "It looks as though you caught more than one fish."

Barb hugged Joyce and Sandy, and then Todd introduced them to Lori.

"When I last saw Lori, she was a teacher. Now she's a wildlife photographer. She's changed almost as much as I have."

Lori needed to know whether they were still a match. "How have you changed, Todd, outside of being a partner in a business?"

Sandy said, "Let me answer that one. Thanks to Todd's insistence on investigating what criminal activities Emma Read was involved in, our group of friends worked together to prevent the overthrow of the government of the smallest nation in the Caribbean and caused a battle between neo-pirate thugs and Mexican drug cartel fighters, killing many on both sides as well as Emma Read, the pirate queen. Does this sound like the Kentucky-rooted tour guide you knew in Chicago?"

Todd said, "We all worked together."

Barb said, "Yes, but you built the group and kept us focused."

"I guess I have changed quite a bit. I rarely even eat pizza, let alone one with bacon, pepperoni, mushrooms, anchovies, and onions. That was once my favorite."

Lori turned and walked away. *I was once your favorite too, Todd. They're right; there's no going back. It's all different.*

As Lori walked away, Barb said, "John Sandy is waking up. Let me carry him for a while." As Todd handed her the baby, she kissed both of them.

-END-

ABOUT THE AUTHOR

Richard Davidson is the author of the self-help guidebook: *DECISION TIME! Better Decisions for a Better Life*. He has written the five-novel Lord's Prayer Mystery Series: *Lead Us Not into Temptation, Give Us this Day our Daily Bread, Forgive Us Our Trespasses, Thy Will Be Done*, and *Deliver Us from Evil*. He has edited an anthology, *Overcoming: An Anthology by the Writers of* OCWW. His Imp Mystery Series, contains five novels: *Implications, Impulses, Impostor, Impending*, and *Impasse*. The Imp novels continue to chronicle the exploits of characters introduced in the earlier series, along with affiliated newcomers, taking their interests in new directions. *Loyalties* is the first in a new series of standalone novels. Mr. Davidson is Past President of Off-Campus Writers' Workshop, the oldest ongoing group of its kind in the U.S. and is the founder of the ReadWorthy Books Book Review Blog. He is also the founder of the Independent Mystery Publishing Society (IMPS). Mr. Davidson is a former Lay Leader in the United Methodist Church. He is an aeronautical & astronautical engineer.

WORKS BY THIS AUTHOR
NONFICTION:

DECISION TIME! Better Decisions for a Better Life,

RADMAR Publishing

ISBN 978-0-9829160-7-0 (2nd edition paperback)

ISBN 978-1-4581-8395-8 (Smashwords eBook)

ASIN B014QFZP68 (Kindle Edition eBook)

Where you are in life today is the result of all of the past decisions you have made or which have been made for you in response to the various situations and events that have impacted your life. The decisions that you will make from this point forward will determine the degree to which your future will be positive or negative. *DECISION TIME!* gives you insight into the subjective decision-making process as applied to both small and large choices you will face. It includes dynamic aspects, cultural effects, and morality as applied to decision-making for individuals, teams, corporations, and societies. *DECISION TIME!* prepares you to face continuous decisions confidently and without hesitation.

Richard Davidson

FICTION:

Lead Us Not into Temptation (The Lord's Prayer Mystery Series, Volume I),

RADMAR Publishing

ISBN 978-0-9976381-0-3 (2nd edition paperback)

ASIN B01GEK7ZZ2 (Kindle Edition eBook)

Arthur Blake, former NASA engineer turned minister, receives an emergency appointment to be pastor of the United Methodist Church in Parkville, a distant suburb of Chicago, following the bizarre sudden death of the church's unusual former pastor. Pastor Blake's attempts to unravel the mystery that shrouds his predecessor become involved with tracking the child of a possibly bigamous soldier in World War II England; art and jewelry treasures plundered by the Nazis and their sympathizers; and the eventual results of childhood sibling conflicts in combined families. Arthur's allies in his investigation include Parkville Police Chief Bobby Andrews, County Medical Examiner Irma Custis, and the married team of Penny and Joe Gonzalez who work for a clandestine government agency. During the course of *Lead Us Not into Temptation,* the reader discovers how seemingly minor historical events lead to major present-day dislocations in church, village, and family relationships.

Loyalties

Give Us this Day Our Daily Bread (The Lord's Prayer Mystery Series, Volume II)

RADMAR Publishing

ISBN 978-0-9829160-5-6 (2nd edition paperback)

ASIN B01H7M47M0 (Kindle Edition eBook)

Arthur Blake, Pastor of Parkville United Methodist Church, has to deal with the aftereffects of a traumatic communion incident. He works to assist the authorities in investigating the cause while doing his best to convince members of his congregation that it is safe to return to church. Working with the police and federal agencies, he discovers that the terror of the initial event is minor compared with the potential chaotic impact of future disasters being planned by the perpetrator. The investigation is interwoven with several relationship situations that affect the final outcome.

Richard Davidson

Forgive Us Our Trespasses (The Lord's Prayer Mystery Series, Volume III)

RADMAR Publishing

ISBN 978-0-9976381-1-0 (2nd edition paperback)

ASIN B01IQ1TJXS (Kindle Edition eBook)

Arthur Blake, Pastor of Parkville United Methodist Church, tries to assist his father to resolve his trauma after learning that his best friend, recently killed in a car accident, may have been an imposter with a heinous background. The investigation reveals that the presumed accident was but one link in a chain of murders. Blake works to determine the true identity of his father's friend, while also discovering the man's past activities and affiliations. Arthur works to solve the murders in conjunction with his colleagues at ABC Consultants. He also draws on assistance from associates at a covert government agency with which he has worked before. The coordinated effort to solve the puzzle examines incidents that span the period between World War II and the present in order to defuse the personal, national, and international dangers resulting from them.

Loyalties

Thy Will Be Done (The Lord's Prayer Mystery Series, Volume IV)

RADMAR Publishing

ISBN 978-0-9829160-2-5 (paperback)

ASIN B009JU6EZM (Kindle Edition eBook)

The sudden death of a young woman attending Parkville United Methodist Church infuriates her brother and leads to congregational outrage over his outburst and subsequent murder. The investigation of that slaying by Pastor Arthur Blake and his associates leads to revelations of a previously undetected criminal organization operating in the area. Unraveling the mystery and scope of this group entangles Arthur and his associated investigators in a web of conspiracies extending from Illinois to both U.S. coasts and through Mexico to Guatemala.

Richard Davidson

Deliver Us from Evil (The Lord's Prayer Mystery Series, Volume V)

RADMAR Publishing

ISBN 978-0-9829160-3-2 (paperback)

ASIN B00EBDUXFY (Kindle Edition eBook)

Arthur and Irma's wedding day has finally arrived, but an unexpected interruption leads to their need to investigate a possible murder committed by someone close to them. With the aid of friends and federal agents Penny and Joe Gonzalez, they follow a series of clues, crisscrossing the United States to learn more about the murder, related subsequent events, and the significance of a rare object brought home by a veteran of the Iraq War. A second murder close to Pastor Arthur Blake's church involves them in a new investigation, assisting Parkville Police Chief Bobby Andrews. Are these murders and the tracking of that strange object connected? Will marriage deteriorate or improve the relationship between Arthur and Irma? Character flaws in many relationships color the outcome.

Loyalties

Overcoming: An Anthology by the Writers of OCWW

Edited and with an Introduction by Richard Davidson

RADMAR Publishing

ISBN 978-9829160-4-9 (paperback)

ASIN B00E80NN4I (Kindle Edition eBook)

This anthology covers many aspects of overcoming life's problems, obstacles, and challenging developments. The contributing writers have used fiction, non-fiction, memoir, poetry, historical chronicle, and drama to highlight our continuing need to overcome our problems, rather than dwell on them. The reader will learn from many talented writers the skills needed to respond constructively, energetically, and sometimes humorously to whatever obstacle bars one's path. Apply their lessons to your own needs and to those of others you cherish.

Richard Davidson

Implications: An Arthur Blake Mystery Novel (Imp Mysteries, Volume 1)

RADMAR Publishing

ISBN 978-0-9829160-6-3 (paperback)

ASIN B00LY9IBWK (Kindle Edition eBook)

Bishop Howard Chandler has assigned Pastor Arthur Blake to investigate the burning of a church in the small city of Amboy, Illinois. He learns from that church's pastor that she had to overcome past improprieties by former members. During the investigation of the fire's cause, Arthur and the other state fire investigators uncover disturbing aspects of the ninety-year-old church's design and history. Arthur calls on his federal associates for assistance, as the investigation of a local church fire expands to seeking solutions to related crimes occurring from the present to recent years and back to the Prohibition Era. Progress in the investigation intertwines with new developments in Arthur's family life.

Impulses: An Arthur Blake Mystery Novel (Imp Mysteries, Volume 2)

RADMAR Publishing

ISBN 978-0-9829160-8-7 (paperback)

ASIN B012LFQXYI (Kindle Edition eBook)

Several disturbing dreams cause Arthur Blake to wonder whether he is trying to do too much for the many people who seek his services. These qualms are complicated by Bishop Howard Chandler's suggestion that Arthur temporarily set aside his official duties and take an extended sabbatical leave. His resulting internal debates about career moves are set aside when the pastor who replaced him at the Parkville church dies in an apparent suicide possibly linked to several deaths at the Parkville Rehabilitation Home. The bishop assigns Arthur to determine the circumstances behind the new pastor's death, while Arthur and Irma, his wife and constant investigative partner, also study a mysterious shipment at his father's antiques shop. The sudden disappearance of a young associate provides another mystery and leads to questions of life after death and reincarnation. Events that initially appear simple become increasingly complex as the true natures of many people come into question.

Richard Davidson

Impostor: A Genealogical Mystery (Imp Mysteries, Volume 3)

RADMAR Publishing

ISBN 978-0-9829160-9-4 (paperback)

ASIN B01FZQZEK4 (Kindle Edition eBook)

When Debbie Danforth discovers a flaw in the genealogy of her live-in boyfriend, Jeremy Hadley, he and his family try to discredit her findings, but eventually admit they must be true. Jeremy and Debbie run a private detective business, the Sandley Agency and commit their skills and resources to learning about the impostor Debbie has discovered in the Hadley ancestry. They are assisted in this effort by Penny and Joe Gonzalez, principals in a covert federal agency, with whom Jeremy has previously worked as a consultant. Their joint investigation uncovers both unique details concerning the mysterious Hadley impostor and little-known facts about events leading up to World War II in both Britain and the United States. Was the person who masqueraded as a Hadley a villain or a hero? Did other Hadleys know he was a fraudulent member of their family? Did his actions assist or impede the British and the Americans as they faced the growing menace in prewar Europe?

Impending: A Genealogical Mystery (Imp Mysteries, Volume 4)

RADMAR Publishing

ISBN 978-0-9976381-2-7 (paperback)

ASIN B072KPHN7K (Kindle Edition eBook)

Young married private detectives, Debbie and Jeremy Hadley, discover that Debbie's family, the Danforths, have a family secret. Grandma Marie Danforth summons them because she fears that alienated family members and underworld characters will attempt to wrest control of the secret from her. The history of the secret begins at the American Civil War Battle of Gettysburg and develops through a century and a half of Danforth family twists and intrigues. Although written as one story, *Impending* actually is effectively two novels in one: the saga of how the secret developed from its inception to the present day, and the mystery of how to counter multiple attempts to hijack it. *Impending* is history and mystery all-in-one. Debbie and Jeremy team with police from two cities to unravel the mystery and reach its surprising conclusion.

Richard Davidson

Impasse: An Arthur & Irma Blake Mystery

RADMAR Publishing

ISBN 978-0-9976381-3-4 (paperback)

ASIN B07BGD6T6Y (Kindle Edition eBook)

The discovery of human bones while excavating a property to build a new church requires all work to stop. Arthur and Irma Blake investigate and find an earlier structure on that lot was involved in illegal activities, requiring FBI leadership of the inquiry. Further research reveals a group of foreign citizens who replaced Americans illegally and an elaborate money laundering scheme. What are the foreigners trying to do? Who killed the people unearthed during construction and others discovered later? How will the killer be brought to justice more than twenty years after the crimes?

Loyalties: Uncertain / Mixed / Fanatical

RADMAR Publishing

ISBN 978-0-9976381-4-1 (paperback)

Todd Weatherford, Kentucky-born Chicago tour guide is seduced by an apparent tourist from the West Indies, leading to the sudden breakup of his marriage. When the seducer abruptly disappears, Todd seeks guidance from his family and learns that his ancestors were Revolutionary War Loyalists who also had West Indies connections. Todd and two friends journey to the Bahamas to track the mystery woman and unravel her suspected evil intentions. What is her ancestral secret? Will she once again derail Todd's plans, or will he and his friends sabotage hers? Is she working alone, or does she have wealthy and powerful associates? The answers to these questions involve Todd and his friends in unexpected adventures.

Richard Davidson

Learn more about the writings, humor, and random thoughts of Richard Davidson at: radmarinc.com davidsonbookshelf.com and at the Independent Mystery Publishing Society (IMPS) https://www.mysteryimps.com and https://www.mysteryimps.net

Richard Davidson's author page on Amazon is located at https://www.amazon.com/author/richarddavidson Follow and *Like* Richard Davidson, Author on Facebook at https://www.facebook.com/richarddavidsonauthor ?ref=hl Follow him on Twitter @mysteryimp